The Adventures of
Bearcub Ironskull

The Adventures of Bearcub Ironskull

by
Gustave Aimard

Translated from the French by
Jean-Marc & Randy Lofficier

A Black Coat Press Book

Acknowledgements: Thanks to Nicholas Waller for his invaluable assistance with respect to the sailing terms used in this book, to Michael Shreve for editing the ms.

English adaptation, annotations & introduction Copyright © 2024 by Jean-Marc & Randy Lofficier.
Cover illustration Copyright © 2024 by Phil Cohen.

Visit our website at www.blackcoatpress.com

TABLE OF CONTENTS

Gustave Aimard

Introduction

Ourson Tête-de-fer, here translated as *The Adventures of Bearcub Ironskull*, was initially published in France by Amyot in 1868, and has been reprinted many times since, due to its status as *the* seminal French pirate novel, predating *Treasure Island* (1882) by fourteen years!

Deeply rooted in popular culture, the world of piracy has given rise to many familiar characters. From Captain Hook to Long John Silver, Captain Nemo to Jack Sparrow, the adventures of pirates have graced the pages of many novels and seen a multitude of film and television adaptations. Simple criminals for many, precursors of great revolutionary movements for others, pirates heralded a wind of revolt across the world's seas. Even today, they are the subject of people's dreams due to the perception of their unwavering devotion to freedom.

Novelists like Daniel Defoe, with *The King of Pirates* (1719) *The Pirate Gow* (1725) and *A General History of the Pyrates* (1724-26), propelled pirates to the rank of heroes of adventure novels from the 18th century onward. Halfway between reality and fiction, they originated with actual historical figures such as William Kidd, Jack Rackham and the inevitable Blackbeard. Against the backdrop of a search for legendary treasure, authors such as Edward John Trelawny, Robert Louis Stevenson and many others gave us different visions of fascinating crooks steeped in ideals, all interspersed with adventures of all kinds. Chief among these, in France, was Gustave Aimard.

Gustave Aimard was born on September 13, 1818, in Paris. He was the author of many adventure novels, often first serialized in newspapers such as *Le Moniteur*, *La Presse* and *La Liberté*. He himself had a turbulent life in which it is difficult to distinguish fantasy from reality.

Aimard was born to unknown parents. As he once said, he was the son of two people who were married, "but not to each other." His first recorded name was Olivier Aimard, but later he chose to change his first name to Gustave. It was only after his death that it was discovered that his biological father was Horace François Bastien Sébastiani (1772-1851), who had been a general, an ambassador and a minister under Napoleon. His biological mother was Félicité de Faudoas-Barbazan de Seguenville (1785-1841), who was married to Anne Jean Marie René Savary, Duke of Rovigo (1774-1833). Born out of wedlock, abandoned by his biological parents, the child was given as a baby to the Gloux family who were paid to raise him.

Young Olivier was reportedly turbulent, to the point of being expelled from several educational institutions. At age 9 (or possibly 12, as the records are not clear), he either ran away or was sent off on a herring ship to serve as a cabin boy. He then spent part of his youth in South America where (he says) he was taken prisoner by the Patagonians, then became a woodsman, a traveler, a gold digger, a hunter, a trapper, a slaver, possibly a thief. In 1835, he enlisted in the French navy where his stormy temper and his multiple escapades earned him harsh corporal punishment. He deserted in 1839 in Chile, where he took part in the struggles against the dictator Rosas, then became a pearl fisherman. He also claimed to have been captured by the Indians, was twice tied to a torture post by the Apache and then married a Cheyenne, with whom he had a child. This might explain the position he established between good and bad Indians, and his fascination for mixed bloods and the wood runners. (Most of this comes from his autobiographical novel, *Par mer et par terre* (1879)).

Aimard returned to Paris in 1847. Coincidentally, that same year, his half-sister, Fanny Sebastiani de Praslin,[1] was murdered by her husband, Duke Théobald de Praslin, who committed suicide soon afterward. He then traveled to Spain, Turkey and the Caucasus. After the revolution of 1848, he was granted amnesty for his desertion from the Navy.

In 1851, after having served for a short while in the Garde Mobile, Aimard left again for the Americas. This time he was among the 150 miners hired by Duke de Raousset-Boulbon (sic), who wanted to mine in Mexico. However, mining permits were not issued, and the duke decided "to free the poor people of Mexico." He took over the town of Hermosillo on 13 October 1852. The duke died from diarrhea on the first night of his conquest, and the villagers retook their village. The miners fled and Aimard again returned to France. He later described this adventure in his semi-fictional novel *Curumilla*. A contemporary history written in 1856 and the official account published in 1935, *The French in Sono-*

---

[1] Sébastiani had been married to the Duchess de Coigny. In 1806 the couple produced a daughter: Alatrice-Rosalba Fanny. Shortly after her birth, the mother died. Fanny was then raised by her grandmother, the Duchess de Coigny.

ra, leave no doubt that Aimard had indeed participated in this reckless adventure.

In 1854, Aimard married Adèle Lucie Damoreau, a lyrical artist, and began his career as a writer, specializing in tales of the American West. Fenimore Cooper's *Last of the Mohicans* (1826) was still hugely influential, North America was in fashion—it was the time of the California Gold Rush—and the recent success of Gabriel Ferry's *Coureur des bois* (1856) helped Aimard to quickly find his niche in that genre. He became as successful and popular in his time as Eugène Sue and Paul Féval. In total. he wrote approximately seventy novels and is still remembered today for such potboilers as *Trappers of Arkansas* (1858) and *Bandits of Arizona* (1882).

Most of his western novels were translated into over ten languages. About 15 of his books were translated into English and can be found on Gutenberg, but strangely not *Ourson Tête-de-Fer*. Their reviews mostly dealt with the question of whether they would harm children or not, or whether they were too bloody or not.

In 1870, Aimard and other members of the literary community participated in the Franco-Prussian war and in the short-lived success at the Battle of Le Bourget. He was at the origin of the creation and the ensuing scandal of the *franc-tireurs de la presse*. He fought during the Siege of Paris. Unfortunately, his novel on the topic, *The Adventures of Michel Hartmann*. was censored by the French government, which at the time did not want to further inflame the Germans.

In 1879, *Jim l'Indien* and eleven other western novels appeared under the double signature of Gustave Aimard and Jules Berlioz d'Auriac at publisher Degorce-Cadot. It turned out that the books had first appeared under the sole signature of Berlioz at another publisher and were unauthorized adaptations of a series of little-known American dime novels. Aimard had agreed to lend his celebrity to Berlioz in exchange for a cut in royalties.

That same year, Aimard left for Rio de Janeiro. The local newspapers heralded the arrival of the famous French author. He rented a suite there and all of Rio's high society came to visit him. He befriended Emperor Dom Pedro II, who had often visited Paris, and loved literature, science and technology. Aimard wrote a diary about his trip to Brazil, *My Last Trip, New Brazil* (1886). Aimard then visited Buenos Aires before heading inland. The Imperial Museum in Petrópolis, Brazil, has a copy of a letter that he sent from Buenos Aires to Pedro II.

In 1881, Aimard returned to France. Two years later, he was admitted to the Sainte-Anne hospital in Paris with erysipelas, eczema and psychiatric troubles. He passed away on June 20, 1883, First buried in the cemetery of Ivry, his body was transferred years later to the family vault of his wife in Écouen (Val d'Oise) where he rests today.

Gustave Aimard is, with Gabriel Ferry, the main representative in France of the western novel. In addition to this type of story, he also wrote maritime novels, patriotic stories and urban mysteries, but the vast majority of his works favor the American continent.

Throughout Aimard's work, we find autobiographical notes. A large number of them deal with his life and his journeys on the American continent. Through all the books he wrote, in most cases through the voice of his fictional alter ego, he bore witness to the search for his biological family. In almost all of his novels, the theme of the abandoned or adopted child is there. In *Les Invisibles de Paris*, he alludes to the death of someone in the Luxembourg prison. It was about the Duke de Praslin, who had murdered his half-sister. In his autobiographical novel, *Par mer et par terre*, he retold the story of her murder.

Between the lines, his books contain many anthropological, and historical facts. Due to his lack of formal education, Aimard seemed to have had difficulty juggling the different roles he had assigned to himself: novelist, historian, anthropologist, etc. For example, in one of his novels, Aimard interrupts the narrative to defend the Indians, saying that, despite what others may have written about them, they are not savages; then, he resumes his story by continuing to describe these same Indians as "red devils."

The stories for which Gustave Aimard is most famous are certainly his westerns. Among these, the most reprinted are *The Trappers of Arkansas* (1858), his first novel, and *The Outlaws of Missouri* (1868). Some are inspired by historical events; others are essentially based on cheap exoticism. There are a few recurring heroes: Valentin Guillois, Coeur-Loyal and Balle-Franche. These works take place mainly in Central America and in the Southern United States, more rarely in Canada or South America.

The second type of stories have the sea and the world of piracy as their settings; this series of maritime sagas takes place in the 17th century, and Vent-En-Panne (but not Bearcub) is a recurring hero. Finally come the minor novels, *Les Invisibles de Paris* and *Les Vauriens du Pont-Neuf*, located in the Parisian underworld, plus a few patriotic novels, and even a robinsonade (*Le Robinson des Alpes*).

It would be ridiculous to claim that Gustave Aimard was a great writer. His style is repetitive, his characters stereotypical, his plots somewhat conventional, and there are often repetitions and continuity errors. The standard Aimard book more or less follows the same structure: a band of Indians and/or bandits, led by a leader who is both noble and perverse, massacres innocent people in a particularly violent way, often eyeing a young girl who belongs to the group of their victims. A woodsman, usually accompanied by a young aristocrat, becomes involved in the matter. He bonds with a band of Comanches (or woodsmen) to fight against the villains. At the end of a particularly violent final combat (and after many scenes of torture and machination), the heroes triumph, the villains are vanquished and violently massacred, and the young aristocrat marries the virgin girl, while the woodsman leaves for more adventures. The traitor always wears deceit on his face (which must be inconvenient!), the Apache are cruel, and the Comanche noble and proud. But despite, or because of, the familiarity of these elements, it is impossible to put the books down.

The fact remains that Gustave Aimard was an important contributor to the history of French popular literature. His works (with Gabriel Ferry's) were the main representatives of what will later be called the western, a new genre of novel based on geographical adventures. His stories bear witness to the hesitations of a genre not yet born. The villains form secret societies and are closer to the criminals of urban mysteries than modern desperadoes. The landscape itself, with its underground passages right in the middle of nature, its forbidden Inca cities, and the disturbing rarity of descriptions of land-scapes, substitutes a kind of abstract no man's land for the more detailed locations. It is akin to the space of a urban serial novel despite the astonishing absence of any actual cities or human habitations. It is a world of no-mads as much as it is a geographical adventure story.

His plots frequently hesitate between a purely his-torical narrative and exotic fantasy. Occasionally, pirates and Indians cross paths, as in J. M. Barrie's *Peter Pan*, and the sentimental romance often holds a considerable place in the story. Finally, by favoring French people, often suspicious of the "Yankees" and foreign to this America which they visit as tourists, Aimard anticipates the tradition of the geographical adventure novel.

Before Aimard, the western novel did not really ex-ist. He was preceded in France by Gabriel Ferry (1809-1852), in Ireland by Mayne Reid (1818-1883) and in Germany, by Charles Sealsfield (1793-1864), Balduin Möllhausen (1825-1905) and Friedrich Gerstäcker (1816-1872). He will be followed by Albert Bonneau (1898-1967) in France, Edward S. Ellis (1840-1916) in Great Britain and Karl May (1842-1912) in Germany and, indirectly, the spaghetti western of Sergio Leone and Segio Corbucci in the Italian cinema of the 1960s and 1970s.

Jean-Marc & Randy Lofficier

Bibliography

1856-57:
Les Compagnons de la nuit (serialized in *La Revue Française* Nos. 58-72)
1858:
Les Trappeurs de l'Arkansas (Amyot).
Le Grand Chef des Aucas (Amyot)
Le Chercheur de pistes (Amyot)
Les Pirates des prairies (Amyot)
1859:
La Loi de Lynch (Amyot)
L'Éclaireur (Amyot)
1860:
La Grande Flibuste (Amyot)
La Fièvre d'or (Amyot)
Curumilla (Amyot)
1861:
Balle Franche (Amyot)
Les Rôdeurs de frontières (Amyot)
Les Francs-tireurs (Amyot)
Le Cœur-Loyal (Amyot)
1862:
Valentin Guillois (Amyot)
La Main ferme (Amyot)
La Grande flibuste (Amyot)
1863:
L'Eau qui court (Amyot)
Les Aventuriers (Amyot)
1864:

Le Guaranis (Amyot)

Le Montonero (sequel to *Le Guaranis*) (Amyot)

Zeno Cabral (conclusion of *Le Guaranis*) (Amyot)

Les Chasseurs d'abeilles (Amyot)

Le Cœur de pierre (Amyot)

Les Nuits mexicaines (Amyot)

Les Aventuriers (Amyot)

L'Araucan (Cadot) (a.k.a. *Le Fils du Soleil*)

Les Fils de la Tortue (Cadot)

Le Lion du désert (Cadot)

Les Flibustiers de la Sonora (5-act play written in collaboration with Amédée Rolland) (Michel Lévy)

La Tour des hiboux (Cadot)

1865:

La Castille d'or (Amyot)

Les Bohèmes de la mer (Amyot)

Un Hiver parmi les indiens Chippewais (short story published in the anthology *Les Plumes d'or*, Dentu)

1866:

Les Gambucinos (Amyot)

Sacramenta (Amyot)

L'Esprit blanc (Amyot)

Une Vendetta mexicaine (Cadot)

1867:

La Mas-Horca (Amyot)

Rosas (Amyot)

Les Vaudoux (Amyot)

Les Chasseurs Mexicains (Degorce-Cadot)

Les Invisibles de Paris (written in collaboration with Henri Crisafulli) (Amyot)

- 1 – *Les Compagnons de la lune*
- 2 – *Passe-partout*
- 3 – *Le Comte de Warrens*
- 4 – *La Cigale*

• 5 −*Hermosa*
1868:
La Légende du saltimbanque (serialized in *Le Monde illustré* Nos.596-602)
La Castille d'or
Les Outlaws du Missouri (Amyot)
Ourson Tête-de-fer (Amyot)
1869:
Le Forestier (Amyot)
Le Roi des Placères d'or (Amyot)
Le Commandant de la campagne (Amyot)
1870:
La Forêt vierge (Dentu)
• 1 – *Fanny Dayton*
• 2 – *Le Désert*
• 3 −*Le Vautour Fauve*
1871:
La Guerre sainte en Alsace (Dubuisson)
1872:
Les Scalpeurs blancs (Dentu)
• 1 – *L'Enigme*
• 2 – *Le Sacripant*
1873:
*Les Titans de la mer (*Amyot)
Les Aventures de Michel Hartmann (Dentu) (a.k.a. *Les Maîtres Espions*)
• 1 – *Les Marquards*
• 2 – *Le Chien Noir*
1874:
La Belle rivière (Dentu)
• 1 – *Le Fort Duquesne*
• 2 – *Le Serpent de Satin*

Cardenio, scènes et récits du nouveau monde, suivi de *Un profil de bandit mexicain, Carmen Frederique Milher* (Dentu)

La Guérilla fantôme (Lachaud et Burdin) (a.k.a. *Dona Flor*)

1875:

Les bois-brulés (Dentu)
• 1 – *Le Voladero*
• 2 – *Le Capitaine Kild*
• 3 –*Le Saut de l'élan*

1876:

Le Chasseur de rats (Dentu)
• 1 – *L'œil gris* (a.k.a. *Les Révoltés*)
• 2 – *Le Commandant Delgrès* (a.k.a. *Le Rapt*)

Les Bisons blancs (Dentu)

Le Pêcheur de perles (Dentu)

Marianita (Dentu)

Le Saut de Sabô (Dentu)

1877:

Les Rois de l'océan (Dentu)
• 1 – *L'Olonnais*
• 2 – *Vent-en-Panne*

Le Baron Frédérick (Dentu)
• 1 – *Une Poignée de coquins*
• 2 – *Le Loup-Garou*
• 3 –*Pris au piège*
• 4 –*Les Fouetteurs de femmes*
• 5 –*La Revanche*

1878:

Les Vauriens du Pont-Neuf (Dentu)
• 1 – *Capitaine d'aventure*
• 2 – *La vie d'estoc et de taille*
• 3 –*Diane de Saint-Hyrem*

Une Goutte de sang noir : épisode de la guerre civile aux États-Unis (Dubuisson)
Les Révoltés (Degorce-Cadot)
La Guérilla fantôme (Degorce-Cadot)
Un Duel au désert (written in collaboration with Jules Berlioz d'Auriac) (Degorce-Cadot)
L'Esprit blanc (written in collaboration with Jules Berlioz d'Auriac) (Degorce-Cadot)
L'Aigle noir des Dacotahs (written in collaboration with Jules Berlioz d'Auriac) (Degorce-Cadot)
Le Mangeur de Poudre (written in collaboration with Jules Berlioz d'Auriac) (Degorce-Cadot)
Les Pieds fourchus (written in collaboration with Jules Berlioz d'Auriac) (Degorce-Cadot)
Rayon-de-Soleil (written in collaboration with Jules Berlioz d'Auriac) (Degorce-Cadot)
Le Scalpeur des Ottawas (written in collaboration with Jules Berlioz d'Auriac) (Degorce-Cadot)
1879:
Œil-de-Feu (written in collaboration with Jules Berlioz d'Auriac) (Degorce-Cadot)
Cœur-de-Panthère (written in collaboration with Jules Berlioz d'Auriac) (Degorce-Cadot)
Les Terres d'or (written in collaboration with Jules Berlioz d'Auriac) (Degorce-Cadot)
Les Forestiers du Michigan (written in collaboration with Jules Berlioz d'Auriac) (Degorce-Cadot)
Jim l'Indien (written in collaboration with Jules Berlioz d'Auriac) (Degorce-Cadot) (a.k.a. *L'Œuvre infernale*)
La Caravane des sombreros (written in collaboration with Jules Berlioz d'Auriac) (Degorce-Cadot)
Les Coupeurs de routes (Dentu)
• 1 – *El platero de Urès*
• 2 – *Une vengeance de Peau-Rouge*

Par Mer et par Terre (autobiography) (Ollendorf)
- 1 – *Le Corsaire*
- 2 – *Le Bâtard*

Le Rapt (Dentu)

Le Fils du soleil (Dentu)

1880:

Une Passion indienne

L'Héroïne du désert

L'Ami des blancs

1881:

Le Rancho du pont des lianes (Dentu)

Les Chasseurs de minuit (Dentu)

Rosarita la pampera (Dentu)

Les Bandits de l'Arizona : Scènes de la vie sauvage (Blériot) (a.k.a. *Les Pirates de l'Arizona*)

1882:

Cornelio d'Armor (Dentu)

Au Bivouac, récits militaires (?)
- 1 – *L'Étudiant en théologie*
- 2 – *L'Homme-Tigre*

Le Souriquet (Dentu)
- 1 – *René de Vitré*
- 2 – *Michel Belhumeur*

1883:

Le Rastréador (Dentu)
- 1 – *Les Plateados*
- 2 – *Le Doigt de Dieu*

Les Batteurs de sentiers (Dentu)

Sacramenta (Dentu)

1884:

Mariami l'Indienne

Don Marcos

1886:

Le Brésil nouveau Mon dernier voyage (Dentu,

1888:
Les Peaux-Rouges de Paris (Dentu)
Le Trouveur de sentiers (Dentu)
Le Roi des Ténèbres (Dentu)
Le Robinson des Alpes (Bleriot)
1891:
Les Pirates des prairies (Dentu)
1893:
L'Oiseau noir, histoire américaine (Dentu)

LE VOLUME COMPLET
65 CENT.

GUSTAVE AIMARD

AVENTURES
EXPLORATIONS
VOYAGES

VALENTIN GUILLOIS

A. FAYARD Éditeur

Dedication

To:
MONSIEUR PAUL GRANIER DE CASSAGNAC
Editor of *le Pays*,
KNIGHT OF THE LEGION OF HONOR

My dear Paul,

We are both members of the great Republic of Letters. This literary fraternity introduced us to each other only a year ago. Such short acquaintanceship has, nevertheless, allowed me to appreciate what is in your heart and mind.

Despite the significant differences that will always exist between our political opinions, it is with real pleasure that I dedicate this book, which serves as a link in our bond, to you. Also, with it, I take the opportunity to call myself, most sincerely

Your friend,

GUSTAVE AIMARD.

Paris, October 15, 1868.

Foreword

A brief introduction, in which the author reveals to the reader how he was led, when he least expected it, to tell this story

On my last trip to America—the date of which, by the way, although not specified here, is not as far in the past as many of my *excellent friends* in the press and others, pretend to believe—the ship on which I had taken passage at Le Havre, battered by several storms in the Lesser Antilles, arrived full windward on the island of St. Christopher,[2] where it took refuge as quickly as possible, in order to empty the bilge, which its pumps could not manage *to drain*, as the sailors say in their picturesque language.

The island of St. Christopher, of which I wrote in a previous work on the *Brothers of the Coast*, these notorious pariahs of the 17th century, although I did not know it then, was in reality the cradle of the freebooters. It was from there that they set out, like vultures, heading for Tortuga and Santo Domingo.

St. Christopher, which the Caribbean natives called *Liamiuga,*[3] is today part of the British West Indies in the Leeward Islands or *Iles sous-le-Vent* in French.[4] It is fif-

---

[2] today called Saint Kitts.

[3] "Fertile island."

[4] Around 1300 AD, the Kalinago, or Carib people, arrived on the islands. A Spanish expedition under Christopher Columbus claimed the island for Spain in 1493. The first English colony was established in 1623, followed by a French colony

ty-six miles WNW of Antigua, and seventy-eight miles NW of Guadeloupe, all near and NW of Nevis Island at 170°, 18° N latitude and 65° W longitude. Its total length is fifteen miles; and it is of volcanic origin, like most of the other islands in the West Indies. It is crossed by a chain of mountains, of which Mount Misery,[5] an extinct volcano 3701 feet high, is the highest point.

This island, which flourishes today and does considerable trade in rum, sugar, coffee, cotton, etc., is well-populated.

The French, in the 18th century, called it *l'Île Douce*; and a proverb widely known throughout the West Indies says: "*Nobility lives on St. Christopher, the Bourgeois on Guadeloupe, the soldiers on Martinique, and the peasants on Grenada.*"

Despite all the vicissitudes experienced by this island for nearly a century, before it was definitively ceded to England by the Treaty of Versailles,[6] a few French families continued to live there and most of them enjoy a

---

in 1625. The English and French briefly united to pre-empt a Kalinago ambush and massacre the natives. They then partitioned the island, with the English in the middle and the French on either end. In 1629, a Spanish force seized St. Kitts. The English settlement was rebuilt following the 1630 peace between England and Spain. The island alternated repeatedly between English and French control during the 17th and 18th centuries. Since 1783, it has been affiliated with the Kingdom of Great Britain, which became the United Kingdom.

[5] Now Mt. Lamiugia.

[6] Not the better-known Treaty of Versailles of 1919, of course. The British were first granted sole dominion under the Treaty of Utrecht in 1713. This consolidation of British rule was further recognized by the Treaty of Versailles (aka the "Peace of Paris") in 1783.

well-deserved reputation for loyalty and intelligence. These families, although living under the protectorate of England, remained essentially French, and although descended from the first owners of the island, they consider themselves foreigners and recognize no authority other than that of the French Consul of Basse-Terre, the capital city of the island.

When we anchored at Sandy Point, the captain of the ship warned me that our stay would be quite long and that we would remain on St. Christopher for at least three weeks.

At first, I was rather upset; but as a life of travels has provided me—thank God!—with a rather strong dose of practical philosophy, I took this setback fairly easily, and tried to arrange things so I could spend these three weeks as pleasantly as possible.

It wasn't easy: the English, who are already difficult to get to know at home, and who do not particularly care for foreigners, are unbearable in their colonies. I must confess in all humility, that I have never felt great sympathy for those selfish, cold, affected, pompous islanders, who profess a profound contempt for all but themselves, and who, whatever they may say, particularly hate the French, who admittedly reciprocate those feelings, especially when they meet each other in Asia, Africa and America, indeed, everywhere these modern Carthaginians have run into each other.

So, I did not for a single moment think about presenting myself to the island's authorities, or asking for an introduction to any English residents. Tea makes my stomach turn and the British arrogance is nerve-wracking.

After rummaging through all my papers, I finally discovered a letter of introduction, which by chance one of my Creole friends from Guadeloupe, who is now the editor of one of our major political newspapers, had given me the day before my departure from Paris.

"You never know what might happen," he had said to me when he had handed me this letter. "Perhaps circumstances impossible to foresee might take you to St. Christopher. I know all about your Anglophobia, so here is a letter for one of my relatives whom, I believe, still lives near Basse-Terre, I don't know exactly where, for I have never met him, never been to that island. But don't worry, just present yourself boldly, this letter in hand, and you will be well received."

I had put the letter, along with many others like it, at the bottom of my trunk and never given it another thought.

But the captain's words and the threat of a prolonged stay in St. Christopher reminded me of that letter I had then foolishly scorned, and it was with a real sense of joy that I finally discovered it under a pile of papers.

It was addressed to Comte Henry de Châteaugrand, landowner on St. Christopher. I carefully placed the precious talisman in my wallet and calmed myself.

My first task, after I had disembarked, was to rent a horse and a guide, for two pounds, which I thought was quite expensive for a trip unlikely to take more than a couple of hours, Then we set out for Basse-Terre, where I arrived at three o'clock in the afternoon.

I didn't exchange a single word with my guide during the entire trip, which probably did not give him a high opinion of me. Instead, I was content to admire the landscape, which was quite beautiful and very mountainous.

One must admit that the English, wherever they gain a foothold, immediately imprint a special stamp on that country, giving it life, movement, and that feverish activity which is the secret of their commercial prosperity. I had rarely seen better tended land, more carefully maintained roads, and more charming cottages, even in Europe.

I was enchanted by the delightful picture of this small island, lost in the immensity of the Atlantic, that exuded such well-being and prosperity. Indeed, it was so overwhelming that I blushed inwardly for us, Frenchmen, are so very clumsy in all that concerns colonization. We have managed within a few short years of occupation, thanks to our obdurate and unimaginative military rule, to turn the most fertile and populated countries into vast and arid deserts.

Upon arriving at Basse-Terre, my guide respectfully asked me if I was staying at the Hotel Victoria. In every English colony, there is a "Hotel Victoria" and a "Hotel d'Albion."

I asked him instead to take me directly to the French Consulate.

Five minutes later, I stood before the consul's house. It was a delightful cottage, set between a courtyard and garden, located on the quay itself.

I trembled with joy when I saw the wide folds of our beloved tricolor flag undulating in the capricious breath of the sea breeze. Abroad, I am *chauvinistic*—I confess in all humility—and I am very much in agreement with our good General Lallemand who said that every Frenchman on foreign soil should represent France and make her respected by his behavior.

The post of vice-consul, on this island was one of the most pleasant sinecures in the world. As there are no more than three French ships arriving in St. Christopher in a year, the vice-consul was reduced to crossing his arms from morning to evening, like the consul general of the King of Siam in Paris. But our representative, an eminently distinguished man and a fanatical naturalist, had managed to create his own special occupation, which did not leave him a moment of leisure.

I will use the pseudonym of M. Ducray for this excellent man, to whom I am indebted for not having died of boredom on St. Christopher. M. Ducray was forty-five years-old; he was tall and well-dressed; his manners were elegant; his open physiognomy was refined and spiritual, and he was essentially sympathetic. He belonged to one of those French families of which I spoke above, and was a well-considered, even by the English authorities of the island.

He received me with great delight, and made me dismiss my guide and my horse, telling me that I would be his honored guest for all the time of my stay in St. Christopher. A black servant took care of my coat, then M. Ducray took me to his private apartments, and led me to a charming room with a stunning view over the harbor.

"Here you are at home," he said with a smile. "You will stay here for the duration of your stay on the island."

As I tried to protest and tell him how much trouble and embarrassment the intrusion of a stranger into his home might cause him, he replied:

"First of all, my dear sir, you are not a stranger, but a compatriot, that is to say, a friend. Besides, you will have complete freedom to come in and go out, and do as you please. No one will think of inquiring about your affairs. I am alone at the moment. My wife and daughter are in Antigua, staying with one of their close relatives, and planned to spend another two months there. I am consequently, if temporarily a bachelor. Therefore, not only won't you disturb me in any way, but you will do me a real service by relieving me of my loneliness and accepting my hospitality."

There was nothing more to say. I shook hands with M. Ducray and he let me tidy up. A little later, I joined him in the salon.

Our vice-consul had been warned the very morning of our arrival, and was waiting for the captain who'd been invited to dinner.

In my haste to go ashore, I regretted not having told the Captain of the excursion I was planning; but the damage was done, and there was no longer any point in berating myself about it.

"I forgot to mention," said M. Ducray with a smile, "that the bell rings four times a day, for breakfast, lunch, dinner and supper, which is at eight o'clock in the evening."

"Oh, but you eat all day long?" I asked him, laughing.

"More or less," he replied in the same tone. "We have adopted English customs. As you know, the English are great eaters—and especially great drinkers. But don't let that worry you; here, we eat and drink only when we're hungry and thirsty; so you have been warned. Besides, when the bell rings, we don't wait for anyone to sit down to the table: you don't have to be more uncomfortable with us than we will be with you. You must resign yourself, my dear sir, I have indeed taken you hostage. What can I say? We don't see enough French folks on this island for us to let them escape when, by chance, a few of them show up. Now, come and see my collections; they are very beautiful and, above all, quite curious…"

I followed him immediately.

What M. Ducray modestly called his "collections" was, quite simply, a museum, which occupied five large rooms of his house. There, he had gathered, with remarkable patience and intelligence, specimens of the flora so rich and so numerous of all the West Indies, large and small. The fauna of these islands was also richly represented there, in both mammalogical and entomological forms; then came minerals of all kinds and Caribbean antiquities, discovered God knows how; and all this was labeled with such order and care that it would have made any employee of our museums in Paris green with envy.

Humboldt, d'Orbigny[7] and a couple of other illustrious scholars had visited this museum, or these "collections," as the reader might prefer to call them, and had been amazed. I had never seen anything so curious and interesting.

Three hours passed with extreme rapidity in the midst of all these marvels, which I did not tire of admiring, and I would have remained there without paying attention to the time, if a servant had not come to announce the arrival of M. Dumont, my captain.

M. Dumont was waiting for the vice-consul in the salon. The brave captain was, at first, quite surprised to see me, as he thought I had remained at Sandy-Point; but soon everything was explained.

Five minutes later, we sat down at the table. The conversation first went on about France and the events

---

[7] Friedrich Wllhelm Heinrich Alexander von Humboldt (1769-1859) was a German polymath, geographer, and naturalist; Alcide Charles Victor Marie Dessalines d'Orbigny (1802-1857) was a French naturalist.

that had taken place there in the last few months; the captain had brought a bundle of newspapers which he gave to M. Ducray, who, completely ignorant of European affairs, was very flattered by this opportunity to get up to date with our national politics. Then, after a chat about a loan which the captain wanted to take to repair the damage to his ship, had been discussed between him and the vice-consul, the conversation took a sudden turn and, quite naturally, fell on the island of St. Christopher.

There, M. Ducray was on comfortable grounds, and, very obligingly, told us of the habits of the island's Creoles, and of the limited number of attractions and resources that it offered to visiting foreigners.

"You have several French families who live here?" asked the captain. "Are they wealthy? Well regarded?"

"Yes, they are in general quite rich, and very well regarded by the British authorities, although they have very few points of contact with them," answered M. Ducray. "All these families have remained French; no solicitations, no flattery, could force them to accept British citizenship; they remain stubbornly attached to their French citizenship. Their children are brought up in France, for the most part, and serve our country either in the army, the magistracy or in diplomacy. Then after their debt has been paid, these soldiers, magistrates or diplomats, come back here to quietly finish their days."

"Do you know, it is simply magnificent, what you just told us!" I exclaimed.

"But not very extraordinary," M. Ducray commented with bonhomie. "Politics has its own requirements, which private individuals are not obliged to follow. It is more or less the same in all the former French colonies. However, I must confess that these prejudices—this is what the British call this stubborn attachment to our

33

homeland—are much more ingrained here than any-where else."

"To what cause do you attribute this fact?" I asked with curiosity.

"In the past, St. Christopher was owned by both the French and the British. By a singular chance, as French adventurers landed on one side, British adventurers arrived on the other at the same time. At first, these adventurers cohabited in good company; then the French pushed the British out and remained sole masters of the island. The British tried, on several occasions, to regain a foothold, but always in vain. But you know," he added, "how stubbornness is the British' most precious quality. The Treaty of Versailles[8] finally settled the question in their favor, but it was stipulated that French families who wished to continue to reside on the island would be free to do so while retaining their own citizenship. These families were all descended from the original French occupants, each of them having, among their ancestors, at least one of those famous freebooters who, for nearly a century, held Europe in check and made Spain tremble, since it was that country at which they struck with their first and harshest blows."

"Thus the present French residents are descendants..."

"...Of the same buccaneers, who later occupied Tortuga Island," he completed, "and of more than half of the island of Saint-Domingue. I, myself, am the great-grandson of a famous Ducray, who, with only a hundred men, took Grenada and ransomed it.[9] The Marquis de la

[8] See Note 6, Page 24.
[9] The Capture of Grenada was an amphibious expedition in July 1779 during the American Revolutionary War. Charles

Motheherbue is closely allied with Monsieur d'Ogeron.[10]
The Baron Ducasse is descended from the famous buccaneer.[11] The Chevalier du Plessis,[12] the Baron du Ros-
sey, the Comte de Châteaugrand, the Chevalier Levasseur,[13] all are descended from freebooters who en-
joyed worldwide fame. You can well understand that
these men, whose ancestors spread the French influence
in the Americas, are jealous of their title of Frenchmen,
and are anxious to stay on a land for which their ances-

Hector, Comte D'Estaing, led French forces against the Brit-
ish-held island of Grenada. If there was a Ducray who took
part in the battle, I couldn't locate his name.

[10] Bertrand d'Ogeron de La Bouëre (1613-1676) was governor
of Tortuga Island and Haiti from June 1665 to the end of 1668,
then, after a short interim, from 1669 to 1673 and from April
1673 to the beginning of 1675, a total of ten years at the head.
of that buccaneering colony.

[11] Jean-Baptiste du Casse (1646-1715) was a French privateer,
admiral, and colonial administrator during the 17th and 18th
centuries. He took part in several victorious expeditions during
the War of the League of Augsburg in the West Indies and
Spanish South America. During the War of the Spanish Suc-
cession, he participated in several key naval battles, including
the Battle of Málaga and the siege of Barcelona. In the midst
of these wars, he was Governor of Saint-Domingue from 1691
to 1703.

[12] French pirate active in the West Indies and the Caribbean in
the 1660s, died in 1668.

[13] Olivier Levasseur (c.1688-1730), was a French pirate, nicknamed La Buse ("The Buzzard") for the speed and ruthless-
ness with which he attacked his enemies. He is known for allegedly hiding one of the biggest treasures in pirate history,
estimated and leaving a cryptogram behind with clues to its
whereabouts.

tors fought under the leadership of the great Montbarts[14] himself."

"Of course, I understand this, and I am proud on behalf of my country of this unbreakable loyalty to our common homeland; but, pardon me, among the people whose names you just mentioned, I believed was that of the Comte de Châteaugrand?"

"I mentioned it indeed, Monsieur," replied the vice-consul with his charming smile, "because it is perhaps the most honorable and revered on this island. This name is dear to us in many ways. Do you know, by any chance, know Monsieur le Comte?"

"How could I, Monsieur, since I have never set foot on your island before?"

"This would not necessarily be an obstacle, Monsieur. You might know the Châteaugrand from the younger branch of the family. They come from the Angoumois,[15] where some of its members still reside."

"Alas no, Monsieur. I merely carry a letter of introduction that, before leaving Paris, M. P*** de C*** from Guadeloupe kindly gave me for Comte Henry de Châteaugrand."

"Oh! Then you will be well received by Comte Henry, and in fact, I shall take it upon myself to introduce you tomorrow."

---

[14] Daniel Montbars (1645–1707?), better known as Montbars the Exterminator, was a 17th-century French buccaneer. For several years, he was known as one of the most violent buccaneers active against the Spanish during the mid-17th century. His reputation as a fierce enemy of the Spanish Empire was matched only by François L'Olonnais.

[15] Historically the County of Angoulême in Western France, part of the parent duchy of Aquitaine.

"Your kindness overwhelms me, Monsieur; but who is this Comte Henry, whose name you appear to pronounce only with reverence?"

M. Ducray smiled and leaned on the table while playing with his knife.

"Monsieur," he said, "Comte Henry de Châteaugrand is one of those elite beings, one of those great characters, that nature only creates every hundred years perhaps. Since you are going to be meet him, it is necessary that I describe him to you in a few words…"

"I would be much obliged."

"Comte Henry de Châteaugrand is now ninety-six years-old; he is a tall man, with energetic, fine and distinguished features; his eyes are lively; his gentle, spiritual physiognomy has an expression of inexpressible kindness, to which his long locks of his silver hair and white beard almost falling on his chest, add a stamp of grandeur and majesty. In spite of his advanced age, the Comte is still robust; his waist is straight, muscular; he rides and hunts as if he were only forty; fatigue and illness have no hold on his vigorous nature; barring unforeseen accidents, he is cut out to live another fifty years. As he is in physique, so he is in character. After having fought in the American War of Independence alongside Rochambeau and the Marquis de La Fayette, he followed his former general and friend back to France.

"In 1789, he was twenty-seven years-old. He was one of the rare gentlemen who greeted the dawn of the new era with sincere enthusiasm. M. de Châteaugrand was a warrior, and so he took his place in our army in 1792. He left as a volunteer for the northern border; he was Pichegru's[16] aide-de-camp during the taking of Wissembourg. In 1795, he was made a general. Later, he followed General Bonaparte to Egypt. The 18 Brumaire[17] saddened him; he understood the abyss towards which the irrational enthusiasm of the masses was dragging France. The hero of Lodi and the Pyramids was taking giant steps towards the goal he had made for himself; the fascinated populace followed him and acclaimed him—he was no longer Bonaparte, he was not yet Augustus, he was Caesar, he only had to extend his arm to seize the imperial purple and confiscate for his own benefit the liberties so dearly won by nearly fifteen years of a gigantic struggle, sustained against all of Europe in arms.

"The last hour of the Republic rang. The Comte de Châteaugrand understood that the role of the real soldiers of 1792 was over, and that from now on, all the aspirations of France would be stifled and absorbed by the glory of a single man. The Comte sadly bowed his head, broke his sword, and forever left France, crying over her and her destiny. He returned to St. Christopher, where he locked himself up as if in an impregnable citadel, and since that day, has never left his mansion. This is who is the Comte de Châteaugrand is. Each new victory in the dazzling imperial epic made him tremble like a

---

[16] Jean-Charles Pichegru (1761-1804) was a French general of the Revolutionary Wars. Under his command, French troops overran Belgium and the Netherlands before fighting on the Rhine front.

[17] The Coup d'état of 18 Brumaire (9 November 1799) brought Napoleon Bonaparte to power as First Consul of France. In the view of most historians, it ended the French Revolution and led to the Coronation of Napoleon as Emperor.

wounded lion. This grandiose utopia of the reconstruction of Charlemagne's throne frightened him. As early as 1809, he foresaw 1814.[18]; His predictions came true; he moaned bitterly, because behind the titan struck by lightning, he saw the dangling body of France, agonizing and struggling in the throes of death; but he remained faithful to his oath and his convictions. Many offers were made to him, but he rejected them all.

"On learning of the revolution of 1848, he smiled sadly: 'Where is the enthusiasm of 1792?' he asked. 'A government does not impose itself, whatever its name; one does not do the same thing twice; the fall then is grotesque or miserable.' Since then, not a word has come out of his mouth about political events. He lives patriarchally in the midst of his family, but his eyes are constantly turned towards this France for which he has shed his blood on twenty battlefields, from which he has voluntarily exiled himself, and which he will never see again."

Captain Dumont and I had listened to this simple and beautiful story with deep emotion.

"*Sacrebleu!*" cried the captain, "your Comte is a great man!"

"Yes," continued M. Ducray smiling, "he is a man whose heart is immense, capable of all sacrifices, but who will die ignored by his country, for which he has sacrificed so much. The ingratitude of peoples is the halo that God puts on the forehead of great citizens. But I will not bore further on this subject. Tomorrow, Monsieur, you will see the Comte and you will judge him for yourself. Now, gentlemen, here are some cigars from Havana. I guarantee you they are excellent!"

---

[18] First abdication of Napoleon (4 April 1814).

"One more question, please, Monsieur, if I may?" I asked as I chose a cigar.

"Of course. Speak up, Monsieur."

"This Comte de Châteaugrand is also descended from a famous freebooter?"

"Perhaps the greatest of all, for his glory was always without blemish. He was neither cruel like Montbarts the Exterminator, his friend, nor a pillager like Morgan[19], nor ferocious like L'Olonnais,[20] nor debauched and vindictive like Beau Laurent.[21] This man, whose exploits made Spain tremble for so long, forced even his enemies to admire him."

"Oh-oh! I think I know his name then," I said, "because in *The Annals of Freebooting*, written by Olivier Œxmelin,[22] there is only one man who resembles the splendid portrait you have just drawn."

"Who?" asked the vice-consul with a smile.

"Captain Bearcub Ironskull."

"Well, my dear Monsieur," replied M. Ducray, rising to take us to the terrace to enjoy the sea breeze,

---

[19] Henry Morgan (c.1635-1688) was a Welsh privateer, plantation owner, and, later, Lieutenant Governor of Jamaica.

[20] Jean-David Nau (c.1630-c.1669), better known as François L'Olonnais, was a French pirate active in the Caribbean during the 1660s.

[21] Louis-Laurent Aubin du Plessis a.k.a. Beau Laurent (1700-?) was another French pirate active during the same time.

[22] Alexandre Olivier Exquemelin (also spelled Esquemeling, Exquemeling, or Oexmelin) (c.1645–1707) was a French, Dutch or Flemish writer best known as the author of one of the most important sourcebooks of 17th-century piracy, first published in Dutch as *De Americaensche Zee-Roovers* [The American Freebooters] in Amsterdam, by Jan ten Hoorn, in 1678.

"Comte Henry de Châteaugrand is indeed the great-grandson of Bearcub Ironskull."

I was literally stunned by that revelation, so unexpected it was.

The entire night passed without me being able to sleep, or even wanting to, despite the fact that the bed that M. Ducray had given me was excellent. However, the curiosity that I felt caused me such nervous excitement that I couldn't rest. I was anxious to meet this man who was so brave and in whom, after four generations, the noble qualities of his ancestor were still present.

For Bearcub Ironskull was an old friend of mine. I had read and reread a hundred times the tale of his wondrous life, his strange adventures, and his extraordinary exploits, written by these few authors who dealt with these great reprobates of the 17th century who called themselves the *Brothers of the Coast*.

But several points had remained constantly obscure to me, in the accounts that I had read so avidly about the life of that famous adventurer. Undoubtedly, Olivier Oexmelin, an otherwise reliable chronicler, who himself had participated in most of the scenes which he narrated with such naive bonhomie, as well as the other authors who had dealt with the same subject, knew only Bearcub Ironskull as the hero, the public man, but had completely ignored the private man. Nowhere had I found any details about the private life of this great man, who was always wrapped up in a glorious halo—or so it seemed to me—and yet, must have loved, suffered and struggled like any other members of our great human family.

It was this dark point that I was burning to clear up, these precious details that I wanted so much to learn.

Someone—I don't know who—said, "No man is great in the eyes of his valet." This saying, more specious than accurate, spurred my curiosity, and pushed me to try to discover by all means possible those intimate details which are so valuable to completely and truly understand a man.

The dawn finally appeared to my great relief. However, I had to be patient again, and not give my excellent host an unfortunate opinion of me by acting in clumsy haste and put him in the obligation of fulfilling the promise he had made to me.

Around eight o'clock in the morning, however, I couldn't hold my impatience any longer and went downstairs. My host was fully dressed and had been waiting for me, smoking a cigar, walking back and forth in the salon.

"Ah!" he said when he saw me. "There you are. It seems to me that you slept well."

"Perfectly," I replied with a smile, despite the fact that I had barely closed my eyes.

"I've been up since six. All the chancery business is done. I want to devote my whole day to you."

"While thanking you again for your infinite hospitality, I regret to cause you this embarrassment."

"What embarrassment are you talking about?"

"But this early morning visit..."

M. Ducray began to laugh.

"You must be joking!" he said. "We get up very early in the colonies in order to take advantage of the sea breeze. Business is done in the early hours of the morning. In the middle of the day, we close the house and everyone rests."

"I should have known!" I muttered dejectedly.

"What should you have known?" asked M. Ducray, puzzled.

"What you just said. My desire to meet Comte Henry was so great that I didn't sleep a wink all night, and didn't get up earlier for fear of disturbing you."

"Ah!" he cried, laughing. "My dear Monsieur, you certainly made a mistake; judge for yourself: since I got up, I arranged for the loan your captain needed, he already left for Sandy-Point half an hour ago, his money in his pocket, and very happy, I assure you."

"I believe you."

"Then, as I have told you, I settled various affairs of the chancery and I even had time to take a tour of the harbor. Furthermore, I sent to the Comte de Châteaugrand a courier to announce our arrival, so that we are now expected to have lunch there. Then, I came back here to smoke a cigar while waiting for you to get up. Now do you still believe me when I say that you wouldn't have inconvenienced me at all by coming down earlier? But let's not talk about that anymore. Instead, let's drink a glass of old rum, let's light a cigar, then let's ride! We have about three leagues to go."

What was said was done, then five minutes later, after having drunk a glass of excellent rum and lit a no less excellent cigar, we were on horseback. Two servants, in livery and on horseback like us, followed us at a respectful distance.

The morning was magical, the air cool, the breeze fresh; we followed a road as perfectly maintained as an alley in a royal park, lined with these magnificent plants of the tropics which spread such a pleasant coolness; thousands of birds were singing at full throat, huddled under the foliage, and we saw, jumping from branch to branch and making the most grotesque grimaces, peculiar little monkeys particular to the island St. Christopher, whose species is found only there.

These animals are, by the way, a real scourge for the settlers who do not know how to get rid of them, and whose crops they devastate.

After about three quarters of an hour, we arrived at the foot of a rather high cliff, at the top of which had been built a mansion, or rather a magnificent castle, surrounded on all sides, except the seaside, by a luxuriant vegetation, almost buried in an ocean of greenery.

"Do you see this castle?" M. Ducray asked me.

"Certainly, I can—and it looks beautiful!"

"It is indeed! Well, my dear countryman, in the same place where this castle stands today, where we are going, there stood, at another time, a small house built by Montbarts himself right after his arrival in the Americas. It was his first residence in the New World, and it was there that he planned the famous expedition that was to give the Brothers of the Coast the island of Tortuga and a good portion of the island of Santo Domingo."

"The position was well chosen, for it's a real eagle's nest."

"Or more accurately, a vulture's nest! This house was given to Bearcub Ironskull, his crewmate, by Montbarts himself, some time after the famous Cartagena expedition."

While talking like this, we had crossed the rather steep ramp that led to the castle and had arrived on a large terraced esplanade, surrounded by walls and lined with trees. After having crossed a wrought-iron gate, curiously wrought, and having for nearly five minutes followed a wide alley lined with aloes and candle-cacti, we stopped in front of a marble porch with double stairs, at the top of which an old man of high stature, with a long white beard and a kind and proud face, was waiting for us.

Because of the description that M. Ducray had given me the day before, I immediately recognized the Comte de Châteaugrand. There was no mistake, the resemblance was striking.

The reception was most cordial. The Comte took my letter of introduction, but barely cast his eyes over it, and after having shaken my hand affectionately and welcomed me, he preceded us and introduced us into a huge salon, furnished entirely in the fashion of the late 18th century, that is to say, the last years of Louis XVI. No one was there when we were introduced.

The Comte invited us to have a drink, according to the Creole custom, which means that, in each house, refreshments are prepared in advance and left there, so that any visitor doesn't even need to formulate a desire. Then, while smoking and drinking, we chatted while waiting for lunch.

I confess that I took very little part in the conversation. As soon as I had entered the room, my attention had been grabbed by a magnificent signed portrait signed by Philippe de Champaigne, 1672, that is to say one of the last masterpieces by this great painter, since he died in 1674.[23]

This painting of colossal dimensions, since it was more than fifteen feet tall, hung alone in the salon; it depicted the rugged landscape of Santo Domingo; on the right, a man on his knees, half-dressed, whose face could hardly be seen, was cooking meat on a barbecue; in the background, one could glimpse. through a clearing be-

---

[23] Philippe de Champaigne (1602-1674) was a French Baroque era painter, and a founding member of the *Académie Royale de Peinture et de Sculpture* in Paris, the premier art institution in France in the 18th century.

tween the trees of a thick forest, several Spanish soldiers, armed with long spears, who seemed to advance cautiously. At the front, almost seeming to step out of the canvas, was a man of about thirty, dressed in a rough blouse and breeches stained with fat and blood, with knee-high, fawn-colored leather boots and a crocodile skin belt tightened his waist. In it were four long knives in sheaths also made of crocodile skin, on the left, and on the right, a bag of bullets and a bull horn.

This man leaned his two crossed hands on the end of the barrel of a long, silver-trimmed rifle, the stock of which rested near his left foot. Beside him lay three hounds with fawn hair speckled with black, broad chests, and long, floppy ears, as well as three wild boars.

The features of this man, except for the difference in age and the blue-black color of his long hair and the beard that covered his chest, bore a striking resemblance to those of the Comte de Châteaugrand. They shared the same expression, spiritual and energetic at the same time, and even the same lightning in their eyes. A ray of sunlight played on this man's face where it cast a shadow that impressed on his physiognomy a stamp of inexpressible melancholy.

This was undoubtedly the portrait of one of those fearsome freebooters of Santo Domingo, who dealt with the most powerful sovereigns of this world on an equal footing. This man must have been one of the Comte's ancestors—probably Bearcub Ironskull himself.

My preoccupation became so great that the Comte finally noticed it; he followed the direction of my gaze, and with a charming bonhomie, said:

"Ah-ah! You like this painting. Well, what do you think of it, my dear compatriot?"

"I think that it is a masterpiece, Monsieur le Comte."

"Yes, Philippe de Champaigne excelled especially in portraits, as you probably know."

"So it is a portrait," I replied with naive hypocrisy.

"Of course!" he said, proudly raising his head. "It is the portrait of my grandfather, Captain Bearcub Ironskull. He wanted to be painted like that, in his buccaneer outfit, when he returned to France after his marriage."

"What…?" I cried, but stopping before saying anymore.

The Comte smiled.

"Don't you know the story of this famous leader of the Brothers of the Coast?" he asked.

"Only a little, Monsieur le Comte, and I regret it very much, because never has history interested me more than in this man's case."

At that moment, the bell rang and the Comte took us into the dining room.

Several people were waiting for us; among them were three ladies, still young and very beautiful, and four men, two of whom were between twenty and twenty-five. The first two were the Comte's sons-in-law; the two youngest, his nephews.

The Comte introduced me, then we sat down at the table.

"I have two other sons," he said, "but they are absent; the first is a Rear Admiral and commands the station in Brazil, the other is a Major General and is, I believe, in Rome at the moment."

I spent two days at the castle; the Comte did not want to let me return to Basse-Terre.

My visits became frequent, so much so that I soon got into the habit of coming every day to dine at the castle and spend the evening with the Comte and his family.

The Comte was a very good talker, which we no longer know how to do today; his memory, which was good and reliable, provided me with a quantity of funny anecdotes about the last years of the reign of Louis XVI and the first years of the Revolution. He had known all the famous people of these times intimately and told some rather strange stories about them.

He had met Danton, Camille Desmoulins, the two Robespierre, Saint-Just, Fouché, and he made me see these men, who had exerted such a great influence on the Revolution, in a very different light than that in which I had perceived them until then.

The Comte neither judged nor criticized; he communicated frankly and clearly what he had seen and heard, and left it to his listener to draw the consequence of what he had told him.

Our evenings went by with extreme rapidity during these charming conversations, intermingled sometimes, but rarely, with music; for the piano, that scourge created for the despair of our ears, has now crossed the seas and penetrated even the harmless island of St. Christopher.

However, one thing tormented me: often I had tried to turn the conversation to the freebooters, but each time the Comte had immediately diverted it back to another topic. He seemed to take a malicious pleasure in teasing me by not wanting to let me formulate the request which was constantly on my lips, without me ever being able to articulate it clearly.

Time passed quickly; I had been in St. Christopher for nearly a month when Captain Dumont notified me that the repairs to his ship had been completed, that he was storing food and water on board, and that he was planning to set sail within the next two days.

I felt sad to leave these hosts who had welcomed me, a total stranger, so warmly. I didn't know how to say goodbye to them. I even hesitated to do so and postponed as much as possible the moment of our separation, which was likely to be forever.

However, I finally had to resolve to announce my departure. The next day, at eight o'clock in the morning, the ship would set sail. I had to return to Sandy-Point and embark immediately.

The captain had been kind enough to let me know me that a dinghy would be waiting for me until midnight. As it was eight o'clock in the evening, I didn't have a moment to lose.

The separation was painful, this charming family having become accustomed to me and already considering me as an old friend. They all wanted to accompany me to the gate, where a servant of M. Ducray was waiting with two horses that this excellent man had put at my disposal.

The farewells lasted quite a long time, then we had to separate, and I left.

At eleven o'clock in the evening, I arrived at Sandy-Point. Just as I was about to step aboard the dinghy that was to take me back to the ship, the servant who had accompanied me respectfully stopped me.

"Excuse me, Sir," he said. "Monsieur le Comte instructed me to give you this, ordering me to tell you that it was a souvenir he was giving you so that you would not forget the family of Châteaugrand."

I took the carefully wrapped, tied and sealed package he gave me, put a louis in his hand, and got into the dinghy.

The next day, when I woke up, we were at sea; the island of St. Christopher appeared only as a bluish cloud on the horizon that was fading away and would soon disappear completely.

Then I remembered the mysterious package, which the Comte de Châteaugrand had given me in such a peculiar fashion. I opened it and suddenly. I let out a cry of joyful surprise and dropped it. I hurried to pick it up. Then, having locked my cabin so as not to be disturbed, I sat at my desk and carefully set the package down in front of me.

It first contained a note with a few lines, addressed to me, that said:

My dear fellow countryman,

Forgive me for the malicious pleasure I seemed to take in hijacking our conversation every time you tried to bring it around to the subject of my noble ancestor. These were but the teasing of an ornery old man which you must not begrudge.

I think, like you, that the freebooters or buccaneers of the 17th century are not known or, worse, are not well known. Buccaneer, freebooter, these two words have become synonymous with thief, murderer and pirate.

Nothing is more false, however; the freebooters had more in common with the pilgrims of Portsmouth; like them, they sought freedom of conscience and wanted the same from the institutions; moreover, they wanted the freedom of the seas, of trade and the end of the odious monopoly which the Spaniards had organized for their own benefit over almost the entire New World.

The freebooters were free thinkers and, above all, groundbreakers.

France owes them her most beautiful colonies, Spain the loss of her power.

The evil they did is now forgotten, but the good remains; France took advantage of them while slandering them with the name of pirates, despite having dealt with them and having protected them.

She owed them this supreme insult; her ingratitude made it her duty to discharge in this fashion the immense services they had so generously rendered her.

You see, my dear fellow countryman, that I have not forgotten any of the informal talks we have had about freebooters, and that I fully share your opinion about them.

Please accept, in remembrance of the good hours we spent together and my sincere friendship, the enclosed manuscript. It is entirely in the hand of my grandfather; it is a kind of diary written by him, day by day, which contains not only precious documents about him, but also about some of his most famous companions.

For what purpose did my grandfather write this journal? I don't know. Perhaps he, too, wanted to write a history of the freebooters, but if that was his intention, he probably gave up the project, because I have not found anything in the archives of our house that relates to it, even indirectly.

I remain yours most sincerely,

Henry, Comte de Châteaugrand

I immediately opened the package. It did indeed contain a manuscript written on parchment. There was no mistaking the date: the yellowed ink, the shape of the letters, the spelling, everything proved that it was indeed from the middle of the 17th century.

On the first page was written:

Notes relating to some of the most distinguished adventurers of Santo Domingo and Tortuga Island; written by Bearcub Ironskull, himself an adventurer, in the Year of the Lord 1650, and up to and including the year 1680.

So the Comte had not wanted me to leave without satisfying my curiosity.

I thanked him from the bottom of my heart, and I immediately began my reading. I only stopped at the last page. Then I pressed the precious manuscript upon my heart.

A few years went by, many events happened that had almost made me forget it. Then, a few months ago, while browsing in my library, I happened to come across it. I reread it and I felt that this second reading was perhaps even more pleasurable than the first.

I immediately placed this manuscript on my table, in front of me, determined to use it as soon as possible.

This is but an excerpt from this manuscript that I am presenting to the reader today. He will judge whether I was wrong or right in trying to bring it out of oblivion.

As for me, when a few years earlier luck led me to St. Christopher, I was far from expecting the good fortune that awaited me on this almost ignored island.

And now, as the Spanish say, forgive the author's mistakes.

Gustave AIMARD.
Paris, August 10th, 1888

THE ADVENTURES OF BEARCUB IRONSKULL

CHAPTER I
Where the reader becomes acquainted with Captain Bearcub Ironskull

On Friday, September 13, 16**, between seven and eight o'clock in the evening, the Tavern of the Rusty Anchor located on the harbor, almost opposite the main jetty at Port-Margot, and the usual meeting place for the freebooters and buccaneers of Tortuga Island, blazed like a furnace in the dark night, and let out, through its windows open to the sea breeze, a deafening noise of shouting, laughter, singing and broken dishes.

A considerable crowd, made up of locals, buccaneers, freebooters, *engagés*,[24] women, children and even old people, curiously crowded the doors and windows of the inn, without concern for the dishes, glasses and bottles which, from the inside, rained almost continuously on them.

They mixed their joyful applause with the frenetic cheerfulness of the twenty-five or thirty guests seated around a huge round table in the great hall.

---

[24] Also "hired hands," in reality indentured servants.

It was a party that night at the Rusty Anchor, a party of buccaneers, without restrictions and limitations, where drunkenness filled all faces, put lightning in all eyes, and madness in all heads.

Captain Bearcub Ironskull, one of the most formidable buccaneers on Tortuga Island, had, that very morning, hired a crew of 473 Brothers of the Coast, chosen with particular care from the most formidable buccaneers who were then in Port-Margot, Port-de-Paix, or Leogane. And that very night, his ship, the *Trickster*, was to leave her anchorage of Port-Margot and set sail for an unknown destination.

But the captain, before his departure, had wanted to gather all his old friends for a last meal and the most famous leaders of the Brothers of the Coast, sitting at his table, toasted with unreserved enthusiasm to the success of Bearcub Ironskull's mysterious expedition.

There were gathered: Montbarts the Exterminator, Beau Laurent, Michel the Basque,[25] Vent-en-Panne,[26] Michel de Grammont,[27] Pitrians,[28] L'Olonnais, Alexan-

---

[25] Born Michel Etchegorria, pirate from the Kingdom of Navarre in Southwest France. He is best known as a companion of L'Olonnais, with whom he sacked Maracaibo and Gibraltar. He died in 1668.

[26] Fictional character, the hero of several other novels by Aimard.

[27] French privateer born in Paris in 1645, lost at sea in the north-east Caribbean in April 1686. His privateer career lasted from around 1670 to 1686 during which he commanded the flagship *Hardi*.

[28] Allegedly an English pirate; he may be fictional too, as he appeared in Aimard's *Les Bohèmes de la Mer*.

dre Bras-de-Fer,[29] David,[30] Pierre Legrand,[31] the Pole-tais, Drack,[32] Roche Braziliano,[33] and so many other Brothers of the Coast, no less illustrious and no less formidable.

M. d'Ogeron, governor on behalf of His Majesty Louis XIV, of Tortuga Island and the French portion of Santo Domingo, occupied the place of honor; at his right sat Captain Bearcub Ironskull; at his left, Pierre Legrand, a young man of twenty-five years of age, with fine and distinguished features, the second in command of the planned expedition.

As for the other buccaneers, they had sat down at random.

A swarm of hired men, poor devils, barely dressed in shorts and tattered canvas shirts, stained with fat and blood, circulated around the guests in a ghostly silence, constantly passing dishes, plates and jugs of wine, which most of the time, as a joke, the freebooters threw at their heads—after having emptied them, of course.

In the opinion of the Brothers of the Coast, who, for the most part, had made this hard apprenticeship, a hired

---

[29] "Iron Arm". French pirate mentioned in Exquemelin's book (see Note 22). He is best known for capturing a Spanish ship after being shipwrecked.

[30] Likely David Williams (*floruit* 1698–1709, last name occasionally Wallin), Welsh pirate best known for sailing under a number of more prominent pirate captains.

[31] Another French buccaneer supposedly active during the 17th century, also according to Exquemelin's book (see Note 22).

[32] Francis Drake? (c.1540-1596) considered as a pirate by the Spanish, who nicknamed him "El Draque" or "El Dragón."

[33] Dutch pirate born in the town of Groningen. His career lasted from 1654 until his disappearance around 1671.

hand was little more than a beast of burden, over which they had the right of life and death during the five long years of their slavery.

Captain Bearcub Ironskull, as he was called, for lack of knowing his real name, was at that time a man between thirty and thirty-two years of age at the most, of almost colossal size and remarkable strength.

His regular features, of uncommon beauty, were enhanced by two black eyes filled with fire. He had an unmistakable stamp of distinction about him. His energetic manner was strengthened by a long, bushy black beard, which covered the entire lower part of his face and fanned out to his chest. His gestures were sober and elegant; his gait noble; his voice, pure and harmonious.

But like most of the Brothers of the Coast, there was a secret in his life that he carefully hid. No one knew who he was, or where he came from; everything about him, down to his name, was a mystery. All that was known of his life was what had happened since his arrival on Tortuga Island.

Although very short, his story was dark and lamentable. He had, for several years, suffered excruciating pain, without a complaint ever coming out of his lips. Never had he let himself be struck down by undeserved misfortune. Unlike other buccaneers, he lived alone.

He had never wanted to bind himself intimately to anyone else, nor enter into this fraternal association called *matelotage* which made the freebooters so fearsome. In short, he was a superior man, and, as we would say today, an eccentric.

We will quote two pieces of evidence in support of what we are saying.

The first testified to an unusual boldness for the age of superstition in which he lived: he was not afraid of setting sail on a Friday 13th with a crew of 473 men.

The second was even more peculiar: wherever he went, he was constantly followed by two *venteurs,* or hounds, and two wild boars of extraordinary ferocity, who nevertheless lived together in perfect harmony and were devoted to him in every way.

At this very moment, sitting amongst his guests, he had his four inseparable companions lying at his feet, and from time to time, he would drop under the table morsels from the best pieces of food served on his plate.

Captain Bearcub Ironskull being one of the main characters of this story, we will say a few more words about what had happened to him since his arrival on Tortuga Island.

Five or six years before the time our story begins, a ship, coming from Dieppe, had arrived at Port-Margot. It was loaded with goods of all kinds required by the colonies; furthermore, it carried eighty-five *engagés*, men and women, whom the employees of the *Compagnie des Indes*[34] had hired in France at derisory prices, supposedly to practice their trades in the colonies, such as masons, carpenters, wheelwrights, painters, and even doctors. Olivier Œxmelin, who later became the historian of

---

[34] More accurately, the *Compagnie française des Indes occidentales* (French West Indies Company), a French trading company founded on 28 May 1664 by Jean-Baptiste Colbert and dissolved on 2 January 1674. The company received the French possessions of the Atlantic coasts of Africa and America, and was granted a monopoly on trade with America, which was to last for forty years. Its headquarters were in Le Havre.

the Brothers of the Coast, had been hired as a surgeon in Paris. When he arrived in Santo Domingo, he was sold at auction and remained a slave of one of the most ferocious freebooters for three years.

According to custom, despite their protests, the poor devils we are talking about were, the day after their arrival, auctioned off as *engagés* for a period of three years to the locals and the buccaneers who presented themselves as purchasers.

One of these *engagés*, a good-looking boy of twenty-six, had sought to protest against that iniquitous act of which he was the victim, but soon realized that he had no protection to expect from the island's authorities; that his complaints excited only mocking laughter and crude jokes.

So he had lowered his head and resigned himself, at least in appearance, and silently followed his new master, a buccaneer from Grand-Fond named Boute-Feu. Boute-Feu was an uneducated man, of brutal and nasty nature, who liked, for no good reason other than his pleasure, to beat up his new *engagés*, subject them to ill treatments, and imposing burdens on them beyond their strength, feeding them only the leftovers scorned by his dogs.

The new *engagé* had suffered everything without complaint, fought cruelty with patience, and redoubled his efforts to satisfy the ruthless master in whose hands his unfortunate fate had thrown him. But the evil buccaneer, far from being moved by such resignation, saw in this gentleness and docility only a kind of bravado, and redoubled his vexations, waiting only for an opportunity to finish this man whom nothing seemed to be able to compel to rebel.

One day, in the torrid heat, the poor devil was bending under the weight of three bull hides, still fresh, which he had been carrying on his shoulders for several hours. Boute-Feu was hurling the nastiest reproaches to him, and, carried away in anger by the obstinate silence with which the hired man reacted to his insults, he struck him on the head with a rifle butt and knocked him down bloodily at his feet.

After a moment, seeing that the *engagé* no longer showed any sign of life, Boute-Feu thought he had killed him, and, without worrying about it any longer, took the skins and went away, leaving him there.

To those who by chance asked him what had become of his hired man, he simply replied that he was *marron*. *Marron* came from the Spanish word *maroon*, meaning abandoning, casting away, and buccaneers used it to let people know that a servant or a dog had run away. So the matter remained there and there were no more questions about the *engagé*.

However, the unfortunate man was not dead; he was not even badly wounded. As soon as his master had left, he opened his eyes, got up, and, although very weak, tried to follow him.

But, being a recent arrival, the poor man was not yet accustomed to the jungles of the New World; he was completely ignorant of the way to get safely through these vast oceans of greenery. He got lost in the woods, and wandered around for a few days, without being able to find his way home or reach the seashore. If he had managed to get closer to the ocean, he would have been saved; but every step he took, on the contrary, took him further away from civilization, for which he searched in vain in the midst of these inextricable thickets.

Hunger was beginning to press him; he ate all the meat he was carrying raw, for he had nothing with which to build a fire. His position was all the more horrible because he was completely unable to find the means of supporting himself.

Only one friend had remained faithful to him in his distress: one of his master's dogs who had not wanted to abandon him and whom Boute-Feu had ended up leaving behind, with no more care about it than his hired man, whom he thought he was now rid of forever.

It was then that, pushed to the limit by despair and necessity, the resolute character, the indomitable energy of this man was revealed, a man who, wounded and deprived of all help, instead of letting himself be overcome by pain and abandoning himself to death, instead stiffened himself against adversity and bravely undertook to fight to the very end to save his life.

His days were spent in the woods, marching in every direction; he didn't know where he was going, but he always hoped to finally break through the thick walls of greenery that surrounded him on all sides and find his way back.

Finally, he managed to climb up to the top of a mountain, and from there, he could see the sea.

His courage was reborn at this sight; he hastened down to the plain; but the first smell of a wild beast that he met soon made him lose, despite himself, the direction he wanted to follow.

While walking through the woods, his dog constantly watched out for wild game and hunted for it. When they had caught something, master and beast fraternally shared the game and ate it raw.

Little by little, the man became accustomed to this diet; the raw meat seemed almost tasty to him; he finally learned to spot the game; hunting became more productive; soon he had helpers in the form of young wild dogs and wild boars that he had found, taught, and whose help soon became very useful.

For about fourteen months, the man led this extraordinary existence. He had almost lost hope of ever finding civilization again when, one morning, out of the blue, he found himself face to face with a group of French buccaneers.

At first, they were surprised and almost frightened when they saw him; it is true that his appearance was neither attractive nor even reassuring.

His hair and beard had grown to extraordinary lengths; his clothing now consisted only in a remnant of underpants and a shirt that barely covered him; his features were tanned, his physiognomy fierce; a piece of raw meat hung from his belt; three dogs and two wild boars, looking as wild as he was, followed him step by step.

However, after the first moment of surprise and hesitation had passed, he told his story, frankly and naively. Some of the buccaneers recognized him and became interested.

Immediately, they assembled in council.

After lengthy deliberations, they declared that Boute-Feu had abused the rights that the customs of the Coast gave him on his *engagés*, and that, by his continuous ill-treatment and especially his odious abandonment, he had implicitly renounced the services of the man, and broken his contract; and that, consequently, he was deprived of all further rights on him, and that the hired man was free in fact, and should be declared as such.

This resolution, taken unanimously, was immediately carried out. Bearcub—for such was the name by which our hero was merrily baptized, and which he accepted with good grace—for, in truth, he resembled a bear more than a man—was welcomed as a Brother of the Coast, and was admitted into all the privileges of buccaneers and freebooters.

The new friends of the former *engagé* did not stop there. They gave him clothes, weapons, powder, lead, and took him back with them to Port-Margot, and there, they renewed their declaration before the governor, M. d'Ogeron, and had it sanctioned by him, despite the strong opposition of Boute-Feu, who was obstinate in claiming his rights, and maintained that the man he had hired had neither been hit nor abandoned by him, but had run away out of malice, and had gone *marron* with the intention of harming him.

Unfortunately for Boute-Feu, his reputation of cruelty was so well established in Port-Margot and surrounding areas, that M. d'Ogeron, without even wanting to hear his arguments, sent him away, threatening him with an exemplary punishment if, in the future, he did not treat his *engagés* with more humanity.

The buccaneer withdrew with his head down, without daring to answer, but brewing plans of revenge in his head. Now that he was free and had the right to defend himself, his ex-*engagé* worried very little about threats from his former master.

A few days later, Bearcub embarked under the orders of Montbarts. He thus took part in several expeditions in the company of the most renowned captains, and, in a short time, not only did he acquire considerable wealth, but he also obtained, thanks to his audacity, his daring and, above all, his intelligence, a great reputation among the Brothers of the Coast.

Since he had been declared a free man, Bearcub had never alluded to the horrible sufferings he had endured during his slavery; never had the name of Boute-Feu passed his lips. If sometimes the dreaded buccaneer's name was mentioned in front of him, he always refrained from taking part in the conversation, either to blame or to praise, although he had often been asked for his opinion. Moreover, in the three years since these events had taken place, the two men had never come face to face.

This old story, especially in a country where every day brought new adventures, had been almost forgotten, and those who, at the onset, had expected a brilliant revenge from the new freebooter, began to nod skeptically, if sometimes they were told about the relentless hatred that these two men felt for one another.

Then, one evening, fate placed Boute-Feu and his former hired hand together at the Tavern of the Rusty Anchor.

Here is what happened.

Two or three days before, a freebooter ship, commanded by Michel the Basque, had returned loaded with gold and prisoners, after a month-long cruise in the Gulf of Mexico. Six Spanish galleons, surprised by the privateers, had been boarded, looted and, according to custom, burned at sea.

As soon as the ship anchored at Port-Margot, the prisoners were unloaded, and then the loot was divided up. The freebooters, with their shares of the loot, had hastened, as always, to spend it in wild orgies. These men valued gold only because of the pleasures it procured them.

Above all else, gambling was their favorite passion. They indulged in it with unspeakable rage and frenzy, risking huge sums of money on a single roll of the dice, and, more often than not, leaving the game only when they had lost all their gold, their clothes, and sometimes their very freedom.

Since the return of Michel the Basque's ship, people gambled everywhere in Port-Margot, in the streets and squares, on overturned barrels, in inns, and even in the very house of M. d'Ogeron, the governor. Quarrels arose on all sides, blood flowed in the streets; both wise and foolish men were similarly affected by this *delirium tremens* almost as terrible and as murderous as the more conventional type.

Perhaps the only one amongst all the Brothers of the Coast to escape this madness was Bearcub Ironskull; he despised gambling, which he considered a shameful passion. His friends often ridiculed him for what they called his streak of "puritanism," but he had always remained steadfast, and nothing had been able to bring him out of the reserve he had imposed on himself.

The evening we are talking about, around seven o'clock, just as the sun was beginning to set behind the blue waves of the Atlantic ocean, Captain Bearcub Ironskull, deaf to the noise of the city, was walking nonchalantly on the beach, cigar in his mouth, his head bent over his chest, his arms behind his back, followed step by step by his dogs and boars.

"What are you doing there, you wild dreamer, when the whole city is in jubilation?"

The Captain raised his head and held out his hand with a smile to his interlocutor, one of the most renowned leaders of the freebooters.

"As you can see, my dear Vent-en-Panne," he replied, "I'm walking on the beach admiring the sunset."

"Nice pleasure!" replied the freebooter laughing. "Come with me instead of staying here wandering all by yourself, like a soul in pain, on the beach."

"What do you want, dear friend, everyone takes his pleasure wherever he finds it."

"I have nothing against that, but why do you refuse to accompany me?"

"I haven't yet; however, if you don't mind, I won't go with you. You're going gambling and, as you know, I hate gambling."

"Does that stop you from watching the others gamble? "

"Not at all, but it saddens me."

"You are mad! Listen to me: it seems that there is, right now, at the Rusty Anchor, a rich buccaneer from Grand Fond or the Artibonite, I don't know exactly, who is gambling like a possessed man. It is said that he has already dried up more than half of Michel le Basque's crew…"

"What do you want me to do about it, my dear friend?" asked Bearcub, laughing. "I don't think it's possible for me to alter his luck."

"Perhaps you can."

"How so?"

"Listen, Bearcub, when I saw you just now, I had an idea: my intention is to gamble against this man; come with me, stand by my side, and since you succeed in everything you do, you will bring me good luck and I shall win!"

"You are mad!"

"No, I'm a gambler, so I'm superstitious."

"Do you really want to?"

"Please."

"Let's go then, and by the grace of God, I hope you're right," replied Bearcub, shrugging.

"Thank you," said Vent-en-Panne, shaking his friend's hand. "For God's sake," he added, happily snapping his fingers, "I'm sure to win now."

Bearcub answered only with a smile.

The two Brothers of the Coast went together to the Rusty Anchor.

CHAPTER II
How Boute-Feu and his former engagé *played dice and what ensued*

When the two freebooters arrived at the door of the Rusty Anchor, they discovered a bizarre spectacle and, in spite of themselves, they had to stop for a moment on the threshold before walking inside.

By the glow of the oil lamps, whose smoke, mixed with that of pipes and cigars, rolled in blackish clouds below the ceiling, one could see, as if through a fog, the energetic and grimacing heads of a throng of buccaneers, whose features, twisted by the passion of gambling and drunkenness, took on a sinister expression with the changing reflections of the lights incessantly agitated by the wind.

In the middle of the room, on a long table set with planks over barrels, piles of gold piled up in front of a man who, with a cone in his hand and a mocking gaze, shook the dice with defiance, calling to the freebooters gathered around the table.

Behind him stood a dozen Spanish men and women, prisoners taken in the last expedition, who had been the last stakes gambled by their former captors.

"This is the man we're dealing with," said Vent-en-Panne. "Follow me."

Bearcub cast a distracted glance at the man his companion had pointed out to him. He recognized him at once: it was Boute-Feu.

At this sight, he frowned, a livid pallor spread over his face, and, in spite of himself, he took a step backwards.

"What's wrong with you?" asked Vent-en-Panne, who noticed his emotion. "Ah!" he continued, after a pause, "I understand: you've recognized your former master."

"Yes," said Bearcub in a hollow voice. "That's him, indeed."

"Well, what do you care? You're free now and you have nothing to fear."

"I'm not afraid," whispered the captain, as if he was speaking to himself.

"So, come on!"

"You're right," said Bearcub with a strange grin. "Let's go! Maybe it's better to get it over with."

"What's your intention?" Vent-en-Panne asked him with a touch of anxiety.

"God is my witness that I was not looking for this man—quite the contrary, I did everything I could to avoid that man. When you met me earlier on the beach and asked me to accompany you here, at first I was reluctant, wasn't I?

"True."

"So it is fate and fate alone that brings us together here tonight."

"The Devil takes me if I understand one word of what you are saying," cried Vent-en-Panne.

Bearcub raised his head and looked at his companion with an undecipherable expression of mockery and triumph. Then, after a moment, he passed his arm under Vent-en-Panne's arm and said:

"Come. You have often reproached me for not gambling before. Well, tonight, by God's will, you will watch a game of dice that you and all our Brothers will remember for a long time."

"You're going to gamble?" exclaimed Vent-en-Panne, surprised.

"Yes—the greatest game."

"Against him?"

"Against this man who has so insolently stripped our Brothers of their fortunes," replied Bearcub, pointing his hand at the buccaneer.

"Boute-Feu?"

"The same. And instead of me watching your game, you will be watching mine," added Bearcub.

"Beware!" said Vent-en-Panne.

"My mind is made up. Come!"

"To the grace of God!" murmured the freebooter as he followed his companion.

They then entered the room, and, making their way through the crowd, which was not difficult, for both were highly regarded by their companions, they soon arrived at the table occupied by the buccaneer, who, with a mocking smile, watched them approach.

"Ah-ah!" said Boute-Feu, with a coarse laugh. "Would you like to try your luck against me, brothers?"

"Why not?" replied Vent-en-Panne.

"You're welcome to try—if you feel like it," the buccaneer sneered. "I'd like nothing better than to take you away to your last doubloon, my comrade."

"First, I'm not your comrade, thank God! Please keep these unseemly epithets for others," replied the freebooter in a gruff tone. "As for taking away my last doubloon, we'll see about that."

"Yours and your companion's, on top of that, if, contrary to his habits," Boute-Feu added ironically, "he has the courage to finally measure himself against me."

"No gratuitous insults, Boute-Feu, against a man who does not attack you," replied Bearcub coldly.

69

"I don't care about your observations," replied the buccaneer abruptly, "and if you're not happy, I'm ready to settle this with you whenever and wherever you like."

"I feel obliged to point out," Bearcub peacefully continued, "that nothing between us has motivated the feud that you are trying to engineer at the moment, and that I have not in any way interfered in your discussion with my friend Vent-en-Panne."

At this sudden altercation, a circle of the Brothers of the Coast had immediately formed around the table, curiously waiting for what was bound to happen. Everyone knew the hatred that Bearcub and Boute-Feu felt towards each other, and the spectators foresaw a terrible conclusion at this skirmish of words so boldly started by the buccaneer.

Boute-Feu was not liked by the Brothers of the Coast; his constant luck at dice, which had been going on for some days now, increased, if at all possible, the general dislike towards him, and most people in the crowd nourished the secret hope that his adversary would finally inflict upon him the harsh punishment which, undoubtedly for lack of a propitious occasion, he deserved and which had been postponed for so long.

Bearcub was calm, cold, and, although a little pale, completely in control of himself.

"All right," said Boute-Feu, shrugging with disdain. "Enough talk. One can't have a bad dog follow a good track. Let's leave it at that. I admire your caution and bow before it."

"By all that is sacred! Enough women's talk! Bearcub's right! You're the one angling for a quarrel! And if he doesn't answer you now, it's probably because he has his own reasons for doing so, and I imagine that you won't lose anything by waiting. Now let's play; that's why we're here!".

"Indeed!" agreed Boute-Feu. "What's your stake?"

"Two thousand piasters," answered the freebooter, taking a hefty purse from the pockets of his pants.

"Stop!" said Bearcub, coldly, putting his hand on Vent-en-Panne's arm. "Let me clear things with that man."

The freebooter looked at his friend,. He saw such a dark flash in the depths of his eyes, that he put his purse back in his pocket and just answered with these three words:

"As you will!"

Bearcub then stepped forward, put his hands on the table and leaned towards the buccaneer.

"Boute-Feu," he said in a short and sharp voice, "when I stepped inside this room, I did not know I'd be meeting you here. I did not want to either, because in my heart, contempt is equal to the hatred I feel for you. But since, driven by an ill-meant fate, instead of imitating my reserved and wise conduct, you don't want to feign an indifference equal to mine, well then, I accept the challenge that you offer me."

"Did it require so many idle words to achieve this ridiculous result?" said the buccaneer, with an evil sneer.

"Perhaps. Listen to me: our Brothers here present will serve as witnesses. We shall play three games of *passe-dix*,[35] not more; not less. You will be required to accept the terms I will ask of you if I win. Do you accept?"

"What if you lose?"

---

[35] Game played with three dice and in which a player must make more than ten points in a single throw.

"I shall not lose," Bearcub answered clearly. "We are engaging in a supreme struggle of which, I am convinced, I will emerge victorious."

"Come on, you're mad."

"Ah! You're afraid! That's good. I won't insist. Apologize to me for the insults you have just hurled at me in front of our Brothers, and I will withdraw at once."

"Me, apologize? Never, as long as I live, by God! Watch your words!"

"I am warning you," said Bearcub coldly, taking a pistol out of his belt and arming it. "At the slightest suspicious gesture, I will kill you like the savage beast that you are."

The other buccaneer, drunk with fury, but held in respect by the long barrel of the gun pointed at his chest, cast a circular glance at the crowd, perhaps to find some courage from a friendly face. But all the freebooters remained somber and silent. The only expression he read on their faces was one of sarcastic joy.

With a violent effort of will, Boute-Feu repressed the fury within his heart that made his blood boil, and, with a calm voice, in which it would have been impossible to detect even the slightest tremor, he replied:

"I accept your proposal."

"Which one? The one where you apologize to me?"

"Never!" shouted Boute-Feu.

"Very well," said Bearcub; then addressing the crows, he added, "You have heard the man?"

"We have," they answered in one voice.

"So, here are the rules of the game," Bearcub continued in a firm and steady voice. "The dice, three in number, and the cup, shall be new to you and me, and will be selected at random from our Brothers here."

"Are you saying that my dice are loaded?" exclaimed Boute-Feu in a threatening tone.

"I'm not saying anything and I don't want to say anything, I'm just exercising my right, that's all."

Boute-Feu violently threw his cup to the ground and trampled it with rage.

All the other games in the room had stopped. The Brothers of the Coast crowded around the table, mounted on benches, tables and barrels, to witness this duel of a new kind and to see better, holding their breath and making such a deep silence that one could have heard the fluttering wings of a fly where nearly two hundred people were gathered.

"Here is a cup and three dice, my friend," said a man coming to take his place beside Bearcub, a man to whom all the Brothers of the Coast bowed with respect.

"Thank you, Montbarts," replied Bearcub, who affectionately pressed the hand of the fearsome freebooter.

Then, speaking to Boute-Feu, he continued:

"We'll each have one throw, and the highest point above ten will win, unless we throw the same number, in which case we'll throw again. Is it agreed?"

"Yes," answered Boute-Feu in a low voice.

"We will play only three games. The best of three wins."

"So be it!"

"And I alone shall have the right to set the stakes."

"Unless I win."

"Naturally. Let's set the first stake. How much do you have?"

"Eight thousand seven hundred piasters."

"How much do you value what you own: houses, furniture, hired help, everything?"

"About the same amount."

"You're quite well off, aren't you?" said Bearcub, laughing.

"Do you want to see my books??" answered the buccaneer brutally. "That's my stake."

At that moment, Bearcub felt a slight touch on his shoulder. He turned around. Behind him stood, humble and desolate, the unfortunate Spanish prisoners.

"For pity's sake, *señor*!" murmured a soft, plaintive woman's voice in his ear.

"That's right," said Bearcub, pointing at the prisoners. "I forgot about these people. At how much do you value them?"

"Ten thousand piasters, not one *real* less."

Bearcub hesitated for a moment.

"In the name of the Blessed Virgin, have mercy, *señor*!" said the same woman's voice with an accent of sorrowful pain.

"Thus. your entire stake totals twenty-seven thousand four hundred piasters," said Bearcub.

"You know how to count, boy," said Boute-Feu, sniggering. "It's a nice number, isn't it?"

"Indeed! I shall gamble thirteen thousand seven hundred piasters for our first game."

A murmur of admiration circulated in the attentive crowd.

"Good! Show us the stake then," replied the buccaneer with a sly smile.

"I don't have that money on me," said Bearcub calmly.

"Then, nothing doing, companion. I won't take your word for it."

Bearcub bit his lips, but, before he had time to reply, Montbarts stopped him with a gesture.

"I shall guarantee the stake," he said, fixing his eagle's gaze on Boute-Feu, who lowered his eyes with a confused look.

"I, too," shouted Vent-en-Panne. "By the Horns of Beelzebub! All that I have, I give Bearcub to him willingly."

"So do I," added Beau Laurent, who stepped out of the crowd and came to lean against the table, a stone's throw from Boute-Feu.

"What do you say?" asked Bearcub, his outstretched hands turned towards his adversary. "Do you think these guarantees are sufficient?"

"Yes, they are! Let's play! A thousand devils! Let's see the end of it!"

"Here is the cup. You may start."

The buccaneer grabbed the cup without answering. He shook it for a few moments with a feverish movement, then threw the dice on the table with a dull sound.

"Nice throw," said Bearcub softly. "Six and six make twelve plus five seventeen. My turn."

He nonchalantly took the cup, shook it and threw the dice.

"Three sixes," he said laughing. "You lose."

"Hell!" exclaimed Boute-Feu, who had become livid.

"It seems that your luck is changing," said Bearcub. "For our second game, I no longer need guarantors. I'll stake what I just won against what you have left."

Boute-Feu nervously shook the cup and rolled the dice.

"Ah-ah!" he shouted with a triumphant laugh. "Perhaps not, boy! Look! Three fours! Twelve!"

"Yes," said Bearcub, "it is a fine throw, but maybe I can do better. What do you think?"

The throw turned up three fives!

"I'm ruined!" cried Boute-Feu, wiping away cold sweat from his face, which had become as pale as a dead man's. "Ruined!" he repeated.

"Yes, you are, companion," said Bearcub, raising his head, "but it's not over yet. You forget that we still have one last game to play."

"I don't own anything anymore."

"Wrong! You still have something left that I want to take from you."

"What is it? "

"Your life!" Bearcub shouted in a terrible voice. "Do you really think that I started this game with you for the miserable pleasure of stripping you of this gold that I despise? No, no, Boute-Feu! It is your life that I want! And to win it, I am willing to not only gamble all your fortune which is now mine, but also my own life. The loser will shoot himself in the head, here and now, in front of everyone."

Upon hearing this strange proposal, a shiver of terror passed like an electric current through the ranks of the Brothers of the Coast.

"Bearcub! It is madness," cried Montbarts.

"Don't do it! Don't do it!" several freebooters shouted loudly.

"My Brothers," resumed Bearcub with a cold smile, "I thank you for your support, but my decision is irrevocable. Furthermore, trust me, I am sure to win. This man is already doomed. Look at him: terror has already almost wiped him out; pride alone still sustains him. But I will agree to give him one last chance to save his life: that he confesses his crimes publicly and humbly asks for forgiveness. On this condition, I shall forgive him."

"Never!" cried Boute-Feu, now at the paroxysm of his rage. "Your life or mine—so be it! One of us is too much on this earth and must go! Let us play this last game, and be cursed if you win!"

He threw the dice with his eyes averted.

A shout of stupor rose from the crowd.

He had thrown thee fives!

"One more than last time," said Bearcub, picking up the dice with indifference and putting them back in the cup. "But don't be in a hurry to triumph. You're closer to death than you think."

"Throw the dice! Throw them!" cried the buccaneer in a whistling voice, his chest oppressed, his eyes haggard, prey to an anguish that no words could express.

"Brothers," said Bearcub, still impassive, "this is the judgment of God. In order to prove to you that this man is irremediably condemned by divine justice, I will not even touch the cup. One of you will throw the dice for me."

"Not me!" exclaimed Montbarts. "That's tempting the Devil!"

"No, Brother! On the contrary, it is to reveal God's infallible power to everyone! Take the cup and throw the dice."

"No, on my soul, I shall not!"

"Please, Brother."

Montbarts hesitated.

"Throw the dice yourself then, or are you afraid?" growled Boute-Feu mechanically, crouching like a tiger on the prowl, his hands clenched, his gaze haggard.

Bearcub almost forced the cup into Montbarts' hand.

"Go, and fear not," he said.

"May God forgive me!" Montbarts murmured and he threw the dice, turning his head away.

At the same moment, a shrill, almost inhuman scream was heard: Bearcub was suddenly pulled back by an unknown hand. A shot rang out and a bullet hit one of the ceiling beams with a dull sound.

It all had happened so quickly that less than a minute had passed between the scream and the shot.

When the buccaneers emerged from the stupor caused by this strange incident, they saw Boute-Feu slammed against the table and held there, despite all his efforts, by the powerful hand of Beau Laurent. The evil buccaneer still held the smoking gun in his clenched fingers.

On the table, everyone could see that the dice had come up with three sixes!

Fortunately for Bearcub, two people had been watching over him: the first was the Spanish woman who had bravely pulled him back, at the risk of becoming herself a victim of the bullet intended for him; the second was Beau Laurent, who had kept a close eye on Boute-Feu and had turned the gun away.

Montbarts made a gesture to demand silence. Everyone fell silent.

"Brothers," the freebooter said, "you have all witnessed what has just happened."

"Yes! Yes," cried the Brothers of the Coast with a single voice.

"So, you agree, as I do, that we have the right to use our privileges and judge the would-be murderer?"

"Yes," replied Vent-en-Panne on behalf of them all. "He must be tried here and now."

"Very well, Brothers," said Montbarts. "What do you say should this man's fate be after the cowardly attack of which he is guilty?"

"He must die," replied the crowd in a single voice.

"Is that your judgment?"

"Yes—death," replied all the Brothers of the Coast.

"Prepare a boat, and take him at once to Shark's rock."

Several men rushed out of the room and immediately left the inn.

It was in vain that Bearcub tried to intercede so that the wretched Boute-Feu would be left to shoot himself in the head, but the other freebooters remained inflexible.

A few minutes later, Boute-Feu, tightly bound, was carried to a small boat with a crew of ten, which then left Port-Margot, under the command of Montbarts, who had wanted to execute the sentence himself.

It was a terrible sentence.

Shark's Rock was located six leagues offshore; at each tide, the sea covered it completely.

The man condemned by the implacable justice of the freebooters was left there without food and weapons, to await death in horrible anguish and torture.

Such was the fate reserved for Boute-Feu.

An hour before sunrise, just as the tide was beginning to rise, the boat returned to Port-Margot. Montbarts and his companions disembarked coldly, as men who had just completed a dark duty.

At that hour, it was likely that Boute-Feu had died already.

CHAPTER III
How Bearcub Ironskull disposed of the
fortune he had won from his former master

The awful, but long-anticipated, denouement of this strange game between two relentless enemies had caused extreme emotion in the crowd gathered at the Rusty Anchor.

The Brothers of the Coast, who had followed with anxiety the singular hazards of the game, now looked at Bearcub Ironskull with fearful admiration.

At this moment, M. d'Ogeron, Governor on behalf of the King of France of Tortuga Island and the French section of Santo Domingo, entered the room, greeted the public, who took off their hats with respect, and coldly took his place amongst the freebooters.

M. d'Ogeron was a man of vast intelligence and a big heart. He had imposed upon himself the perilous and almost impossible mission of rehabilitating these lost souls, and bringing back into the great human family these rebellious children who had been brutally separated from it by the impetuosity of their character and their ardent love for freedom. He tried to accomplish this mission with unparalleled devotion.

Tolerated rather than really accepted by the freebooters, who nevertheless all loved and respected him, M. d'Ogeron was considered much more as an equal than as a leader. Except in grave circumstances, he never interfered in the affairs of the freebooters. He was content to intervene merely through advice and persuasion for these exalted people had never suffered any restrictions, however slight they might be.

Being told of what was happening at the Rusty Anchor, he had immediately rushed, not to prevent the execution of the sentence pronounced against Boute-Feu, but to prevent any more acts of violence.

The Governor's presence was greeted by general acclaim, and everyone hastened to respectfully open the way for him.

When M. d'Ogeron was seated, he leaned over to Bearcub Ironskull and whispered a few words that only he heard.

"Rest easy, Monsieur," replied the freebooter. "Our goals are the same, and I will try to fulfill your intentions."

The captain then turned toward the audience, and, in a voice that was slightly shaking, but which gradually became firmer, he spoke.

"Brothers of the Coast," he said, "freebooters of Tortuga, buccaneers of Santo Domingo and inhabitants of Port-Margot, you have, witnessed in this room, only a few moments ago, not a terrible game played between two men who had long hated each other, but a true judgment rendered by God himself. I was only the instrument chosen by the Divine Wrath, driven to act as I did despite myself. I did not doubt for a moment that I would succeed; the conditions I set, the words I spoke, all prove it to you. I therefore have no right to the wealth I have gained, and I renounce it heartily. I hope you will approve of this resolution. We are lions, not tigers; and if we like to throw away our gold without care in wild and merry feasts, it is because that gold is the price of our worth, our audacity, and because our blood has gloriously bought it."

Frenzied bravos covered the captain's proud and vibrant voice.

When calm returned, Bearcub resumed, with a smile on his face:

"I thank Monsieur d'Ogeron, our esteemed Governor, a man whose paternal solicitude has always watched over us, for having deigned to come here. He will thus sanction by his very presence the resolution I have taken. Here is my intention: the gold which is on this table and the estate of Boute-Feu, which is now mine, will be, through the care of M. d'Ogeron, shared equally among the poorest among us, without distinction of class or origins, whether they be buccaneers, or local residents. May this objective remove from these ill-gotten riches the mud they were soiled with! Does any of you know how many *engagés* Boute-Feu had under his control?"

"I do," said Beau Laurent. "He had five."

"We're all here!" cried a man from the middle of the crowd.

"Come closer," said Bearcub.

Five poor half-naked devils, pale and thin, stepped forward timidly.

"I hereby declare you to be free men, according to the privileges granted to me by the customs of the Brothers of the Coast," said Bearcub. "Further, I will give to each of you, as is customary, a gun, three pounds of gunpowder, three pounds of bullets and five hundred *écus*, which you will share among yourselves."

The poor *engagés*, dazzled by such sudden good fortune, did not dare to believe what they had just heard. They cast frightened glances around, and finally broke down in tears.

"Come on," said Bearcub with an accent of sweet pity. "Come on, friends, now your miseries are over, you are free and Brothers of the Coast."

Cheers burst out again from all sides with such force that the oldest buccaneers themselves, those steel-hearted men that nothing could move, felt touched. It was more than enthusiasm, it was a frenzy.

"Well done, Captain," said M. d'Ogeron, pressing Bearcub's hand with emotion. "You are setting a noble example. This is how we will succeed in rehabilitating these lost but generous souls. You are making my task easier."

"I am but trying to follow in your footsteps, Monsieur," Bearcub respectfully replied. "I couldn't have a better model."

"Captain, with ten men like you," said M. d'Ogeron in a low voice, "in one year this magnificent colony would be entirely rehabilitated."

"Or lost," Bearcub murmured pensively.

"Oh! Do you believe that?"

"Alas, yes! We're not men like the others. It's fire that runs in our veins, not blood."

"Would you be abandoning our common purpose?"

"Not in the least! You will soon have proof of it."

The Governor smiled and shook Bearcub's hand. The Brothers of the Coast waited impassively for the end of their conversation.

"I have not finished, Brothers," resumed Bearcub after a moment's silence. "I still have to decide the fate of the Spanish prisoners. Is it right that these unfortunate people should remain slaves, when we all share in the inheritance of the man we have condemned? Although these prisoners belong to a nation that we abhor, we would be committing an unspeakable injustice by leaving them in slavery. To those proud Spaniards who treat us so haughtily as *ladrones* and hunt us down like wild beasts, let us show that we despise them too much to fear them! Let us set these prisoners free! Let us let them return to their relatives and friends, who no longer hope to see them again. By knowing us better, the Spaniards will fear us more. Do you approve of this resolution, Brothers?"

There was a visible hesitation in the crowd. For a moment, Bearcub Ironskull feared that his noble resolution might fail in the face of the hatred of his companions. A law of the freebooters forbade, on pain of death, a Brother to grant his freedom to a Spanish prisoner, man, woman, child or priest, without the general consent of all.

M. d'Ogeron judged the situation at a glance. He understood that Bearcub, in his generosity, had exceeded the limits of prudence, and that if he did not intervene, all might be lost.

"Captain Bearcub Ironskull," he said, standing up, "on behalf of all the Brothers of the Coast, I thank you for the generous initiative you are not afraid to take. Freebooters are too strong to fear their enemies. They attack them bravely to their face, overthrow them, and after they have defeated them, their hearts must then be open to mercy. To whatever nation they belong, let us remember that these unfortunate are also our brothers and sisters. It is up to us, banished from society, to give this example of humanity to a world that rejects us. I repeat to you, Captain, in the name of all the freebooters, I thank you. These prisoners are yours; you are their master and therefore free to return them to their families if you so wish."

"Yes, yes!" cried the freebooters driven by the noble words of M. d'Ogeron. "Let them be free! Long live the Governor! Long live Bearcub Ironskull!"

Once the initial momentum had been given, enthusiasm quickly spread. The Spanish prisoners were saved.

"It is my turn to thank you, Monsieur," replied Bearcub with emotion, "for without you, I would have failed in my purpose."

"Do not believe that, my dear Captain," said the Governor with a smile. "These men are like children, whose hearts have remained good. It is only a question of knowing how to make their generous nature respond to you."

The gold, which had remained on the table until then, was given to M. d'Ogeron, who was charged with distributing it;. He then left the tavern of the Rusty Anchor.

The crowd accompanied Bearcub Ironskull to the house where he lived, shouting with joy, and did not leave until he, two or three of his closest friends, and the Spanish prisoners, had finally disappeared inside.

The city remained in extreme turmoil throughout the night. Large groups roamed the streets, singing and cheering in honor of Captain Bearcub Ironskull and M. d'Ogeron.

The Spanish prisoners were eighteen men and two women. Bearcub ordered his *engagés* to prepare rooms for these foreigners, whom he now considered as his guests. After reassuring them that nothing bad would happen to them, and that the next day, he would see to it personally that they could leave Tortuga and return home, he took leave of them, abruptly cutting short their assurances of eternal gratitude. He then joined his friends, who, comfortably installed in the living room, were drinking and smoking while waiting for him.

"Hey-ho!" said Beau Laurent, "you were playing a dangerous game by wanting to free the prisoners."

"True, Brother," replied Bearcub, "but I had to do what I did. When Boute-Feu tried to murder me, one of the prisoners, a woman, I believe, resolutely threw herself in front of me, with the obvious intention of saving my life."

"I saw her," said Michel the Basque. "It was a woman indeed; young it seemed to me. She was so well wrapped up that it was possible for me to see only the tip of her nose."

"If it is so," said Beau Laurent, "you did the right thing, Bearcub. It would not have been proper for a *gavacho* to have been more generous than a Brother of the Coast."

"That's what I thought too," replied Bearcub gently.

"What I see most clearly in all this," said Beau Laurent, "is that you have made a charming Spanish conquest—at least I suppose so."

"You are crazy!"

"Yes, yes," said Beau Laurent with a mocking smile. "Your reputation is well known, but what do you intend to do with your guests?"

"I don't know how to get them to leave, especially at this time, when all the ships are away."

"*Pardieu!* Nothing could be easier," said Vent-en-Panne. "One of my close friends is a buccaneer. No doubt, you have heard of him, for he enjoys a great reputation."

"Who are you talking about?"

"The Poletais."

"Of course! Who among us doesn't know the Poletais, at least by reputation?" Bearcub.

"Good! He is a bull hunter and despises boars, which he hunts only rarely and when forced to. He is a stalwart companion, totally devoted to his friends."

"Yes, yes," said the other freebooters, "the Poletais is a true Brother of the Coast. So what?"

"He's the man we need," explained Vent-en-Panne. "Right now, he must be hunting in the Artibonite region. Let's go find him. He will tell us how to reach a Spanish town or village, without having to fight their soldiers. Does this suit you, Bearcub?"

"Perfectly. When shall we leave?"

"That's your call, I'll do what you decide."

"Then let's do it tomorrow, if you agree?"

"Tomorrow's perfect! Let's leave at dawn. I'll come here with two of my *engagés*. Take two of yours as well. That should be enough."

"Are the roads passable for the horses?" asked Bearcub with some hesitation.

"Why"

"By the Devil's Horns! You are very naive, Vent-en-Panne," exclaimed Beau Laurent with a big laugh. "Have you forgotten that there are ladies among the Spanish prisoners?"

"You have a nasty mind, Beau Laurent," replied Bearcub in good humor. "However, in this case, you are right. It would not be humane to force the women to walk perhaps twenty leagues on foot through jungle paths."

"Yes. that would be inhumane indeed," replied Beau Laurent with a sarcastic smile.

"The paths are good," Vent-en-Panne continued, "and the horses will travel easily."

"Then I will take two horses."

"As you wish. See you tomorrow then."

"At dawn. And thank you!"

The buccaneers got up, drank a last glass of liquor, cordially shook Bearcub's hand, and left, leaving him free to go to sleep.

But, in fact, he didn't sleep. A strange feeling crept slyly into his heart; a mysterious curiosity that he didn't even try to acknowledge kept him awake all night.

In spite of himself, the words of Beau Laurent still rang in his ears.

The next morning, at dawn, as planned, Vent-en-Panne, a punctual man per excellence, accompanied by two of his hired men, armed to the teeth, knocked on Bearcub's door.

The captain opened it himself and came to meet his friend, his hand outstretched.

"We're ready," he said.

"So let's get going," replied Vent-en-Panne. "If we press hard, perhaps we will meet the Poletais at his place around eleven or twelve o'clock. If not, we will not have the opportunity to see him before six, when he comes home."

Bearcub immediately had the Spaniards come down.

Ten minutes later, the caravan left the freebooter's house and, turning its back to the sea, headed for the mountains.

Vent-en-Panne and Bearcub, followed by his dogs and wild boars, which, as we have said, he never left behind, took the lead.

Then came the two women on horseback. They had wrapped themselves in their clothes, mantillas and rebo-zos, so that all that could be seen of their faces were their large black eyes, shining like carbuncles, casting anxious glances to the right and left.

A few steps back, the prisoners followed on foot, their wide-brimmed *sombreros* folded over their faces, wrapped up to their eyes in the thick folds of their coats.

Spaniards, whatever the weather, rain or shine, cold or hot, in Europe or in America, never left their *capa* behind; it was for them the indispensable garment per excellence.

The four *engagés* of Bearcub and Vent-en-Panne, their rifles on their shoulders, with pistols hanging from their belts, carrying axes and crocodile skin holsters filled with knives and bayonets hanging from the side, walked along the flanks of the column.

The few inhabitants that the freebooters met in the streets greeted them respectfully and wished them a good trip, but without showing any indiscreet curiosity.

The guards at the city gate raised the portcullis and lowered the drawbridge as soon as they saw them, and soon the caravan was in the open country.

CHAPTER IV
How the freebooters met the Poletais,
who was busy surrounding fifty Spaniards
all by himself.

It was still dark; the cold was intense; on the horizon, the waves of the Caribbean Sea were beginning to take on bloody red hues as the Sun was about to rise from the waters.

The travelers followed a narrow, rocky path bordered on each side by the green tufts of the sassafras. Here and there, groups of coconut trees sprang up and, with the last breaths of the exhaling breeze, swung their bushy heads.

In the distance, one could see the dark and imposing mass of the thickest forest of the Artibonite region[36], dominated by the high peaks of the *Massif du Nord*

The jungle was beginning to awaken and all its mysterious inhabitants were greeting the return of the day, each in their own way.

Horrible *pipas*, ox-voiced toads, roared at the edge of some forlorn swamp, above which myriads of *mapires* and mosquitoes swirled and buzzed. The *campanero*, or bell-bird, would toss its vibrant and monotonous note at equal intervals; the monkeys would squeak; the *peccaries* and *conocushi* would growl loudly in the

---

[36] Artibonite or Latibonit is one of the ten departments of Haiti located in central Haiti. With an area of 4,887 km² it is Haiti's largest department. As of 2015, its estimated population was 1,727,524. The region is the country's main rice-growing area. The main cities are Gonaïves and Saint-Marc.

thorny bushes; and great bearded vultures with enormous wingspan flew in wide circles in the air, making hoarse and jerky cries, mixed with the strident meows of the wild cats and the joyful songs of thousands of birds of all species and colors, all huddling under the verdant foliage.

The travelers were walking briskly, both to warm themselves up, as mornings are cold in Santo Domingo, and to make up for lost time spent in the preparations for this expedition.

Since leaving the city, no words had been exchanged.

The freebooters smoked their short pipes. As for the Spaniards, they probably reflected on the happy and unexpected event that had given them back their freedom, when all that loomed for them was the sad prospect of slavery.

However, when the shadows had completely disappeared to make way for the bright tropical light, before which the most beautiful days of our old Europe seem dull and foggy, the travelers gradually drew closer to each other, and a few words were exchanged between the different groups that made up the caravan.

Bearcub Ironskull, so calm, so cold, and usually so much in control of himself, seemed preoccupied, even worried. He was constantly looking back, either to the right or to the left, answering questions his companions were asking of him, sometimes even stopping short for no apparent reason, and then starting to walk again, seemingly in a bad mood.

"I don't know what has bitten you," said Vent-en-Panne finally, "but you are not pleasant this morning. I have asked you the same question four times without you deigning to answer me."

"I hadn't heard you," replied Bearcub in the tone of a man who's just woken up with a start.

"Then you must be going deaf."

"Deaf, me?"

"Sure—since you can't hear. Beware, my friend," added Vent-en-Panne, bending over to better reach the captain's ear, "if this goes on, I shall believe that Beau Laurent was right last night."

"What has Beau Laurent to do in all this?" replied Bearcub, annoyed in spite of himself.

"*Pardieu!*" said Vent-en-Panne. "Didn't he say that your interest in the Spanish prisoners had its source in the black eyes of one of the *señoras*—perhaps even both of them?"

"So far I haven't even seen their faces."

"All the more reason, friend."

"You are crazy."

"Of course, and you are wise—it is agreed. Only, however crazy I may be, if I were in your place, instead of letting an opportunity that perhaps may never come again slip out of my reach, I would approach these ladies and resolutely start a conversation with them."

"What's in it for me?"

"The pleasure of hearing a soft and melodious voice caressing your ear—isn't that something?"

"But what would I talk about?"

"*Pardieu!* So your tongue is tied now? Talk to them about anything, day, night, the weather, the birds… It doesn't matter!"

"That doesn't sound interesting at all!" said Bearcub, shrugging his shoulders with disdain.

"It's more interesting than you think, and I'll give you the proof right now."

"How?"

"It won't take long, you'll see."

Vent-en-Panne stopped and, when the ladies had reached the place he stood, he said politely to the woman whose horse was the closest:

"Excuse me, *señora*, I think that your horse has been badly harnessed. Allow me to make sure."

"Thank you, *señor*," replied the lady softly.

Vent-en-Panne made a serious examination of the straps.

"Ah, well, I was wrong," he said after a moment. "Everything is in perfect condition."

"Thank you for your attention, *señor*."

"Would you be kind enough, *señor*," said the second lady in a low and almost inarticulate voice, "to allow me to ask you a question?"

"I am at your command, *señora*," replied Vent-en-Panne, saluting her respectfully, "as well as my companion," he added, pointing to Bearcub, who was walking beside him and who, seeing himself so suddenly dragged into the conversation, did not know how to react.

"Will we be traveling for a long time yet?" the lady continued.

"It is impossible for me to answer, *señora*, for the simple reason that I am as ignorant as you are."

"You know, however, where you are taking us?" asked the woman insistently.

"More or less, yes, *señora*."

"Is that more or less?" the Spanish woman said with a fresh and melodious laughter.

"You are becoming indiscreet, Lilia! You should be more careful," said her companion.

"Me, indiscreet?" exclaimed the first lady. "What makes you say this, my dear Elmina?"

"Because you should understand that these men probably have serious reasons for not responding otherwise."

"You misjudge us, *señora*," said Bearcub softly, suddenly jumping in the conversation. "What my friend told you is, I assure you, the exact truth."

"Then I believe you, *señor*," Doña Elmina replied with emotion. "Your behavior towards us has so far been too noble and generous for us to question your words for a moment."

"Excuse me, *señora*, but if you allow me, I will explain to you in a few words this matter which, for good reason, intrigues you. You know that we are in a state of continuous war with your compatriots?"

"Yes, I do know that," answered Doña Elmina with a slight tremor in her voice.

"Therefore, you understand that we have to be extremely careful when approaching the Spanish borders if we don't want to risk falling into an ambush."

"But," interjected with animation Doña Lilia, "with us being with you, this danger does not exist. If we were attacked..."

"Silence, Lilia, in the name of Heaven!" cried out Doña Elmina, putting her hand on her companion's arm.

"Also, we are sailors, and therefore, we know very little about this area," Bearcub continued, smiling. "So we are looking for one of our friends, who is a buccaneer who hunts in the area, and who will undoubtedly provide us with the means to reach any Spanish city or town without any trouble. That's your answer, *señora*."

"I thank you, *caballero*. The matter is indeed quite simple, and I recognize that your friend couldn't have answered me other than he did."

The other Spaniards had come close without affectation and they listened to the conversation with a rather disgruntled air, as if their intractable Castilian pride had been wounded to see that the two *señoras* had consented to talk in this way with the *ladrones*, even though these same men had just rendered them an immense service.

The freebooters thought it useless to pursue a conversation in which too many people would soon find themselves involved, so they respectfully saluted the two ladies and returned to their positions at the head of the caravan.

"So," said Vent-en-Panne laughing to his friend, "you can see that it wasn't very difficult."

"True, but what good did it do to us?"

"Well, first of all, we learned the names of these two ladies, names that, by the way, I find charming—what about you? Then, we also discovered that our ex-prisoners are much more important than they like to pretend..."

"And how did you make this beautiful discovery?" asked Bearcub ironically.

"Very naturally! When Doña Lilia was abruptly silenced by her companion, just as she was probably going to let her secret out."

"Yes, I remember it now. Indeed, it struck me as odd at the time..."

"But I see that we're now entering the Artibonite plain," Vent-en-Panne remarked. "In an hour, perhaps less, we should be meeting the Poletais."

It was about half past ten in the morning. The caravan had been traveling for more than six hours. The path it had followed, instead of leading it deeper into the forest, had taken it to the center of a vast savanna covered with tall grass, thick groves of trees, and cut through by swamps and streams that were wide but shallow. The *Massif du Nord*, a little to their right, dominated the whole plain with its dark and imposing mass.

The heat was becoming overwhelming. The Spaniards, no doubt rich people accustomed to all the refinements of luxury and comfort, seemed to be suffering a lot from fatigue. They now moved forward only with difficulty, stumbling at every step on the stones of the road, but silent, resigned, not letting a complaint escape.

As for the freebooters, long accustomed to this life, used to overcoming the greatest obstacles, they continued to walk with an equal and sure step.

"I believe," said Bearcub, "that, despite their Castilian stoicism, our ex-prisoners wouldn't mind if we stopped for an hour or two, what do you think, friend?"

"I agree," replied Vent-en-Panne. "They're having trouble following us. Let's look for a suitable place to set up camp."

The caravan was now passing through a very dense forest that seemed to extend quite far in all directions.

"We will stop in the shade," continued the freebooter, "when we reach the edge of this forest. It wouldn't be prudent to stop here. I'd much rather like to see clearly all around me. I'm wary of these walls of vines and leaves; you never know what lurks behind them."

No sooner had Vent-en-Panne uttered these words than a shot rang out at a fairly close distance and a loud male voice cried out in a threatening tone:

"I forbade to shoot under penalty of death, damn it! By the Devil, what's the use of wasting powder like that! These cursed *gavachos* are surrounded and they can't escape us!"

The travelers stopped instinctively.

They feared to come across a scene of struggle and perhaps carnage, as was all too often the case in the depths of this uncharted jungle, where Spaniards and buccaneers were all too likely to meet.

"I recognize this voice! It's the Poletais," said Vent-en-Panne in Bearcub's ear. "There must be some devilry going on down there. Let's watch out!"

Some sounds, such as could be made by the heavy march of an armed detachment, were then heard coming from the woods.

"We are not fooled by your ruse," replied a haughty voice in Castilian. "The people you talk to exist only in your imagination."

"I repeat that you are surrounded by a considerable force. You better watch out! At the slightest movement, my men will fire on you from all sides at once!"

The Spaniards seemed to take the threat seriously because the sounds of the detachment on the march ceased immediately.

"At least, show yourselves," the Spanish officer impatiently replied. "Let us know who we're dealing with."

"You will see us sooner than you think," replied the Poletais in his mocking voice. "You've got yourselves into quite a pickle here, my good friends! There's only one way out for you, I warn you, and that is to put down your weapons immediately and surrender at once!"

"We won't surrender to an invisible enemy," said the Spanish officer who was commanding the Spanish *Cincuenta*.[37]

"As you please! I'll give you five minutes to make up your mind."

---

[37] A brigade of 50 soldiers.

Then, there was silence. The still invisible actors of this scene probably consulted with each other.

Bearcub said a few words in a low voice to Vent-en-Panne; the latter replied with a gesture of assent. Then he blew a softly modulated whistle to call their four *engagés* and gave them orders, while Bearcub approached the ex-prisoners.

"*Señores*," he said, "strange things are happening all around us, as you have heard. Some of our companions are struggling with a *Cincuenta*. Give me your word of honor to remain neutral and, whatever happens, not to utter a word, not to make a gesture that could reveal our presence here. If you refuse, the need to protect our safety would force us to take measures that would offend our sensitivity, especially considering our current relations with each other."

"*Señor*," replied one of the prisoners nobly, "your conduct towards us has been too chivalrous for us to hesitate to make the commitment you ask of us. In the name of my companions and my own, I give you my word of honor that, whatever happens, we will maintain the strictest neutrality. We will only come out to help you, in case fortune should declare itself against you, and your liberty or your life be in danger."

"I accept your word, *caballero*," said Bearcub.

After courteously saluting the Spaniard, he rejoined Vent-en-Panne.

At his command, the four *engagés* had disappeared under cover, slithering like snakes through bushes and scrub.

"Your five minutes are up," said the Poletais. "Do you surrender, yes or no?"

"We shall not surrender to invisible enemies," the Spanish officer replied immediately.

"Ah! Then we're going to have some fun!" shouted the buccaneer in his most mocking tone. "Get ready, my braves!"

"We're ready, Captain!" suddenly shouted threateningly several voices coming from various sides at once.

A tremendous sound of broken branches could then be heard in the brush. It was Vent-en-Panne's and Bearcub's *engagés* who had just spoken.

"Should we start shooting?" cried Vent-en-Panne loudly.

"Not yet!" replied the Poletais, without showing any surprise at this help which had literally come out of nowhere unexpectedly. "Take twenty men with you, Vent-en-Panne, and close the *gavachos'* retreat."

"Bearcub Ironskull already occupies this position with fifteen of his men," replied Vent-en-Panne immediately.

"Well, then, no quarter! Bearcub, can you hear me? We must punish these people as they deserve," said the Poletais imperturbably.

"Rest assured, brother, not one will escape!" shouted Bearcub in a firm voice.

The Spaniards, dismayed to hear so many individuals speaking at once, when they thought they were dealing with only one, and terrified by the names of Vent-en-Panne and Bearcub Ironskull, whose fearsome reputation froze them with terror, now thought they were lost and did not try to resist any further.

"We surrender!" shouted the officer. "We beg for mercy in the name of the Holy Trinity, *señores ladrones*!"

"Throw down your weapons," said the Poletais. "I'm sending four of my men to pick them up!"

Vent-en-Panne, Bearcub and two *engagés* moved toward the Poletais, who, hiding behind a bush, was laughing like a madman.

"Who do you have with you?" asked Vent-en-Panne.

"No one. I'm alone," replied the Poletais. "These *gavachos* surprised me while my three hired men were on a hunt. All the same, Brothers," he added, reaching out to shake the two freebooters' hands, "if you hadn't showed up when you did, my position was beginning to be, if not bad, but at least rather embarrassing."

"Your idea of pretending to surround the *Cincuenta* was magnificent," cried Vent-en-Panne enthusiastically. "To me, it's the highest form of audacity!"

"That was the only way I could think of to get out of that mess. Still, when I heard your friendly voice, I was quite relieved! Now, let's not give the *gavachos* time to change their minds. Let's go and collect their weapons."

They then left their hiding place and moved towards the Spaniards, rifles armed, fingers on the trigger and ready to fire at the slightest suspicious movement.

But these precautions were useless. The Spaniards did not think of picking up a fight.

CHAPTER V
What happened next between the freebooters and the Spaniards

The *Cincuenta*, as its name indicates, was a detachment of fifty soldiers commanded by an *alferez*, or second lieutenant, especially created to protect the Spanish borders and hunt down the French buccaneers, who were continually trying to cross it.

These detachments were normally armed with rifles, which were later replaced by long spears.

The reason for this apparently illogical change was the very terror that the French buccaneers inspired in their enemies. As soon as the Spanish soldiers entered the savannas, they began to unload their rifles and set fires while they had any powder left, with the aim of warning the buccaneers of their presence and thus forcing them to flee, which they did, not out of fear, but in order to not to be disturbed in their hunting.

This precaution of arming with spears soldiers trained to fight enemies with excellent rifles, and such renowned skill, that they could cut the tail of an orange on the branch with a bullet at five hundred paces, made both the soldiers and their government ineffective.

Indeed, what trust could be placed in such men in the event of hostile encounters; and what could one think of the humanity of a government that coldly sent these poor devils to a certain death?

The *Cincuenta*, led by its *alferez*, were lined up in good order about ten paces from the woods, in a fairly open area, but surrounded by thick bushes on all sides—

bushes which the terror of the Spaniards had filled with invisible enemies. Spears and swords lay gathered in heaps before them on the ground.

The Poletais was walking a little ahead of his companions. He first cast a sneering glance at the Spaniards, and, after a moment of silence that sent a shiver of fear through their veins, he finally decided to speak in his mocking voice:

"Ah! ah! My *caballeros*, have you finally made up your mind?"

"Your Lordship," said the *alferez* humbly, "our duty as soldiers prevented us from surrendering to an inferior force."

"And now," said the Poletais sarcastically, "have you admitted your mistake?"

"Yes, Your Lordship. And, as you can see, we did not hesitate to lay our arms."

"I see," said the Poletais brutally, laughing unceremoniously in the nose of the *alferez*, "that you are fools and cowards."

"Your Lordship!" said the offended officer who rose to his feet.

"*Pardieu*! Are you now going to take back your air of *matamore*?[38] I warn you that they are out of season. You have surrendered to only six men," he continued with incredible effrontery. "However, it is true," he added with superb pride, "that these six men are Brothers of the Coast, and that each of them is worth ten of you."

"Curses!" cried the officer enraged.

---

[38] Matamore (from the Spanish *mata moros*, Moorish killer) is a character from the *commedia dell'arte*. He is a swaggering soldier, boasting of exploits he has never achieved and who is basically just a coward.

"No moaning; it won't do you any good," said the buccaneer dryly. "*Señor* lieutenant, have your men tied up."

"What are your terms?"

"None. You have surrendered at your discretion. I will dispose of you as I see fit."

What could the unfortunate soldiers who had fallen into this trap, so skillfully set, and now disarmed, do?

The freebooters stood between them and their spears and swords; they had only one resource left: to try by prompt submission to soften the hearts of their terrible conquerors; that is what they did.

Five minutes later, the whole *Cincuenta* was firmly garroted. Out of consideration for his rank, only the *alferez* remained free. The Poletais picked up his sword and presented it to him.

"Take your weapon back," he said to him with irony. "You use it too well, *señor*, for me to deprive you of it."

At this terrible insult, the young officer became pale as a corpse; his whole body shivered with a nervous tremor. He suddenly grasped the sword with a feverish hand and, making it whistle above his head, he cried out in a voice strangled with anger:

"You are a coward, a wretch and a *ladron*!"

And, with the flat of the blade, he struck the buccaneer.

The Poletais roared like a tiger and, rushing at the young man, he knocked him down with his axe.

"Thank you," said the officer. "Thanks to you, I will die like a soldier!"

A last convulsion agitated his limbs, his eyes closed, and he fell back, dead.

This bloody episode, which had ended this comedy in such a tragic way, darkened all faces.

"You were too quick," said Vent-en-Panne.

"I admit it," replied the Poletais frankly.

"He was a good man."

"He proved it; I don't hold a grudge against him."

"That would be the last straw!" says Vent-en-Panne, smiling in spite of himself at the strange logic of the Poletais.

"Now," said Bearcub, "let's talk business, shall we?"

"What business?" asked the Poletais.

"The business that brought us here."

"Ah yes! I wasn't thinking about it anymore. What is it all about, Brother?"

"First and foremost, we should have breakfast," interrupted Vent-en-Panne. "We're starving; where's your cabin?"

"Not far; a stone's throw away. Follow me."

"We have some Spaniards with us," said Bearcub.

"Prisoners?"

"No, they are people to whom we have given back their freedom."

"Where are they?"

"In the wood, under cover."

"What to do?" said the Poletais, thinking. "Ah, I've got it!" he resumed after a moment. "Vent-en-Panne, go get your prisoners; you, Bearcub, stay here with the *engagés* and watch these rascals. In a quarter of an hour, I'll be back. Instead of going to the food, it will be the food that comes to you."

"Good idea! Go!"

The Poletais threw his rifle under his arm and walked away, while Vent-en-Panne went into the woods.

Bearcub Ironskull, left alone, wasted no time; with the help of the *engagés*, he dug a grave in which the body of the unfortunate officer was laid with his sword beside him. Then, the pit was filled in, and large stones were placed on it as a guarantee against desecration by wild animals.

The soldiers of the *Cincuenta*, dazed by fear, had attended this gloomy, sad and silent ceremony. The tragic end of their commander gave them much apprehension about the fate that awaited them.

When the Spanish prisoners arrived, led by Vent-en-Panne, the pit had been refilled, and the traces of the murder so well concealed, that they completely escaped even the more clairvoyant eyes amongst the newcomers.

Bearcub Ironskull and Vent en-Panne helped the ladies to set foot on the ground and politely led them under an *enramada*[39] that the *engagés* had improvised with a few strokes of the axe, and which offered sufficient shelter from the burning rays of the sun.

The men sat down as they wished, on the sole condition that they remain at a certain distance from the soldiers of the *Cincuenta* and not engage in any conversation with them.

As the buccaneers greeted the two women, they saw them exchange a quick look between them and made a movement as if to hold back.

"What do you want, *señoras*?" asked Bearcub, who understood that they wanted to talk to them.

They hesitated a second longer.

"*Señores*," said Doña Elmina, "perhaps the opportunity to exchange a few words with you will never come again. Before a separation that will undoubtedly

---

[39] Arbor.

last forever, allow us to express our most sincere thanks and offer you the expression of a gratitude that will never end. We owe you both our life and honor, the most precious goods for a woman. Thanks to your generous compassion, and your courageous devotion, Captain Bearcub Ironskull, we have regained our freedom. In just a few hours, we will be back amongst our compatriots."

"Madam," interrupted the captain with a nobility and dignity that caused them extreme surprise, "I only acted as my duty as a gentleman commanded me."

"Well, Captain," said Doña Elmina, "I will not insist any further. I now know what to think of those buccaneers whom I was constantly told were savages without faith or honor. I take with me a memory of them that will always be sweet to me, and when they are slandered before me, I will now know how to defend them."

"Madam, your indulgence and kindness are too high a reward for me."

"It is forbidden for us to reveal our names and rank, but we think that we would be lacking in the respect we owe you if we parted without letting you see the faces that you will never see again, but of which you may keep the memory. Look at us then."

Speaking thus, Doña Elmina pushed back the *rebozo* that veiled her, a movement immediately duplicated by her companion.

The two adventurers gave a cry of admiration at the sight of the two beautiful faces that suddenly offered themselves to their eyes.

Doña Elmina and Doña Lilia were barely seventeen years-old. In them, the Moorish and Castilian types had mixed to make up the most dazzling beauty that only the dreamy soul of a poet could have imagined.

But unfortunately, this delightful vision lasted only as long as a flash. Almost immediately, the two women, with a charming smile, put the folds of their *rebozos* back in front of their faces.

"Already!" whispered Bearcub.

"Now, *señores*, farewell!" said Doña Elmina.

"One more word, *señora*," said Bearcub.

With some deliberation, he took a ring hanging from a steel chain from his chest and broke the chain. He then offered the ring to Doña Elmina, saying:

"The future belongs to no one. As God is my witness, my dearest wish is that you be happy; but if misfortune should ever come upon you again, and if you ever need a safe, devoted, and brave friend, take this ring. It bears my seal. Anytime, anywhere, send me the imprint of that seal, and you I will come at once. Show it only to one of our Brothers. All of them know it, and it will also serve as a safeguard if you yourself are forced to come to me."

"I accept it, *caballero*," replied Doña Elmina with emotion. "You have accustomed me so well to your delicacies, that one more blessing cannot increase my debt to you."

Vent-en-Panne, despite his rough and uncultivated nature, was as moved as his companion. He cut short this scene, which threatened to become embarrassing, by abruptly taking Bearcub away.

The Spaniards, immersed in their own reflections, had not noticed, or at least pretended not to notice the long conversation between the freebooters and the two women.

An hour later, the Poletais rejoined the Brothers of the Coast. He was accompanied by three more *engagés*, and followed by a dozen sailors who, upon seeing the

Spaniards, first wanted to jump at their throats, and whom they had great difficulty in containing.

The *engagés* carried on their broad shoulders all the elements of a gigantic feast. It took only a few minutes to set up the tents and cook the meat.

By order of the Poletais, who was a good man at heart, in his own way, abundant food was served to the former Spanish prisoners and soldiers, whose hands were untied to allow them to eat.

The best pieces were naturally reserved for the ladies, who had remained under the *enramada*; then, the Brothers of the Coast and their *engagés* sat down in a circle, and vigorously ate the food.

While eating, the freebooters explained, in a few words, to the Poletais the reasons for their presence in the savanna and made him aware of their plans.

The buccaneer did not object, sometimes merely nodding his head, but he reserved his right to act as he saw fit with the soldiers of the Cincuenta, who were his own prisoners, which his companions found perfectly fair.

After the meal, which was soon dispatched, the Brothers of the Coast lit their pipes and, on the order of Bearcub Ironskull, the former Spanish prisoners were brought before them.

"*Señor*," said the Captain to the one of the prisoners that his companions seemed to acknowledge as their leader, "it is here that we separate. As I promised you, you are free to go. You will be taken to a Spanish outposts by one of the Poletais' men, who will be your guide. You are only a few leagues from it and will reach it before sunset. For the price of the service I have rendered you, I ask only one thing: a little humanity for the next Brothers of the Coast that fate would make in the future fall into your hands.

"I shall never forget, *señor*," replied the Spaniard with dignity, "that it is to you that we owe our liberty. This debt that I have contracted towards you, I promise to pay it off by treating any French prisoner whom I shall be master of, with the consideration due to misfortune."

"I accept your promise, *señor*, and declare myself amply paid."

"Do not forget, *caballero*," added the Poletais, interrupting unceremoniously the conversation, "that the lives of ten soldiers in your *Cincuenta* will answer for any evil that may befall my guide."

"Will these poor soldiers remain your prisoners?" asked the Spaniard earnestly.

"Yes, unless you agree to pay their ransom."

"I understand, *señor*. How much do you demand?"

"Fifty piasters per man," replied the Poletais.

"I accept, *señor*. Only you understand that I do not have this money with me; but on my honor and my faith as a gentleman, tomorrow, two hours after sunrise, I swear to you that a man of mine will give you the agreed price, that is, two thousand five hundred piasters."

"As soon as that sum is received, your soldiers will go free."

"Do you doubt my word, *señor*?" cried the Spaniard with height.

"Not at all, but I prefer money. No piasters, no soldiers."

"How about settling this business between us, Brother?" said Bearcub, intervening.

"What do you mean?"

"I'll give you my guarantee, if you agree, for this gentleman's word."

"You're mad; you'll be robbed!"

"I don't think so, but that's my business."

"O.K.! Do as you wish then; but as for me, I wash my hands of it."

"Excuse me, *señor*," said the Spaniard, intervening in turn. "I thank you for the guarantee you are willing to offer me, but I do not need it. Instead, I will show this gentleman that I have more confidence in him than he has in me."

He then took a small case from under his tunic.

"Here," he continued, "are several diamonds that I have managed to hide from the eyes of your freebooters. Take them, *señor*. You will give them back to the person who will bring you the agreed price."

The Poletais opened the case and examined the diamonds as a connoisseur.

"These are worth more than a hundred thousand piasters, do you know that, *señor*?" he said.

"Four hundred thousand piasters, in fact," replied the Spaniard coldly.

"And you would entrust them to me like that?"

"Why not? I have faith in your honor."

"Take this case back, señor," said the Poletais, returning it, ashamed of the lesson he had received. "The prisoners are hereby free. You will pay me their ransom whenever you want."

"That's very honorable! Thank you, *señor*!" said the Spaniard.

A moment later, the ladies got back on their horses and the ex-prisoners, after having silently saluted the Brothers of the Coast, set off, preceded by one of Poletais' men.

Passing by Bearcub, Doña Elmina leaned slightly on her saddle and whispered this one word:

"*Recuerdo*!"[40]

The Captain bowed respectfully without answering. He followed the march of the procession with his eyes as long as he could see it.

When at last the Spaniards had disappeared in the meanders of the road, the freebooter choked a sigh and thoughtfully went to join his companions.

That same evening, the Poletais' man brought five thousand piasters back to his master—twice the agreed upon ransom.

The next day, Vent-en-Panne day and Bearcub Ironskull, after cordially taking leave of the buccaneer, returned to Port-Margot.

Weeks, months, a year, and then another year, passed without Bearcub Ironskull, despite his searches, obtaining news of Doña Elmina. His already dark and intense character darkened even more. The hope that he had kept until then—a very weak hope to tell the truth—was then completely extinguished.

He thought that Doña Elmina had forgotten him, and yet, when she had parted from him, she had thrown him that word so sweet and full of such seductive promise:

"*Recuerdo*!"

However, one evening, as he wandered sadly and pensively on the beach of Port-Margot, as was his wont, a man he thought he recognized, without being able to remember where he had seen him before, stopped in front of him and greeted him.

---

[40] I remember.

"Who are you and what do you want?" asked Bear-cub.

"Captain Bearcub Ironskull," replied the man, "I am one of the Poletais' *engagés*. My master has charged me to give you this note, which he received for you yesterday, an hour after sunset."

A secret premonition gripped the Captain's heart. He took the paper with a trembling hand and unfolded it. A glance was enough to tell him that he had not made a mistake. On this note was a black wax print of his seal with these three words: *Cartagena. Luego. Peligro.* Which meant: *Cartagena. At once. Danger.*

"Your master didn't say anything?" asked Bearcub.

"Your pardon, Captain! He added: '*Where Bearcub goes, you tell him that I will go too. Tomorrow at the latest, I will be near him.*'"

"Thank the Poletais for me and tell him that I shall wait for him. This is for you."

And digging in his pocket, the freebooter gave the *engagé* a few coins. The man saluted and left.

The next day, which was a Thursday, the Poletais arrived, as he had promised.

Bearcub immediately began to hire a crew. The task was completed on Friday morning. The buccaneer did not know what danger was threatening Doña Elmina, but it had to be very great for her to ask for his help. So, without even giving himself time to think, he put the greatest celerity in selecting his armaments.

First of all, it was necessary to arrive; later, it would be time to think about what action should be taken. Moreover, the circumstances would undoubtedly force him to adopt some kind of plan.

Bearcub Ironskull had suffered too much not to be a great believer in the power of Fate.

He had hope! What kind of hope? He would not have known how to spell it out. He merely hoped, perhaps for the impossible!

Besides, isn't it always like that with men in love? And, without admitting it to himself, Bearcub Ironskull was in love!

He loved this young girl whom he had met for only a second and whose image had remained forever engraved upon his heart.

His whole life was focused on this love, whose intensity frightened him, and whose impossibility—all too real alas!—made him angry with himself.

And yet, as we said, he hoped!

So he acted accordingly.

But as his race for armaments had caused great commotion in Port-Margot, he resolved to cut short the gossip, and to impose silence on all inventors of more or less absurd rumors about his expedition.

He found only one effective way to close the mouths of all these garrulous bystanders: to fill them!

This was the method he adopted, and he had every reason to congratulate himself for having taken this approach.

On Friday, Bearcub invited all the leaders of the freebooting community to a big lunch, his intention being to set sail immediately afterward.

That is why, as we said at the beginning of this true story, a feast was held at the Rusty Anchor on September 13, 16**.

And now that we have reported all the relevant facts that preceded this *Haulte Beuverie,* as Rabelais would have said, we will resume our story at the point where we had stopped.

CHAPTER VI
How the Trickster *set sail and what Bearcub Ironskull asked of his crew*

Bearcub's guests did honor to his lunch; the glasses clinked with magnificent spirit; joyful words circulated uninterruptedly from one end of the table to the other; songs and laughter dominated the private conversations; and sometimes, an empty dish or bottle, thrown through the window, would break in the midst of the crowd gathered outside in front of the tavern, who greeted the fall with a Homeric laugh.

However, thanks to the presence of M. d'Ogeron, the party came close to the limits of *bienséance*, but never went beyond them. A few freebooters rolled under the table where they snored like organ pipes, but their fall went unnoticed; they had slipped out of their seats without causing the slightest scandal, and the other guests had only taken advantage of these incidents to move their chairs and become more comfortable.

Some of the leaders of the freebooters, on their own, had kept their cool: they were, with M. d'Ogeron, Montbarts, Vent-en-Panne, the Poletais, Michel the Basque and of course, Bearcub Ironskull, who only ever drank water; but the Captain had long been known as an eccentric, and this infraction of the freebooters' customs had been accepted all the more easily since, if he did not drink himself, he did not prevent the others from drinking—quite the contrary.

It is well known that nothing makes one thirsty like talking, and God knows if the Brothers of the Coast were having a good time! Sometimes, they even spoke all at once without any concern for the answers given to them. Also, that day, the weather was stormy, the atmosphere heavy, charged with electricity, the heat stifling… So many excuses for drunkenness, as if for drinkers drunkenness needed an excuse!

"By Jove!" cried suddenly Beau Laurent, raising his glass. "Listen to me, companions! I drink to Captain Bearcub Ironskull and to the success of his projects! Join me if you will!"

"To Captain Bearcub Ironskull!" cried out all the freebooters without exception—those who could still stand, of course.

"And may he meet on his way the galleons of the viceroy of New Spain!" Montbarts the Exterminator cheerfully added.

"To his prompt and happy return among us!" said the Governor with a smile, before bringing his glass to his lips.

Captain Bearcub Ironskull, for a few minutes, seemed to be immersed in deep reflections; however, hearing the toasts that his friends were so enthusiastically making, he raised his head. His pale face lit up with a charming smile, and, seizing his glass, he shouted:

"Bring some of your best French wines! It is not with piss that I want to answer the toasts of my Brothers!"

"Bravo! Long live Bearcub Ironskull!" cried the freebooters, clapping their hands joyfully at this unexpected statement so out of the Captain's habit.

The wine was brought and immediately poured into the glasses of the guests. Captain Bearcub Ironskull then stood up, and greeted the crowd:

"Brothers!" he said in a vibrant voice, "as Beau Laurent said earlier, listen to me, companions! First, I drink to the prosperity of all freebooters!"

"To the prosperity of all freebooters!" repeated the guests.

"Then," said the Captain, holding out his glass again, "I drink to France, our common mother, and to the freedom of the sea, since the land is denied to us!"

This toast, too, was greeted by frenetic clamors of joy.

"And lastly," said the Captain, suddenly breaking his glass on the table, "I won't drink anymore. Brothers, receive my farewells! The hour of separation has come. I am leaving. In a month, I will be back successful—or I will be dead!"

"Why such somber thoughts at this time, my dear Captain?" asked M. d'Ogeron softly.

Bearcub nodded with melancholy.

"You're right, Monsieur," he said. "I am wrong. I sadden you all, and I should not have ended a merry feast like this that way. Forgive me, Brothers. At this moment, I am gambling my life on the roll of the dice. All odds are against me. On the verge of leaving you, forever perhaps, the memory of our fraternal friendship tears my heart—If it does not weaken my will."

"Why leave today?" asked Montbarts.

"On a Friday the thirteenth, too!" added Vent-en-Panne, pensively.

"Wait until tomorrow, Captain," shouted all the freebooters. "Wait, Brother! It is to tempt God to brave him like this!"

"There's a storm in the air," added Beau Laurent.

"You are all correct, my friends," replied the Captain in a firm voice. "Unfortunately, I can only answer by saying this: Because I must!"

"So be it then, since it is so," stated M. d'Ogeron. "We shall ask no more, Captain, for you are one of those men whom nothing can turn back when it is a question of doing one's duty. It is not without reason," he added cheerfully, "that you were nicknamed Ironskull, but we will not leave you like that. We will accompany you all the way to the docks!"

"Yes! Yes!" cried the freebooters clapping their hands. "To the docks!"

"Thank you, Brothers, I accept," Bearcub Ironskull simply replied.

He stood up. All the Brothers of the Coast imitated him.

They then all left the tavern of the Rusty Anchor and slowly headed towards the harbor between two rows of freebooters who, from the street, had witnessed the whole scene and joined in the general emotion.

They finally reached the docks. A boat mounted by ten men swung at the foot of a ladder.

The farewells began.

Captain Bearcub Ironskull and his friend, the Poletais, shook hands one last time with M. d'Ogeron and the leaders of the freebooters; while Alexander, one of their *engagés*, took the animals, i.e. the dogs and the wild boars, Bearcub's faithful companions, down into the boat, where they settled immediately under the benches.

The two Brothers of the Coast then embarked, and they pushed the boat off the wharf. The air was fresh, the sea lapping; a few clouds glided swiftly across the dark blue sky, enameled with stars as bright as diamond dust;

the Moon, almost in its full glory, lit up the night with its pale clarity. The sea was calm.

The rowers, bent over their oars, covered in less than a quarter of an hour the distance that separated them from the ship moored in the bay.

The boat, hailed and recognized by the sentry standing upon the stern, docked the ship by the starboard quarter.

Pierre Legrand, the frigate's first mate, respectfully waited for his captain to step on board, and when he appeared, he gave him the honors due to his rank.

Captain Bearcub Ironskull, while putting his foot on the deck of his ship, cast an inquiring glance around; then, after a moment, he looked pensively at the lights of the town which sparkled in the shadows.

"Is everything ready?" he asked Legrand.

"The anchor's apeak, capstan bars shipped and ready, and the sails furled only with rope yarn," the first mate replied.

The Captain then climbed on the bridge, inspected the horizon for a moment, and grabbed his megaphone:

"Everyone to his station ready for departure!" he shouted in a powerful voice, which was heard everywhere on the ship.

The tanned and energetic faces of the sailors appeared immediately through all the hatches, and within seconds, they were on the deck and lined up for the routine maneuvers.

"Are we ready?" asked Bearcub again.

"Yes, Captain," replied the first mate who had taken up his position on the stern.

"Then, heave, men! Heave and wake the dead!"

About a hundred men threw their weight on the bars of the capstan, and heaved the anchor up.

"Helm to starboard! Sheet in topsails! Sheet them home! Hoist the standing jib! Brace the courses to larboard!"

These various maneuvers were carried out with extreme skill and speed.

"Port breeze forward, starboard aft; starboard side the big jib!"

The vessel paid off majestically to starboard; when it reached four points off, the Captain again raised the megaphone. The men at the capstan were still heaving to bring the anchor to the cathead.

"Haul!" shouted the Captain. "Keep the helm centered."

The *Trickster* was on her way.

The Captain then stepped down from the bridge and handed the megaphone to Pierre Legrand, who, as soon as they were out of the harbor, was in charge of setting the anchor and hoisting the smaller boats tied against the hull.

Twenty minutes later, the freebooter vessel was slipping through the night like a ghost, under double-reefed topsails, outer jib, foresail and spanker.

Despite the fresh breeze offshore, conditions were reasonable and the vessel was making good progress with the wind on her quarter.

A whistle blew, and as soon as the departure was completed and the maneuvers were ready, the crew started to pray.

The buccaneers were very religious; a prayer was said morning and evening on board their ships; the first mate read the prayer, which the sailors repeated after him; often it was while singing hymns that they leaped like tigers as they boarded enemy ships.

This peculiar custom is good to point out when it comes to such men.

An hour later, except for the watch, which stood on the deck ready to maneuver, the crew slept with the carefree attitude that characterizes sailors.

Bearcub Ironskull's ship was an eighteen-hundred-ton vessel, which had just come out of the Ferrol shipyards a year ago.[41]

The Spaniards had armed it with thirty cannons, gave it a crew of five hundred men and sent it to the Gulf of Mexico to protect the passage of their galleons.

It was then called the *San-José*, slim, slender, low on the water, easy to maneuver, and had an upper bridge.

Unfortunately for the *San-José*, she had hardly arrived in the West Indies when she was surprised, by a beautiful night, between midnight and one o'clock in the morning, and captured almost without a fight, by five boats of freebooters commanded by Bearcub Ironskull.

The Spanish captain and his crew, who had attempted to fight back against all odds, were hanged, and the *San-José* was taken to Port-Margot, and its crew sold into slavery to the locals and the buccaneers.

After having given his companions their shares in the catch, Bearcub bought the *San José* for his own account, which he immediately renamed the *Trickster*, a name which, was appropriate in every respect for this fine, light, dashing, and even coquettish ship.

Since the *Trickster* had acquired a new captain, it was the first time she had been back at sea.

---

[41] A harbor city in the Province of A Coruña in Galicia, on the Atlantic coast in north-western Spain, in the vicinity of Strabo's Cape Nerium (modern day Cape Prior).

Around two o'clock in the morning, the Captain went back to the deck. The breeze had continued.

Bearcub said a few words in a low voice to the man keeping watch. It was the Poletais who was as experienced as a sailor as he was daring as a buccaneer.

He had had a lantern lit and affixed at the top of each mast, another at the prow, and masked the grandhunier. The ship then remained stationary.

They were no more than five or six cables from the coast, along which the ship had been sailing since its departure from Port-Margot, which could still be seen clearly, thanks to the brightness of the night.

About half-an-hour passed.

Bearcub was walking around the back of the ship, his head lowered, his arms behind his back, seemingly immersed in serious thoughts.

"Captain," said the Poletais respectfully, for discipline was strict on freebooters' ships, "I see lights on our port side."

"How many?"

"Four."

"That's the count! Be ready to cast a line to the dinghies, when they dock after being recognized."

The Poletais saluted without asking for an explanation and went back up to his watch.

About twenty minutes passed. The lights were rapidly approaching the *Trickster*, and now one could distinguish the shape of four small boats.

"Ahoy!" cried a loud voice from below.

"Ahoy!" replied the Poletais. "Who are you?"

"Brothers of the Coast!" cried the same voice.

"Who's your Captain?"

"L'Olonnais!"

At this name, famous among all freebooters, the sailors on watch trembled.

"Come on up!" the Poletais replied.

A line was thrown, then seized, and two hundred and fifty freebooters, armed to the teeth, climbed aboard the *Trickster* with a monkey's skill. In a few minutes, they found themselves together on the bridge, without the slightest concern for the boats that had brought them there, and which they let adrift.

"Here I am!" L'Olonnais said simply to Bearcub.

"Thank you, Brother!" replied the latter, cordially shaking his hand. "You are a man of your word; besides, as you can see, I was waiting for you. No one suspects anything over there?"

"No one."

"Not even M. d'Ogeron?"

"He doesn't have the slightest suspicion."

"So much the better! The crazier our mission, the more it must remain secret. Are you sure of your men?"

"As of myself! I chose them one by one. Even the most timid of them is like a demon incarnate!"

"Again, so much the better! My lads," added Captain Bearcub Ironskull, now raising his voice and addressing the newcomers who had gathered on the portside deck, "in three hours, it will be daylight. Until then, berth as you can in the gun posts and in the dinghies, and sleep. At sunrise we shall talk again."

The buccaneers withdrew without answering, and as they were all true sea wolves, a few minutes were long enough for them to settle either in the dinghies or under the forecastle, so as not to hinder the maneuver.

The *Trickster* had set off again.

"Come, Brother!" said Bearcub to L'Olonnais. "I must talk to you."

Both went down to the cabin, where they locked themselves in and talked for more than an hour.

Then Bearcub wished his companion good evening and threw himself all dressed on his bed. As for L'Olonnais, he simply lay on the floor, rolled up in his coat. Soon, the two men were soundly asleep.

Around half past four, the sun rose in a cloud. During the night, the breeze had become increasingly cool. The sea was rough, with short, deep waves; the land in the distance appeared only as a bluish cloud.

The *Trickster* was pitching and rolling from side to side, even though she only carried her topsails at half-mast reef; the small jib, the foresail and the brigantine, had been reduced by half. However, she was making good progress.

The Captain went up on deck, followed by some of his closest friends, among whom were L'Olonnais, the Poletais, and Alexandre, his favorite *engagé*.

Pierre Legrand, in his capacity as first mate, had taken over the watch at four o'clock in the morning.

The Captain, after carefully consulting the compass for a few minutes and looking at the sails, approached him and said a few words in a low voice.

Legrand saluted, blew his whistle, leaned over the railing and shouted in a stentorian voice:

"All upstairs! Everyone ready for the chase!

Five minutes later, the crew was standing on the deck and the catwalks.

The sailors stood motionless, silent, with the stocks of their rifles resting on the deck, their hands folded over the end of the barrel, their eyes on their captain, who stood with his arms folded a little behind the main mast.

It was a strange sight to see these men with their tanned features, their energetic physiognomy, calm and carefree on this ship beaten by a furious sea.

Their attires added a touch of picturesque singularity to this extraordinary gathering by their naive simplicity and parsimony.

All they had for clothing was a small canvas shirt and underpants that only came halfway down their thighs; one had to look closely to determine whether the garment was, in fact, made of canvas, since it was soaked in blood and fat, which made it waterproof.

Some had spiky hair, in the form of a hat with the edges cut off, except at the front as a visor; others wore it tied. All grew beards, some of them very long.

Each freebooter had at his belt, on one side, an axe and a short sword with a straight and broad blade, called an ox-tongue, a gun bag and a gourd full of gunpowder; and on the other side, a crocodile skin holster holding four knives and a bayonet. In addition, they each bore a rifle, as mentioned above, and carried a piece of fine, rolled up canvas over their shoulders, which they used as a camping tent.

The rifles deserve a special description: they were made in France by Brachie, in Dieppe, and by Gélin, in Nantes; their barrels were four and a half feet long; the stock was almost straight, massive and loaded with silver ornaments; these rifles shot bullets of sixteen to the pound[42] and were of a remarkable accuracy, especially in the hands of the buccaneers, whose skill was proverbial.

The Captain climbed on his watch bench and, with a gesture, ordered the men to approach.

---

[42] 17.5 mm caliber in today's parlance.

This movement was performed in the highest order. A strident and prolonged whistle demanded silence.

Then Bearcub Ironskull took off his hat, greeted the Brothers of the Coast and began speaking. His voice then rose, calm, accentuated, sonorous, mixing with the high-pitched whistles of the breeze in the ropes and the rumblings of the furious sea against the sides of the ship.

His dogs and wild boars, his inseparable companions, had laid down at his feet, letting themselves be carelessly rocked by the roll of the sea, and looking at the freebooters with that expression so naively melancholic that God put in the eye of the animals created to live with, or for, man, a tacit and instinctive reproach they address to him about his cruelty towards them.

Bearcub passed his hand on his forehead, and, proudly raising his head, casting a lightning glance around, said:

"Brothers of the Coast, we are old acquaintances, you and I. Amongst you, there isn't a man who hasn't sailed with me before. So, not only do you know who I am, but also what I am capable of, and by setting foot on the deck of my ship, your mind was made up. You knew that I was going to lead you to one of those conquests that only the freebooters of Tortuga Island know how to try and accomplish! You were not mistaken, companions! A new expedition is indeed beginning, but, I must tell you frankly, it is one that is more daring and more insane than any carried out up to now! In a word, we are going to surprise the Spaniards in their supreme refuge! We're going to take away their galleons in the very middle of the port which, in their Castilian pride, they claim to be invincible, because the idea had not yet occurred to us to take them! Brothers, we are going to take Cartagena!"

"Cartagena! Cartagena! Long live Bearcub Ironskull!" exclaimed the freebooters, brandishing their weapons with wild enthusiasm.

"I am not going to bother," the Captain continued, "mentioning all the perils that we will have to face, the countless difficulties that will arise! What does that matter to us? We are the Brothers of the Coast! The eagles of Tortuga! We shall triumph!"

"Yes! Yes!" shouted the freebooters whose enthusiasm was redoubling at hearing these proud words, whose full significance they understood.

"Certainly," continued Bearcub with a biting irony, "it would have been easy for me to follow Morgan's example, from his expedition to Porto Bello,[43] and to arm a squadron; but if the geese fly in a troop, the eagle is always alone, and we alone will be sufficient for our task! The enemy, who does not suspect our plan, will be struck as if by thunder and knocked down before he has even had time to think of defending himself!"

"Long live Bearcub Ironskull!" once again interrupted the freebooters with a cry that almost reached the limits of frenzy.

"But, as you know," the Captain continued, "the more glorious this expedition is, the greater our perils, the more severe our discipline must be. I have written a *chasse-partie*;[44] listen carefully when it is read, for it will have to be signed by all of you."

---

[43] Henry Morgan attacked Porto Bello (now in modern-day Panama) on 11 July 1668. The city was the third largest and strongest on the Spanish Main, and on one of the main routes of trade between the Spanish territories and Spain.

[44] A pirate code, or a code of conduct. A group of freebooters would draw up their own code or articles, which provided

"The *chasse-partie*! The *chasse-partie*!" shouted the crew.

The Captain took a sheet of paper folded in four out of his pocket, asked for silence with a gesture, then he unfolded it and read it:

"Article 1: All the Brothers of the Coast embarked on the frigate *The Trickster* swear to Captain Bearcub Ironskull, leaders of the expedition, and to the officers composing his staff, complete obedience under penalty of death."

"We so swear!" cried the crew in a single voice.

"Article 2: The Captain alone will appoint the officers intended to command under his orders up to the ranks of boatswain and master gunner."

"We so swear!"

"Article 3: Whoever removes the enemy's flag from a fortress to fly the three-colored French flag of the freebooters, will receive, in addition to his share, fifty piasters."

"We so swear!"

"Article 4: Whoever takes a prisoner when we need information from the enemy, in addition to his share, shall receive one hundred piasters; whoever takes a superior officer prisoner, two hundred piasters; and for each grenade thrown into a fort, one hundred piasters."

"We so swear!"

"Article 5: The Captain shall receive one prisoner for every hundred prisoners taken; the other officers one for every two hundred. The King's share will be one tenth of the total booty; another share of one tenth will

---

rules for discipline, division of stolen goods, and compensation for injured men.

127

be set aside for the widows and orphans of the Brothers of the Coast who die during the expedition."

"We so swear!"

"Now, Brothers, here's the part that has to do with the wounded and maimed. These allocations will be taken from the total loot before the sharing."

"Bravo! Long live the Captain! Let's listen, let's listen!" cried the freebooters, who were especially interested in that last article.

"Article 6: He who loses both legs will receive fifteen hundred piasters or fifteen slaves, at his choice; for the loss of both arms, eighteen hundred piasters or eighteen slaves; for the loss of one leg, without distinction of right or left, five hundred piasters or six slaves; for one arm or one hand, the same; for one eye, one hundred piasters or one slave; for both eyes, two thousand piasters or twenty slaves; for one finger, one hundred piasters or one slave. Any person crippled in an arm or leg shall be compensated as if that limb had been cut off; any person seriously wounded in the body shall receive five hundred piasters or five slaves."[45]

"Good!" the buccaneers said "The Captain has thought of everything. Long live Bearcub Ironskull!"

"So the whole *chasse-partie* is approved?" asked the Captain.

"Approved and sworn without hesitation by all," cried the freebooters cheerfully.

"Now, Brothers," resumed Bearcub, "listen to the names of the officers to whom I have surrendered some of my power over you. I hope that the choice I have made will meet with your approval."

---

[45] The terms of this *chasse-partie* are rigorously historical and taken from Olivier Œxmelin's book. (*Note from the Author*)

Silence was restored as if by magic.

"First mate of the *Trickster*," continued Bearcub, "Pierre Legrand; second mate, David; first lieutenant, L'Olonnais; second lieutenant, the Poletais; boatswain, Alexandre; master gunner, Tributor. Do you swear obedience to these officers?"

"We so swear!"

"Now, Brothers, appoint yourselves your quarter masters and petty officers; divide yourselves into two teams. From this moment on, I declare the expedition in progress. As soon as the elections are over, the ship's bursar will have you sign the *chasse-partie*. Dismissed!"

The crew immediately retired to the bow, and the elections began with the calmness and composure that one would have expected from such men, but which proved how conscious they were of the act they were accomplishing.

The Captain and his officers remained alone in the rear. It was eight o'clock in the morning, the helmsman struck eight on the bell and David took the watch.

"Brothers," said Bearcub to his officers, "do me the honor of lunching with me. While we eat, we shall talk. I shall tell you the plan I have formed to seize the city which we are preparing to attack, and we shall discuss it with a glass in hand."

The officers bowed respectfully and went down with him to the council chamber, where a table had been set.

The wind was getting cooler and cooler and turning into a storm, but no one on board the *Trickster* seemed to care. Bearcub Ironskull and his officers were not men to be concerned about the strength of the wind.

The *Trickster* was a new ship, built with the same care that the Spaniards then brought in their naval constructions. At that time, the French navy existed, so to speak, only in name. Colbert was barely a precursor to this armada which was soon to become so formidable; the British navy was already strong, to tell the truth, but was still neither numerous nor well established enough to be a threat. The Spanish navy, we say, had passed the Dutch navy to become the first in the world, first by the number of its ships, and then by their state of armaments and their incontestable nautical qualities.

This frigate, the *Trickster,* whose rigging was new, whose frames were solid, which ran like a racehorse and maneuvered as if it were endowed with intelligence, had nothing to fear from even a strong squall, and therefore, there was no need to worry about it.

The officers, presided over by their captain, sat down around the rolling table on, or rather in which the meal was served.

These brave freebooters were very hungry, for they hadn't eaten since their banquet at the Rusty Anchor. So much business had taken so much of their time that they had barely found a few seconds to hastily swallow a few bites and take a sip of brandy.

So they ate and drank merrily, talking about all sorts of things, more or less interesting, and then, when the appetite of these powerful natures was finally satisfied, bottles of brandy were placed on the table, the pipes lit, and the conversation slowly took on a more serious tone.

"It's a beautiful city, Cartagena, isn't it?" asked L'Olonnais.

"They say so," replied Bearcub. "I can't rightly say, having never seen it."

"That's right," laughed L'Olonnais. "Neither of us have, I suppose."

"The Spaniards are so jealous of their colonies," said the Poletais, "that one can only visit them with a rifle in one's hand."

"Eh!" said Pierre Legrand with a smile, "I rather like that. It's more lucrative!"

"You're not wrong," laughed L'Olonnais. "Only I wonder why, wanting to go on an expedition, our friend Bearcub chose Cartagena in preference to any other city on the coast."

"You don't understand anything," said the Poletais, secretly exchanging a look of intelligence with Bearcub. "However, it's quite easy to grasp."

"Do you think so?"

"For God's sake, it's obvious!"

"Well, tell us then!"

"I would like to. Besides, if I'm wrong, Bearcub is here to correct me."

"Go on, friend," said the Captain.

"Yes! We're listening!"

"Ah, it won't take long," laughed the Poletais.

"Then, go on, talk!"

"So here it is in a few words: all the cities on the coast have been more or less, er, visited by us, that is to say, taken, plundered and burned. Only a few have escaped our, er, visits."

"I like your use of the word 'visit.' It is charming," said Pierre Legrand, laughing.

"Isn't it? Now these cities, of which there are at most ten, have been ignored until now, either because they are too poor, and, as they say, it wouldn't have been worth the risk, or because they are too well fortified for us to have dared to try to, if not visit them, which would have been easy, but to actually take them, which would be quite dangerous. Two or three of them especially are

131

considered really impregnable. Montbarts and Morgan took Porto Bello, Panama, Maracaïbo, and God knows what else, all expeditions of incredible daring. Bearcub Ironskull is an excellent comrade, true, but despite that, these great feats, so skillfully executed by his friends, have saddened him inwardly—not that he is jealous, of course, but the glory of Montbarts, Morgan, Beau Laurent and others keeps him awake at night. So he, too, wanted to organize one of these expeditions that frighten our enemies, and make their wealth pass into our hands. The city that passes for the most fearsome of all those that we haven't visited is Cartagena, so naturally, Bearcub had to choose that one. Four days ago, he came to find me at my cabin and said: 'I want to organize an expedition. I need you, will you come?' And I replied, as any one of you would have: 'Where are we going?' 'To Cartagena,' he answered. 'OK, we'll go to Cartagena,' I said, and I followed him, without further explanation."

"The fact is that there was no need for it," said L'Olonnais.

"Yes, that was enough," added Pierre Legrand.

"So friends, that's why we ended up here, on our way to take Cartagena, isn't that the truth, Bearcub?"

"That's the God-given truth," replied the Captain smiling.

The explanation was clear, simple, and above all, it seemed very logical to these men who didn't even need excuses to attack Spaniards.

"Brothers," said Bearcub after a moment, "the night is coming on, and we all need rest before we fight. I want to discuss an urgent measure that we must take without delay with you first."

Silence was immediately restored.

"We are listening, Captain," said the Poletais.

132

"This is what I want to discuss with you, gentlemen," continued the Captain;. "Our supplies were so keenly selected that our men have only the standard three pounds of flour and five pounds of smoked meat, which they are obligated to bring with them. The stores at Port-Margot were so badly supplied, and the merchants' prices so high, that I was forced to refuse to deal with them. As a result, our galley is mostly empty. We have gunpowder, bullets and cannonballs in abundance, but we are very much short of food: no meat, no bread, no wine, no liquor; only water. Now we have to plan for this state of affairs which, if it is to continue for more a day, might lead to serious complications. Moreover, it is indispensable for us to find a guide, a man who knows Cartagena and can point out its weak spots. This is a frank and honest assessment. Now, what say you?"

"Forgive me," said L'Olonnais. "According to you, we must have food and a guide. For that, I see only one solution."

"Which one?"

"Take them from where we're sure to find them, pal! It seems to me that we have an embarrassment of riches. We're here in the middle of the Spanish Main, full of rich islands, provided for with abundance. Let's pick the nearest one, take it, and ransom it. It's not more complicated than that."

"L'Olonnais is right," said the Poletais. "The coastline of Santo Domingo is also full of hamlets and villages where we can easily find what we need."

"No, that would delay us too much," said Bearcub. "We can't waste any time. I agree with L'Olonnais; taking an island is the best solution, but I didn't want to make this determination without first consulting you."

"Your decision is yours, Captain," replied the officers with one voice.

"Which is the nearest island?" asked the Poletais.

"The closest one is Cuba," answered Pierre Legrand.

"Hum," said L'Olonnais, "that is a hard target to swallow."

"You shouldn't even think about it," said the Poletais.

"Perhaps, perhaps not," said Bearcub.

"Huh?" cried the freebooters, surprised.

"The very audacity of our enterprise," the Captain replied, "will ensure its success. The speed of our attack makes this infallible. By the time the Spaniards pull out of their stupor, we will be gone and safe from their vengeance. Listen to me: Cuba has only one major city, Havana, which has six or eight thousand inhabitants. The many ports scattered along the coast are nothing but fishermen's hamlets, unable to resist a skillfully executed attack. In four hours, we can have all the supplies we need and be sailing again. Do you trust me?"

"*Pardieu*! We do!" cried the freebooters.

"Then, let me do it my way and we shall succeed."

"You are the master here, and free to act as you please," replied the Poletais. "We rely on you as you rely on us. Give your orders, and rest assured that they will be carried out."

"Good! Then, go and rest. It's now ten o'clock in the evening. At three o'clock, the attack shall take place. And by tomorrow night, I promise you, we will have plenty of food. Pierre, lower our sails by three quarters; the wind seems to have softened a little."

Pierre Legrand went up to the bridge to execute the order he had just received. Soon, they noticed at the more accentuated movement of the ship that this order was being executed.

Bearcub Ironskull stood up:

"Now, good night, Brothers!" he said. "Remember that we rise at three."

Five minutes later the freebooters were asleep as if they were never to wake up. The expectation of the danger they were about to face had not in any way affected their peace of mind or their sleep patterns. For what was danger to these fearless sea lions!

CHAPTER VII
How Bearcub Ironskull got the supplies he needed and found a guide

The details of the enlistment, organization and discipline of the crews on board the freebooters' ships are singular enough to deserve to be mentioned here.

Every Brother of the Coast had the right to mount an expedition; all he had to do was to own a ship.

That ship was often—even most of the time—either a large pirogue or even a humble rowboat; these frail craft were enough to board the proud Spanish vessels.

When an expedition was being planned, its captain would summon the freebooters to a tavern to the sound of drums and trumpets.

He would then reveal his plan to those he wanted to enlist, agree with them on the duration of the mission, and a contract would be made.

Each man was required to sign, or to make his cross if he could not write—which was rare—at the bottom of a document prepared by one of the clerks of the *Compagnie des Indes*; this act, deemed authentic, was then countersigned by the captain and the governor.

Each man was required to have: a rifle, an axe, a straight sword, a dagger, fifteen charges of gunpowder, an adequate number of bullets, and a camp tent, a piece of fine cloth that the Brothers rolled up and carried in a sling. Furthermore, they had to carry a gourd full of brandy, and enough smoked meat and flour for three days.

These conditions were strictly mandatory.

As soon as they were enlisted, the Brothers of the Coast had to obey their captain blindly and show him the greatest respect at all times, even if these officers had been their subordinates on previous expeditions. For it often happened that today's captain was a simple sailor tomorrow; it depended on how he spent his loot, and consequently, on his fortune.

Discipline on board was relentlessly severe. Only two punishments were used: dry dock and death. These two were, in fact, one and the same, under different names. It happened but rarely that someone didn't die from dry dock, but remained crippled for life.

Upon embarking on the ship, the enlisted men were required to pair up with a comrade. Here's why:

At sea when one deckhand was on watch, the other rested, or took care of the domestic tasks, i.e. cooking and cleaning the weapons, or cared for his mate when he was sick and even replaced him, if necessary, in his service.

Ashore, the two seamen walked side by side, helping each other along the way, and hunting for food for each other; if one was wounded, the other could not abandon him; he was required to rescue him, carry him back to the ship on his shoulders, and watch over him, carrying his weapons and ammunition until his mate's strength had fully returned; moreover, he had to protect him, even at the risk of his own life during battles.

This system had the advantage of tripling the strength of the crews and making these men nigh invincible; these fraternal bonds, forged in the midst of peril and deprivation, almost always became indissoluble, and often did not even break upon the death of one of the two; the survivor continued his task by adopting the family of his deceased mate, and sometimes pushed self-sacrifice to the point of marrying his widow, whom he had often never seen or whom he did not love, with the sole aim of giving a father to her children.

This was the seamanship among the buccaneers; this tradition has remained almost intact until today in our navy. The officers, who all recognize its usefulness, and who know how much it benefits the discipline and orderliness of the service, take great care to maintain and encourage it on the ships of the Republic.

This system is more generalized and has put deeper roots on the ships of the merchant navy, because there, the men have known each other since childhood, are almost always from the same country, and have almost always lived together.

Expedition leaders were required to have a surgeon on board when the crew exceeded thirty-five men. This surgeon was almost always an unfortunate rifleman or a former apothecary clerk, as ignorant as a donkey, whose entire science was contained in some medical book he consulted as best he could, and who administered the drugs wrongly and carelessly. He cut, cut, and sliced the poor devils whom a bad fate had made fall into his hands with all the aplomb of a skilled butcher, and only by a miracle might they escape the effect of his treatments, as eccentric as they were merciless.

The freebooters were very afraid of these so-called surgeons; they preferred to be killed rather than have the problematic fate to be healed by them.

The sharing of the loot was usually effected when the ship was back, either at Tortuga, Leogane, Port-de-Paix, or Port-Margot, in the presence of the Governor and the chief agent of the *Compagnie des Indes*.

The procedure was as follows:

First, the King's share, which amounted to one tenth of the loot, was subtracted from the total; then, the dead and the wounded men's share were taken and the Governor was instructed to distribute them accordingly. Then the proper division was made according to the terms of the *chasse-partie*, which had been signed by all the men before departure, and a duplicate of which had remained in the hands of the Governor.

The loot mostly consisted of jewelry, gold and silver, more or less precious fabrics, goods such as spices, trinkets, etc., and, finally, slaves—men and women taken during the expedition. The Spanish priests and monks were not, despite their habit, immune from such fate. These unfortunate people were usually given a period of time to "make amends," that is to say, pay a ransom. Such ransoms were set at three times the amount they had been sold to their masters, all of whom were locals or buccaneers.

Once the division of the loot was over, the freebooters, often very much taken with the wealth that had just fallen to them, and which they did not know how to invest, became the prey of these low-level speculators who swarmed in these lands, and who bought everything for a third and often a quarter of its real value.

After that, the celebratory feasts began and lasted until the freebooters had spent, or rather wasted, their last doubloon.

When there was nothing left, they would happily set off on a new expedition, the results of which would almost always be the same. But what did it matter to them, these men who lived only in the present! They were happy like this. Were they wrong? Maybe!

This is how simply and, at the same time, vigorously the association of the Brothers of the Coast was organized, when, as they said, they went on an expedition. It was to this organization that they owed the successes they had achieved and the extraordinary actions they had accomplished.

At three o'clock in the morning, just as the helmsman was preparing to ring the bell, Bearcub Ironskull appeared on the bridge. His officers were already waiting for him.

The Captain glanced around him; the night was clear, the sea a little rough, for the wind was steady. On the starboard bow, there was a dark mass toward which the frigate was rapidly advancing—it was the coast of the island of Cuba, which was no more than two leagues away.

"Get ready," said the Captain "Everyone on deck!"

The boatswain blew the whistle vigorously. Five minutes later, all the sailors were gathered around the main mast. They had not taken long to wake up. The Brothers of the Coast slept lying in a jumble in the steerage, or in the gun posts; a hammock was a luxury that the freebooters did not allow themselves.

The Captain called his officers.

"Gentlemen," he told them, "remember this: this is a surprise attack, not a battle! Let us try, if possible, not to fire a single shot. Our business at the moment is not to fight, but to steal supplies. Is this well understood?"

"Perfectly, yes, Captain," answered the officers.

"We are heading right towards the port of Guantanamo. There is a colony of fishermen there that has been established for about twenty years. These people are rich; their port trades with the city of Santiago, which is not far away, and to which it supplies cereals, pigs and oxen brought there from the interior. We shall find everything we need there. The Poletais and

L'Olonnais, each with 150 men, will go ahead of the frigate in canoes, whose oars will be muffled so as not to awaken the locals. The Poletais will surround the village on the right, while L'Olonnais will surround it on the left. Then you will both remain there, each at his post, making sure that no one escapes into the wilds to sound the alarm. I will enter straight into the harbor. If you act with caution, our raid will be over before the *gavachos* have time to even suspect our presence. The sun will not rise for another hour at least; that's more time than we need to surprise them in their beds. Let's get going, gentlemen!"

The Captain had the frigate slow down; six canoes were brought up; L'Olonnais and the Poletais embarked with their men, and soon they disappeared in the shadows cast by the high mountains of the island.

Bearcub was pacing at the back of the ship, consulting the compass, looking at the coast and inspecting the sail.

About half an hour had passed when Pierre Legrand approached the Captain.

"What is it?" asked Bearcub.

"Captain," replied the other, "the man on watch at the starboard spotted a small boat that seemed to be sailing along the coast. I made sure of the fact, and I, too, saw this boat."

"Take the little canoe, Pierre, and go check out what this prowler is with ten men. I, for my part, am going to set the frigate on its way again."

Pierre Legrand saluted and withdrew. A moment later he was gone. As the wind favored him, he began a desperate search for the small boat spotted earlier by the look-out.

But then, something strange happened. The suspicious boat, instead of trying to escape as expected, just turned around and went straight toward the freebooters. Either it was an act of great boldness, or rare stupidity from the part of those who manned this frail pirogue.

Pierre Legrand had the weapons prepared and continued to advance.

Soon both boats were only at half pistol range.

As the freebooters got ready to board the smaller boat, they saw that it carried only two men: a European and a native.

A grappling hook was thrown to capture the board.

"Who are you and where are you going?" asked Pierre Legrand in his purest Castilian.

"Dear lord," humbly answered the European, "I am a pilot. I spotted a large ship an hour ago. I assumed it was a ship from Santiago coming to dock here, and I set out to sea to pilot it to the harbor. If I was wrong, I am happy to leave and go home."

"No, by the Devil, no!" Pierre Legrand laughed. "On the contrary, you couldn't have come at a better time. We need you."

"But it seems to me, esteemed captain, that you are not..."

"...Spaniards?" interrupted Pierre Legrand. "Forgive me, but we are not! We are *ladrones*."

"Jesus! Maria!" cried the pilot, struck by his misunderstanding, joining hands in despair.

"Do not worry, however," continued the freebooter amicably. "We don't want to hurt you, and maybe it'll be good for you to have met us—who knows? Let's go! I want four men in this pirogue, and let's wait for the frigate."

They didn't have to wait for long. Almost immediately the *Trickster* was upon them. Pierre Legrand climbed up the ladder with his two prisoners. After he had reported to Bearcub what had happened, he made the pilot approach.

"Are you a pilot?" the Captain asked, looking the man in the eye.

"Yes, Excellency, I am," the other humbly replied. "Not only on the islands, but also, if necessary, on land."

"Ah! ah!" said Bearcub, smiling. "And can you be trusted?"

"Yes, Your Excellency."

"Is the entrance to Guantanamo difficult?"

"No, Excellency. It is only a matter of staying straight in the middle of the channel."

"What is the size of the city?"

"It's only a village, Excellency."

"Very good. Are there any soldiers?"

"About fifty, stationed in an earthen fort."

"The Devil!"

"But," hastened to add the pilot, "this fort is not yet finished, and the guns haven't yet arrived from Santiago. They are expecting them soon."

"That's better! That begs another question: do you think our approach has been reported?"

"About that, no, Excellency. I only saw you an hour ago and everyone is sleeping soundly."

"Very well. Now, listen to this: you know who we are, don't you? So, beware: if you deceive me, you will hang from that mast you see there, above your head; but if you serve me well, I will give you ten ounces of gold. I never break my word. What do you choose?"

"The ten ounces of gold, Your Excellency," cried out the pilot whose eyes shone with covetousness.

"Good! We have a deal then! Now take command and guide us into the harbor."

The pilot bowed and began to obey.

The Spaniard had brazenly chosen his side in his misadventure. The ten ounces of gold so generously promised by Bearcub now made him, temporarily at least, a member of the Brothers of the Coast.

He guided them with great skill through the channel, and soon the frigate found herself in cannon range of the village, still plunged in complete silence.

It would be a rude awakening!

The Captain dropped the anchor and set the sails; then, giving command of the frigate to Pierre Legrand, he went ashore, taking the pilot with him.

Three smaller boats, manned by about a hundred freebooters, followed him. The four boats reached the shore with a few strokes of their oars.

Bearcub, fearing a bad surprise, as soon as they had disembarked, ordered his men to stand offshore; then, turning to the pilot, he asked:

"Who are the village authorities?"

"There is only one, Excellency," the man replied. "An *alcade*."

"Where does he live?"

"In that big house right in front of you."

The big house in question was actually more like a hovel, just a little less miserable than the others.

"Better and better," said Bearcub. "Is this *alcade* a brave man?"

"I don't know, Your Excellency. I only know that he is a stingy, mean man, and hated by everyone; but as he is the nephew of the governor of Santiago, he pretty much does what he wants."

"Ha!" said Bearcub, laughing. "Who knew that to-night, I would be called to play the role of Providence here! That is really very funny!"

"Oh, Excellency," cried the pilot in a pleading tone, "the town would be very happy to be delivered from this wicked man! There is no atrocity he does not commit daily."

"Well then, I'm going to go and say hello to this worthy man right now. As for you, follow me and don't be afraid."

The *alcade*'s house was only a few steps from the shore. Bearcub had it surrounded, then pulling a pistol from his belt, he fired it into the lock, which shattered. Nevertheless, the door did not open, as it was solidly barricaded from the inside.

"It seems that we are dealing with a cautious man," said the Captain while reloading his pistol. "Two blows of the axe in there!"

At the same moment, a window opened and a man in a night shirt, armed with a long harquebus, showed his pale and frightened face, shouting in a shrill voice"

"Ah! You wretched men! You want to murder me! But wait! Wait!"

"Silence that bawling," said Bearcub coldly.

A rifle shot was fired, and the harquebus, broken by the bullet, fell to the ground.

The *alcade* had retreated into the interior of his bed-room.

However, the shots and the axe blows against the door had awakened the inhabitants. The doors opened timidly; pale faces with blinking eyes appeared in the gap, but no one ventured out.

The front door finally yielded under the repeated blows of a vigorous Brother of the Coast.

"Bring that joker down here," ordered Bearcub. "And you," he told his men, "form your ranks and keep your eyes open!"

The *alcade* was half-naked, in his night shirt and underpants; he was trembling with all his limbs, more from terror than cold, although the wind was quite strong, and the nights very cool in these parts. The two freebooters who brought him did not spare him the blows of their sticks to speed up his walk.

"Are you the *alcade*?" Bearcub asked in a stern voice.

"Yes, Your Lordship," the man replied in a strangled voice.

"Tie his hands and put wicks between his fingers. At my command, you will light them."

This order was executed with a speed and skill that testified to the long experience of the freebooters.

As the *alcade* understood what this was all about, his terror redoubled.

"Now, answer my questions and, above all, be careful not to deceive me. If you do, I shall be angry with you," said Bearcub with a cruel smile, tapping his hand with his fingertip.

"Yes, Your Lordship, ask away," the *alcade* replied immediately.

"Your village is in my power. You and all the inhabitants are my prisoners. It is now a question of ransoming you."

"Alas! We are very poor..."

"I see. But perhaps you have meat and grain supplies? Where are they?"

"Your Lordship, I swear on the place that I hope to gain in Heaven someday, that all our supplies are nearly depleted."

146

"Still—where are they stored?"

"There," the *alcade* replied, pointing to two large woodsheds.

"Check them out," ordered Bearcub, laconically.

About twenty freebooters went away; after a quarter of an hour, they came back.

"Nearly empty," reported one of them.

"Are there any other stores?" asked Bearcub.

"None," murmured the *alcade*. "Your Lordship, I swear to you on my place..."

"All right, all right," said the Captain. "You said that already... Still..."

"But, Your Lordship, I promise you I told you the truth," said the *alcade* who began to feel reassured.

But, all of a sudden, he made an abrupt backward movement.

"By the Devil!" he cried.

He had just seen the pilot who, until then, had remained hidden amongst the crowd of the Brothers of the Coast.

"This man is deceiving you, Excellency," said the pilot sharply, "and he is deceiving you knowingly."

"Explain."

"The stores are empty—it is true; but it is because he has confiscated all the goods they contained, notwithstanding the wishes of their legitimate owners, and put them in stores of his own on order to sell them later for his own profit."

"Ah! Is it true?" asked Bearcub, questioning the ever-growing crowd of locals who, though standing at a distance, had nonetheless become emboldened enough to leave their homes, seeing that the freebooters did not seem to have any evil intentions towards them.

"It is true, Your Lordship," they replied with one voice.

"So this man, who by his position should be your protector and defender, is, on the contrary, robbing and persecuting you? "

"He starves us, takes away everything we own, and those who dare to complain, he has them tortured."

"Where are his stores?"

"Your Lordship!" begged the *alcade*, moaning.

"Silence, wretch!" cried Bearcub in a terrible voice.

"His stores are behind his house," the pilot said. "They are full, Excellency, not only of smoked beef, salted pork and cereals, but also of wine and liqueurs."

"It is good then! Justice will be done to this man. Listen, all of you: I could impose a ransom on you, but I don't want to. The only thing I demand of you is that you help my men get the supplies we need aboard my ship. And since I don't want to take what belongs to you, who are poor, I'll leave you to plunder this house. And furthermore, for your help, you will receive five thousand piasters that you can share between you."

Great cheers of joy answered the Captain's speech, Yet, the most joyful cheers were uttered by the very soldiers who had shown up with a combative look under the command of an *alferez*. But when they saw what it was all about, they gave up their weapons and went wild.

The *alferez* was a brave soldier; the cowardice of his men outraged him and made his face turn red. For a moment he stood motionless, frowning, looking with contempt at those under his command, shamelessly rushing to plunder the *alcade*'s house. But this hesitation did not last long. He stood up proudly and stepped forward with a sure step towards Bearcub Ironskull.

The Captain watched him come; a kind smile played on his lips.

"Señor Captain, or whatever your title may be, *caballero*," said the officer greeting him with a haughty courtesy, "I do not come to surrender to you."

"What are you coming to do then?" asked Bearcub, whose eye sparkled.

"Alone, any resistance is impossible," the officer coldly replied. "So I come to protest loudly in the name of my country against the unspeakable aggression of which we are victims. As for my sword..." he added, drawing it from the scabbard and raising it above his head.

"Stop, lieutenant," said the freebooter, grabbing the man's sword and putting it back in its sheath, while the officer let him do so, in the midst of the greatest surprise. "You are a brave soldier! If the government you serve counted many like you, we might not be so strong. Keep your sword—if you lost it, I would be forced to give you mine, and I confess that I am very fond of it."

These words were spoken with such a sympathetic accent that, in spite of himself, the officer felt moved.

"What kind of men are you?" he murmured.

"We are only men like you," replied Bearcub, intentionally. "But now, you must withdraw, Lieutenant. Things are going to happen here that you must not see."

"Captain, is that poor man..." said the officer in a pleading tone, pointing to the *alcade*.

"Don't think about him, don't intercede for him," interrupted Bearcub sharply. "He's a wretch; he's doomed."

The *alcade* felt his blood freeze in his veins at this word.

The officer realized that any prayer would be useless; so he slowly moved away with a pensive air. Soon he disappeared at the corner of a street.

During that time, the entire village population had begun work with an eagerness that showed their desire to win the promised reward and to be freed as soon as possible from the daring invaders who held them under threat from their cannons and rifles.

The sight of the armed groups commanded by L'Olonnais and the Poletais, which Bearcub had recalled when he became certain that he had no resistance to fear, had further increased the general ardor, proving to the inhabitants of the port of Guantanamo that nothing but complete obedience could save them.

The inhabitants were all fishermen, each with his own boat; while some carried the goods to the beach, others loaded them, and finally others took them to the frigate.

Pierre Legrand was amazed at the considerable quantity of supplies that poured aboard; it was like a flood; he struggled to keep up with the inventory.

In less than three hours, everything had been hoisted on board the frigate and secured in her holds; the ship now had provisions for more than six months: it was prodigious!

The Captain watched calmly, cold, impassively, as this operation was being carried out.

When the last bundle was finally stored safely aboard the *Trickster*, and there was absolutely nothing left in the stores of the unfortunate *alcalde*, who watched in panic as this immense disaster engulfed his entire fortune, Bearcub sounded a trumpet call.

The inhabitants gathered around the pirates in a tumultuous manner.

"Good people," said the Captain, "you have so far worked for me, for which I thank you. Now work for yourselves: loot this house, I leave it to you."

The Spaniards did not need to be told twice. They rushed to the *alcade*'s house, broke in, and soon, it was full of relentless plunderers, breaking the furniture and probing walls and partitions.

When finally nothing remained of the house but its four walls, Bearcub set fire to it. Since it had been built of cedar timber, it soon burned in a way that was very pleasing to the eye.

The Captain then took from the hands of a buccaneer a heavy pouch which he had sent the man to fetch on board the frigate, and gave this satchel full of gold to one of the notables, saying in a loud and firm voice, addressing the crowd at the same time:

"You are now paid; I don't owe you anything anymore, do I?"

"Yes, Captain," replied the man to whom he had handed over the pouch, "you still owe us something."

"What do I owe you then?"

"Justice."

"Justice?"

"Yes, Captain," replied the Spaniard. "You have promised us justice."

"I don't understand."

"This man has long been for us the most terrible of oppressors," replied the Spaniard, pointing to the *alcade*. "That wretch has plagued us with his insults, robbed us without shame, and tortured us at will... Will you now give him back to freedom, so that, after you're gone, he can make us all pay for what took place tonight, by your order and under the pressure of your army? Would that be just? Answer, Captain! We have faith in your word as you have had faith in ours. We have faithfully accomplished our task, now it is up to you to accomplish yours."

"So be it!" replied the Captain in a deep voice, "but this man cannot be killed just like that; it would be murder. He must be judged, and you, yourselves, will be his judges."

"May his blood fall on our heads.

"Are you well resolved?"

"Yes," cried the crowd.

"Good! Now answer: what crimes do you attribute to this man?"

"Greed pushed to the point of cruelty, simony,[46] and perjury."

"Do you find him guilty of these crimes?"

"We do!"

"What punishment does he deserve?"

"Death!" the entire population cried out with one voice, panting with hatred and anger.

"Thy will be done then. This man shall die. Pray for his soul so that God may take mercy on it."

But a storm of shouts, jeers, and curses were the only answer to these last words.

The Captain made a sign.

In a few minutes, a gallows had been erected on the beach, in front of the smoky ruins of the house.

The unfortunate *alcade* was seized, garroted, and the rope was put around his neck; but by then, he was no longer aware of what was going on, and it was only an inert mass, already half-dead, that was hoisted to the gallows, to the cries of joy of the entire population.

---

[46] The buying or selling of a church office or ecclesiastical preferment.

At Bearcub's order, a sign was placed on the chest of the condemned man. On it were written in Spanish and French these words, which explained the terrible sentence:

HANGED, NOT AS A SPANIARD, BUT AS A THIEF. BEARCUB IRONSKULL.

When the last convulsions of agony had died out, and the corpse gained that rigidity from which it would not emerge, the Captain saluted the crowd and headed towards the beach.

A few minutes later, the freebooters had returned onboard the *Trickster*.

When the frigate was out of the port, Bearcub called the pilot:

"This island is no longer good for you," he said. "Come with me and when my expedition is finished, I will disembark you wherever you like, and you will be rich for the rest of your days. Does this offer suit you?"

"Yes, captain, but on one condition."

"Which one?"

"That you'll provide me with the means to get to Europe—France, perhaps. In the Americas, like in Spain, my life would not be safe."

"That's good! You have my word: serve me loyally and you won't regret the commitment we make to each other."

"I shall be devoted to you, captain."

The frigate, carried by a good wind, soon lost sight of the coast of Cuba and set sail towards the city of Cartagena, which her Captain was so eager to reach.

CHAPTER VIII
How two girls' conversation ended with a tear

Cartagena de las Indias, or Cartagena, as the French simply called it, was one of the happiest cities in the New World.

The Spaniards possessed an infallible instinct for choosing the location of the cities they founded at each of their harbors on the American coasts; and, apart from a few mistakes of no importance, almost all the cities they founded in this way during their search for gold—the sole purpose of their daring expeditions—still thrive, all rich and powerful for the most part, still attached to their original locations, despite all the changes that have since taken place.

Cartagena was founded in 1533 by Don Pedro de Heredia,[47] on a sandy island in the strait formed at its mouth by the Rio Magdalena. This city had one of the most beautiful and safest harbors in all of the Americas. It served for a long time as a refuge for the Spanish galleons which, loaded with the riches of the Pacific Ocean, transported by mule across the isthmus of Panama, were not deemed to be safe in Porto Bello, especially after the first Panama was destroyed and plundered by the Brothers of the Coast and rebuilt on the Rio Grande, but still on the Southern Sea.[48]

---

[47] Pedro de Heredia (c.1505-1554), Spanish conquistador and explorer of the northern coast and the interior of present-day Colombia.

[48] The city of Panama was founded on 15 August 1519, by Pedro Arias de Ávila. Within a few years, it became a launch-

Like all Spanish cities of the Old and New Worlds, the appearance of Cartagena is sad, although the streets are wide, cut at right angles and refreshed by numerous springs of running water. This air of sadness is due to the long galleries supported by low and heavy columns, a kind of cloister that lines both sides of the streets, and the wide projecting terraces that steal most of the daylight and the sun.

At the time of our history, the population of Cartagena amounted to slightly more than thirty thousand; the city and the port were defended by five fortresses, one of which, the most important of all, that of Boca-Chica, had a battery of sixty cannons.

The Spanish garrison consisted of 5,200 men of old troops formed in the European wars and commanded by a brigadier, a rank roughly equivalent to the modern rank of brigadier-general. If necessary, in a few hours, about 3,500 militiamen, well-armed and all the more brave because they fought *pro aris and focis,*[49] could be added to these troops.

It was this city, so formidably armed, so fortunately situated, that Captain Bearcub Ironskull, with a single ship armed with thirty guns and a crew of seven hundred and twenty-three men, had resolved to take.

---

ing point for the exploration and conquest of Peru and a transit point for gold and silver headed back to Spain through the Isthmus. In 1671, the freebooter Henry Morgan attacked and looted the city, which was subsequently destroyed by fire. The ruins of the old city still remain and are known as *Panamá Viejo* (Old Panama). The city was rebuilt in 1673 in a new location approximately 5 miles southwest of the original city. This location is now known as the *Casco Viejo* (Old Quarter) of the city.

[49] For hearth and home.

It is true that these seven hundred and twenty-three men were amongst the elite of the Brothers of the Coast, and that Captain Bearcub Ironskull used to say that everything that the eye of a freebooter could embrace in his visual range should, if he so wished, belong to him; a fact which, until then, he had always personally proved possible.

But never before had any of the leaders of the freebooters conceived such an audacious expedition, especially with such weak means of execution.

Now, taking advantage of the faculty that has always been granted to novelists to go as they please on the wings of the *djinns* and cross the longest distances in a few strokes, not with wings, but with feathers, we will leave the *Trickster* and her brave crew in the Caribbean, a few hours after the success of their bold *coup-de-main* at Guantanamo, and, beg our beloved reader to follow us to the American coast and go to Turbaco.

Turbaco is a charming little village of seven or eight hundred souls at the most, a village built on the green slope of a hill, just a few leagues from Cartagena, leaning against a majestic and almost impenetrable forest, whose last buttresses come to die on the very edge of the Rio Magdalena.

Six or eight leagues away from the sea, this village serves as a refuge for the wealthy inhabitants of the city and for European Spaniards who are not yet acclimatized, against the excessive heat and diseases that, during the summer, reign on the coast.

This village is really enchanting; it emerges, so to speak, from the middle of a huge mass of greenery, rising in an amphitheater almost to the top of the hill. One can see its large and elegant houses built of bamboo and covered with palm leaves from very far away.

Clear springs gush out of many limestone rocks filled with fossil polyp trees and shaded by the lustrous foliage of the *anacardium caracoli,* which gives them a somewhat strange appearance.

The *anacardium caracoli* is a tree of colossal size, to which the Indians attribute the property of attracting the vapors spread in the atmosphere; a fact whose accuracy we would not dare to verify.

The village being more than 900 feet above sea level, the nights were extremely cool; on the other hand, the days were always stiflingly hot.

We will enter Turbaco, and, after taking a few steps in its main street and passing in front of a monumental fountain that had only one flaw, that of never spouting any water, we will enter a house that was one of the main and most beautiful of the *pueblo.*

This house, divided into two main buildings separated by an immense, luxuriant garden, full of shade and mystery, was almost adjacent to the forest on its rear side, while its façade was almost opposite the fountain we have mentioned.

It was about half past three in the afternoon; the great heat of the day had passed; the streets of the village, deserted since eleven in the morning, were beginning to be populated by a few passers-by; the doors were gradually reopening; the inhabitants were waking up; in a word, the *siesta* was over and life was resuming its course.

In a rather coquettishly furnished living room, with walls made of spaced bamboo, but entirely covered with a fine cloth, to let the air circulate freely, and also thwart any indiscreet curiosity, two young women, or rather two young girls, half lying on hammocks that they themselves were swinging from the tip of their pretty feet, were talking in restrained voices, while smoking thin corn straw cigarettes, whose fragrant smoke was spiraling upwards towards the ceiling.

These two young girls, beautiful in that pure, majestic and simple beauty that both denotes the race and yet ignores itself, were Doña Elmina and Doña Lilia, whom we have already had the opportunity to present to the reader.

As we enter the living room, Doña Elmina, with a gesture of bad grace, had just thrown away the cigarette she had just started.

"What's the matter, *querida*?" asked her companion, surprised.

"What do you think, *niña*?" answered Doña Elmina, trembling, "I am suffering, I am unhappy, and you, wicked as you are, instead of feeling sorry for me, instead of complaining with me, you laugh, you sing and even make fun of me."

"Oh-oh," said the other girl, standing upright with a slight frown, "here is a very sudden and sharp attack, so you must be in great pain indeed, Elmina, to speak to me in this way—not your cousin, but your friend and your sister."

"Forgive me, Lilia, I am unfair indeed, but if you knew..."

"Knew what? Why don't you talk straight to me, Elmina? For almost a month now, a total change has taken place in you. You are pale, somber, nervous, your eyes are downcast. Sometimes on your cheeks, I have seen traces of tears that have barely been erased. Do you think that I am blind, or that I don't love you? No, no, *querida*, I have seen everything since the first day. It was after a long conversation with your father that you suddenly became like that."

"It is true," Elmina whispered, lowering her head.

"But friendship must above all be discreet, so I've kept silent. I saw that you were containing your sorrow in your heart, and, perhaps out of pride, did not want to say anything to me. I have waited until your heart finally overflowed and you are pleased to share with me the heavy burden of your pain."

"Thank you, Lilia, you are good and you do love me."

"Yes, I do love you, Elmina—much more than you know. As for the cheerfulness you reproach me with..."

"I didn't blame you for anything, *querida*," interrupted Doña Elmina with a certain liveliness, while a slight redness filled her charming face.

"This cheerfulness that you reproach me with, I say, is false," Doña Lilia strongly reiterated. "I was pretending, with a feigned joy, to bring back a fleeting smile on your lips. But since I did not succeed, I was wrong to try. Forgive me, Elmina! From now on, my laughter will no longer disturb your pain."

These last words were pronounced by Doña Lilia with such an accent of sweet sympathy and true tenderness that Doña Elmina flinched, and she threw herself into her friend's arms, bursting into tears.

There was a long silence; the two girls were crying.

"You're right," Doña Elmina continued, "I'm suffering terribly. My heart is broken. You've guessed part of my secret already... Well, so be it! Listen to me, you'll know everything."

"Are we alone?" asked Doña Lilia. "Wait..."

And carrying to her mouth a golden whistle hung on her neck by a chain of the same metal, she whistled.

A few minutes passed; then a heavy step resounded on the floor. A door opened and a forty-year-old woman appeared smiling on the threshold.

She must have been very beautiful in her youth; her intelligent features exuded gentleness and kindness, mixed with a certain expression of energy.

"Mama Quiri," said Doña Lilia in a warm voice, "my cousin Elmina and I have some serious matters to discuss, but we are afraid of indiscreet ears, and we don't want to be heard. Can you make sure that no one comes near this salon without us being warned. We will be most grateful."

"Rest assured, *chicas*, that no one will approach. I will take care of it myself. So, little *niña* Lilia, at last try to learn the secret of your sister Elmina. It's not good for a young girl to have secrets of her own."

"I'm working on it," Lilia said laughing. "I'm really working on it, Mama Quiri."

"Well, little girls, chirp fearlessly away like the birds of the good Lord, which are neither purer nor better than you. I will keep watch."

And the woman walked away with a sweet smile.

The two cousins followed her with their eyes until the door closed after her.

"My dear Lilia!" said Doña Elmina. "First of all, promise me not to make fun of me; for you will hear the story of my personal feelings rather than that of serious events that could legitimately sadden or worry me."

"Speak, *querida*! Am I not your other half?"

"Yes, it's true. Then, listen. You know my father, Don José Rivas de Figueroa? I will not tell you anything you don't know already about his haughty, dark, proud character, and his domineering will before which all others must bow. Deprived from birth of my poor mother,

160

who passed away giving birth to me, my early childhood was spent sadly, abandoned to the care of unintelligent and sullen servants. As soon as I was old enough to understand what was going on around me, these injustices, these irrational tantrums, these punishments that nothing justified, frightened me and completely distorted my instincts and aspirations What can I tell you at last, Lilia, my darling? I am afraid that I do not love my father!"

"Oh, Elmina, what an awful thought! It is not possible!"

"Alas! On the contrary, *querida*, this is all too true. In vain, I have tried to erase this fatal impression of my early years, but nothing has worked. I'm afraid of my father; his gaze alone makes me tremble. Sometime after our crossing from Cuba to Santo Domingo, the crossing during which our ship was taken by the *ladrones* of Tortuga Island, when we were so generously and miraculously saved from a terrible fate by Captain Bearcub Ironskull—as you can see, I have not forgotten the name of our liberator…" here, she smiled through her tears. "…You remember, my father was appointed by the King as Governor of Cartagena de las Indias, while Don Lopez Aldoa de Sandoval, your father, was promoted to the rank of brigadier, and at the same time received the command of the garrison of that same city. Your father and mine accepted these promotions. Then, a fortnight later, we left for Cartagena. I don't know why, but when I saw the high mountains of Santo Domingo fade away on the horizon, I suddenly felt my heart tighten, tears came to my eyes and I cried. You asked me the cause of this sadness, but I couldn't explain it to you, for I didn't know it myself. I had only spent a few days in Santo Domingo; nothing attached me to it, the life I had led there had been sad and dull! So why was I sad? Perhaps it was one of those presentiments that sometimes in his kindness God sends to his creatures…"

"What do you mean, *querida*?" asked Doña Lilia with astonishment. "I don't understand you."

"You will. You probably remember the ceremony of intronization of my father as Governor of the city of Cartagena; the notables came to the *cabildo* to pay their respects to the great Don José Rivas. These notables, all very rich merchants, were thirteen in number; the thirteenth was called Don Enrique Torribio Moreno; he was this rich Mexican merchant who had arrived a few days earlier from Vera-Cruz…"

"Don Enrique, who is today your father's close friend?"

"The same one, Lilia."

"He has a dark face, that man," said the other girl, pensively.

"Doesn't he? Well, do you know who he looks like, this Don Enrique? And in such a surprising way that I was struck by it the first time I saw him? "

"No."

"I'll tell you. This man resembles the miserable bandit who, at Port-Margot, would have made us all slaves had not Captain Bearcub gambled for our freedom."

"That is strange," Lilia murmured.

"Oh yes, very strange!" she exclaimed with feverish animation. "And despite his beard, cut in the Spanish style, his Andalusian accent, and his air of false bonhomie spread like a mask over her features, I wasn't taken in by it for a minute. From the very first moment, I understood that this man would be fatal to me."

"But…"

162

"Let me finish, *querida*, and you will see if my presentiments have deceived me. Don Enrique Torribio Moreno, by the way, is a man of perfect elegance, high manners, and, in appearance, at least, hugely rich. Gold flows like water through his fingers."

"And he is a frenetic gambler, and moreover a lucky one."

"This is what I wanted to get to. My father is not rich, but you know that he has a passion for gambling. Every night, they play in his house, and often considerable sums of money are committed either to dice or to the cards."

"Gambling is the scourge of the Americas, *querida*! It is through gambling that the Spanish colonies will perish."

"And the families of their settlers, too. About a month ago, my father arrived here unexpectedly, called me and locked himself with me in this very living room. He made me sit down next to him, looked at me attentively for a few minutes, and then, speaking in a harsh voice, he said, 'Elmina, you are beautiful, you are eighteen years-old; the time has come for you to get married. I have chosen a husband for you; this husband is a very rich *caballero*, my closest friend, so prepare to receive him and to look good; I have given him my word, and you know that I never go back on a resolution taken, and especially on a word given. You have two months to prepare yourself for this union. In two months, to the day, Monsignor the Bishop of Cartagena will bless your union in the Church of the Mercy. The man you are now engaged to, Elmina, is Don Enrique Torribio Moreno.' That was all he said."

"And what did you say to your father in return?"

"Nothing. What could I have said in response to such a peremptorily formulated will? I was aghast, without strength, almost fainting, unable to utter a word. From the very first word, by a sort of secret intuition, I had sensed, or perhaps guessed, that my father would end our conversation with the name of this accursed man. Don José Rivas then stood up, gave me a long glance, and left without saying goodbye, as coldly as he had entered. After the door had closed on him, I fell unconscious on the floor. It was my maid who lifted me up. It has been a month since this conversation took place, Lilia."

"What are you planning to do?"

"I don't know. All I know is that I will never marry this man."

"But why this marriage? How did your father, so proud of his nobility, agree to…?"

Doña Elmina smiled bitterly.

"My father is ruined, Lilia. He doesn't have a maravedis left. Today, all his fortune belongs to Don Enrique Torribio, do you understand now?"

"Oh, that's awful... What hope do you have left?"

"God!" cried Doña Elmina, raising her eyes fervently to the Heavens. "God, who will not abandon me when everything else is against me."

At that moment, the door opened and the man returned.

"Your father is here, *niña*," she said. "And Don Enrique Torribio Moreno is with him."

"Hush!" the young girl said painfully, putting a finger over her mouth and turned to her cousin. "Silence, I beg you, Lilia."

"Courage, Elmina," the other girl replied, kissing her.

CHAPTER IX
Where Don Enrique Torribio Moreno is not being advantageously portrayed

Don José Rivas de Figueroa, governor for His Catholic Majesty of the city of Cartagena de las Indias, was a man of about forty-eight years of age, although he looked five or six years younger; his waist was high, his gait majestic, his gestures elegant; his features, without being handsome, had those broad, angular lines characteristic of blue blood families; his black and lively eyes, deeply sunken in their orbits, bore a majestic expression of arrogance and mocking disdain.

The character that accompanied him, who called himself Don Enrique Torribio Moreno and who passed for Mexican, formed the most complete contrast with him.

His vulgar features, his grey, slanting and flashing eyes, like those of a nocturnal bird of prey, his almost blond chestnut hair, his height barely above average, wide and stocky, gave him at first glance the appearance of a Breton or Norman sailor rather than that of a Spanish nobleman; but there was so much finesse in his gaze, such real vigor in his knotty limbs, that, in spite of oneself, one was forced to recognize in him a most unusual man. His manners were those of a man of the world.

The two cousins had left their hammocks and sat on cushions to receive their visitors; when they heard the door open, they stood up.

Don José Rivas was frowning, a mocking smile on his lips; he seemed to be in a bad mood.

"Good morning, *niñas*," he said with a hint of irony. "I come as a dutiful father to pay you a visit."

"Welcome, father," answered Doña Elmina in a trembling voice.

Doña Lilia brought some chairs.

"I took the liberty," Don José continued, still in the same tone, "of bringing with me Don Enrique Torribio Moreno, my best friend, who has done me the honor of asking for your hand."

"But, father..."

"Please do not interrupt me, *niña*."

The girl fell silent, all trembling.

"Sorry, *señorita*," said the Mexican, bowing respectfully. "Don José Rivas, your father, was about to add that, if I dare to aspire to the supreme happiness of being your husband, it is but on one condition."

Doña Elmina raised her head and stared at Don Torribio with an astonished look.

"Yes," said Don José Rivas in a gruff tone, "I was going to tell you about this condition, however absurd it may be. To put it simply, Don Enrique Torribio Moreno is asking you, my daughter, for permission to court you."

"Sorry, but that's not all, my dear Don José," the Mexican added gallantly. "Yes, *señorita*, I aspire to have the honor of being occasionally admitted in your presence, because, however keenly I desire to become your husband, I want you to know me before granting me your hand. My ambition is, above all, to owe my happiness only to your free will."

"Why, thank you, oh! thank you, sir," cried the young girl with impetus.

And, in a spontaneous gesture, she held out her pretty hand to him, which the Mexican respectfully touched with his lips.

"Bravo!" cried Don José Rivas with a cold irony. "What a charming sight! On my soul, here we are back to the most beautiful time of the Round Table and the court of King Arthur or Emperor Charlemagne. By God! I am moved."

The girl bowed her head, blushing with shame, and, in a voice that emotion made almost indistinct, she murmured:

"I will abide by your will, father."

"Who speaks of my will, *niña*?" Don José Rivas retorted with restrained violence. "I made the foolish mistake of promising your gallant suitor that you will be free to accept or refuse his request, so free you will be, I swear. No influence, not even mine, will come between you and your timid worshipper. So please abandon this air of resigned victimhood, which does not suit you, for you are free, I repeat."

"You heard him, *señora*," exclaimed Don Enrique Torribio Moreno, respectfully nodding to the girl, "your father confirmed my words."

"By God! I had to," Don José Rivas resumed with a disdainful shrug. "Do you still have something to say to my daughter?"

"Nothing more, no, my friend, except to renew to the *señorita* my humble prayer to present myself before her."

Doña Elmina bowed without answering.

"Are you happy now?" Don José said abruptly. "Now, it's getting late, come, Don Torribio, and let's leave these little girls to their toys and dolls."

"I am at your service, my friend."

"Farewell, *niñas*."

"Aren't you going to kiss me before you leave, father?" asked the girl, leaning timidly towards him.

Don José, without even looking at her, put a cold kiss on her forehead.

"Come on, let's go," he said.

The Mexican respectfully saluted the two girls and the two men went out.

At the gate, a dozen horsemen, armed with spears and floating banners, and commanded by a non-commissioned officer, stood motionless like statues.

The Governor made a sign: a black slave brought two magnificent horses, harnessed with the coquettish luxury and sumptuousness used in the Spanish colonies.

The two men got into the saddle and placed themselves at the head of the detachment, which immediately followed them.

When they were no more than a hundred steps away from the house, Don Enrique Torribio Moreno spoke:

"Are you going back to Cartagena?" he asked.

"Where else do you expect me to go?" replied Don José Rivas, looking at him in amazement.

"I will frankly confess that I did not expect to get back to town so quickly. I thought your visit to the ladies would last longer and that, while you were taking some rest, I would have time to push on to the rancho I own here in the vicinity."

"I hadn't thought about it! I think I'd heard that you had bought some charming property, two or three rifle ranges away from the village."

"Oh, it's only a miserable shanty," Don Enrique Torribio exclaimed, "almost in ruins. This is why you must excuse me for leaving you now. I'm having some repairs made at the moment, and I think I'd like to surprise my workers."

"Since there's no hurry, do you want both of us to go there as a company?"

"No, I don't think so."

"And why not?"

"Because first of all, my friend, I have a certain reputation for luxury to maintain; a reputation that I don't care to lose if you were to see the property. And secondly, I confess that I'd hardly know where to put you. Everything is upside down. So, my dear Don José, believe me, continue quietly on your way to the city, and let me go about my business."

"Well, so be it, then! But you know that I am expecting you early this evening at the Citadel. We have a big meeting."

"I shall not miss it."

"Come and ask me for dinner without ceremony, it will be easier."

"I won't say no to that. Wait for me until seven o'clock. Maybe I'll introduce you to someone."

"Who?"

"The captain of my schooner, the *Santa Catalina,* which arrived this morning from the Vera Cruz."

"Is he a man of the world?"

"He's a sailor, but he's rather decent and very good looking."

"Then do bring him along—especially if he is rich," Don José laughed.

"I hope so. Wait for us until the appointed time."

"So it's agreed."

The two *caballeros* saluted each other, then Don José Rivas trotted out of the village, followed by his escort, while Don Enrique Torribio turned his horse towards Turbaco. But, after taking a few steps in that direction, he looked back, making sure that the Governor and his escort had disappeared in the meanders of the road, and that, as far as he could see in all directions, no one was watching him. Then, he made a sudden turn to the right, and another one a few moments later to the left.

Soon, he found himself at the edge of the jungle and galloped down a hollow path, lined on either side with bushy trees, whose thick foliage formed an impenetrable vault above his head.

After barely a quarter of an hour, he reached a miserable *jacal,* made of intertwined dry branches, as hunters and jungle dwellers are accustomed to build, in order to shelter from the burning rays of the sun or furious showers.

At the sound of the horse's gallop, a tall lad, with pale features and emaciated by misery and deprivation, but with fiery eyes and a dark and energetic expression, suddenly appeared on the threshold.

This man, in the prime of life, was proudly draped in sordid and indescribable rags; he had a long knife and an axe at his belt and both hands crossed over the end of the barrel of a buccaneer's rifle, whose butt rested on the ground. He watched with a mocking air as Don Enrique Torribio Moreno came to him.

The Mexican stopped his horse just in front of the *jacal.*

"Are you coming in?" the man said to him in French for all greetings.

"Yes," answered Don Enrique Torribio in the same language. "At least, if you have a place where I can hide my horse. I don't care to leave it here like that in full view on the road."

"Don't worry about it," said the other man, grabbing the animal by the bridle. "Get down and go in."

Don Enrique Torribio obeyed this double injunction. His strange interlocutor then took the horse and disappeared with him into the thicket.

The inside of the *jacal* was, if possible, even more miserable than the outside: in a corner, there was a pile of dry grass serving as a bed; in the middle, a hole with three stones as a hearth, two or three bull skulls as seats, an old sailor's chest, perfectly empty and with the lid missing, an iron pot, and two or three wooden dishes or plates: that was all.

Don Enrique Torribio cast only an indifferent glance at this interior that, probably, he had already known for a long time. He sat down on a bull's skull, chose a cigar from his *cigarera,* lit it and began to smoke quietly, waiting for his host to return.

The man came back almost immediately.

"By the Devil!" he said with a sneer. "What a delicious perfume! You smoke expensive cigars, now. What it is to be rich!"

"Here, take one," replied Don Enrique Torribio, nonchalantly handing out his *cigarera* to the stranger. "And my horse?"

"In the straw up to its neck," replied the other, "and in front of a bale of alfalfa."

Then, after having picked and lit a cigar, he returned the *cigarera* to Don Enrique Torribio and sat down in front of him.

There was a moment of silence. The two men examined each other slyly; but seeing that his guest was obstinate in not saying anything, the owner of the *jacal* finally decided to speak up first:

"It's been a long time since you came here," he said.

"I've been buried under business."

"Poor friend! And yet you remembered your old comrade."

"Weren't we both sailors?"

"True; but a long time ago, and much has happened since. It was under Montbarts, during the Maracaibo expedition. Do you remember?"

"By Jove! How could one forget!"

"But, no doubt, you haven't come to talk about the past? I imagine, you'd rather talk about the present, or possibly the future?"

"Ah! You guessed right, Barthélémy!"

"Oh!" replied the other with a smile of disdain, "I don't have to be a magician to guess that, if you've come to me, it's because you need me."

"Well, to speak frankly, my old friend, yes, I do need you."

"Right-ho, brother! I'm your man, for I'm bored to death doing nothing here. However, I must warn: my help will cost you dearly."

"What are your terms?" said the other man coolly.

"Is the business worth it?"

"Yes."

"You've always been a man of mystery, always hatching some dark schemes. When the Spanish ship, on which I was a prisoner, encountered you swimming in the open sea, and took you on board, you only gave rather confused and unclear explanations about your strange situation. Then you pretended to be Mexican, and I pretended not to recognize you…"

"You've rendered me a great service that day. I've not forgotten it."

"Hum! That was only to be expected between freebooters and especially between sailors. But what was less usual was that, after disembarking at San Francisco

172

de Campeche,[50] instead of coming to my aid, as I was entitled to expect, you abandoned me. You were free, and well considered by the Spaniards. I even believe that a certain knife wound that I received on a certain night on the harbor soon after was a present from you."

"Oh! How can you think that, Barthélémy?"

"I know you so well! But I eventually broke the chains that bound me—for I was tied up like a wild beast—escaped and, after much wandering, I don't know how I got to this coast, but I took refuge in these woods. One day, fate brought us together again, You were rich, I was poor; you could have helped me, but you did not..."

"Barthélémy, you seem to forget..."

"...That you offered me to be your servant, right. But I refused! I, Captain Barthélémy, the famous free-booter, servant of a... Well, let's skip over that, too. On-ly," he added after a while with an ironic smile, "I must grant you that you didn't rat on me and sell me out."

"Ah, you see!"

"I don't thank you for it, however, because if you had done so, you'd have been lost too, for you knew very well that I would not have hesitated to reveal your real name, and the Spaniards knew it, a little more even, than you would have liked. Now, after three months, during which you did not worry for a moment whether I was dead or alive, you come to me and you say to me: 'I need you.' I conclude that this need must be very press-ing, so I make my terms, and I say to you: It will cost you dearly."

"And I answered: I accept."

"So, let's talk. And give me another cigar."

"Take it."

---

[50] Today, Campeche.

173

And Don Enrique Torribio held out his *cigarera* again.

Barthélémy opened it and chose a cigar. That worthy captain was extraordinarily suspicious of his companion. He had known his guest for a long time, so his conduct with him, after all the betrayals of which he had been victim, was fraught with great wariness.

So, while smoking his second cigar, Barthélémy promised himself, in his heart of hearts, to be on his guard, and to play things close his vest, while trying to anticipate any future betrayals.

CHAPTER X
Two sailors talk and what ensued

Let's explain in a few words who this new character that entered our story, and who is called to play a rather important role in it, was.

Captain Barthélémy had a great reputation for courage and daring among the freebooters of Tortuga Island. He was known for his fabulous daring; the most incredible stories were told about him; moreover, he was an excellent sailor and was known by his friends, and especially by his enemies, to have been lucky in almost all the expeditions that he had undertaken.

There was much truth in all that was reported about Captain Barthélémy; gifted with intelligence, an unfailing courage, an unalterable composure, and an unrivaled presence of mind, no matter how bad the position in which he had been unexpectedly thrown by chance, he almost always managed to come out of it safe and sound, by means that any other than him would have found impracticable.

Moreover, he was proverbially loyal, and for nothing in the world would he have consented to break his word once he had given it.

This was the man that Don Enrique Torribio Moreno—we shall continue to call him by that name for the time being—had come to find in a miserable *jacal*, to offer him what he deemed to be a worthwhile business proposition.

While the freebooter was smoking his cigar with the casualness of a real gentleman, the fake Mexican was scrutinizing him, calculating in his mind how it might be possible for him to break the other's shield of seeming indifference.

"Let's talk," he finally said in a false cheer, "what are your terms, brother?"

"First, make me an offer. It's up to the merchant to present his wares. I'll judge on a sample," Barthélémy replied, snickering.

Don Enrique Torribio understood that he had to be candid.

"Did you unsaddle my horse?" he asked.

This question, asked out of the blue, seemed so extraordinary and so out of place to Barthélémy that he looked at his interlocutor in amazement.

"Why are you asking?" he replied.

"Because if I knew where my horse was, I would go and get a suitcase that you probably noticed on his rump."

"Yes, I did notice it; it is quite heavy."

"Indeed. Do you know what's in it?"

"How could I?"

"Well, first, it contains—listen to this—a complete new set of clothes for you—a rich, elegant suit, such as a gentleman must wear. Then, there are a hundred and fifty ounces of gold, which I beg you to accept as a token of my gratitude, and which do not commit you to anything, since we are brothers—or at least we were once."

"By the Devil!" Barthélémy laughed. "If you give me a new suit and twelve thousand pounds, because I am or was your brother, what will you give me then when I will be your accomplice?"

Don Enrique Torribio tried a smile that looked more like a grimace.

"Go and get the suitcase," he said, "and while you clean up, I'll explain what it's all about."

"Are you going to take me with you?"

"Certainly."

"But then I will be horribly ridiculous."

"How so?"

"How do you want me to follow you, if I'm on foot, dressed as I will be."

"Don't worry about that, ye man of little faith," Don Enrique Torribio said, laughing. "When the time comes, I'll find you a horse."

"Well, I can see that you have thought of everything. By the Devil! This business must be important. Now, my curiosity is awakened and my imagination working overtime."

"Let them! I have enough to satisfy both. But hurry, time is running out!"

Barthélémy went out and returned a few moments later with the suitcase. Don Enrique Torribio opened it and pulled out a suit, which he displayed with complacency. It really was magnificent and in the best of taste: jacket, shirt, silk stockings, shoes, gaiters, hat, belt, expensive jewelry, and these thousand things essential to the toilet of a man of the high society, as they used to say at that time.

"Now, get dressed," said the fake Mexican. "Here is a mirror, combs, razors, soap, everything you need. As for the few things you're missing, they'll come with the horse."

"Fine! I'll get dressed. In the meantime, talk."

Barthélémy began his metamorphosis. From a caterpillar, he was going to become a butterfly.

"Your name will be Don Gaspar Alvarado Bustamente," Don Enrique Torribio began.

"What kind of name is that?"

"You are the captain of a two hundred and fifty ton schooner, the *Santa Catalina* from Vera Cruz," continued Don Enrique Torribio, "which arrived this morning at low tide in Cartagena, sailing directly from Mexico, with a full load of European goods consigned to Don Enrique Torribio Moreno."

"Who's that?"

"That's me. That's my name."

"Ah! So that's your name here?"

"Yes. Do you have any problem with it? "

"None whatsoever. Go on. It sounds like a fairy tale," replied Barthélémy laughing.

"Tonight, I will introduce you to the Governor of the city, Don José Rivas de Figueroa, with whom I am intimately connected, and to Don Lopez Aldao de Sandoval, the commander-in-chief of the garrison."

"Do I have to meet them?"

"Yes. It's part of my plan."

"Very well then. What's next?"

"That's it."

"What do you mean, that's it?"

"That's it—for the time being."

"I'll be damned if I understand anything about the scheme you're hatching!"

"You don't need to understand," replied Don Enrique Torribio sharply. "Once your position is well established in the eyes of these folks, nothing will be easier for us than to talk whenever we like. Our business affairs will provide us with a most plausible pretext for this."

"True, true... Our business affairs... By the Devil!" said Barthélémy laughing. "But I am more than a little concerned..."

"Why?"

178

"Well, all these complicated schemes might lead us to some terrible catastrophe."

"Explain yourself."

"I presume that the Governor of the city, Don José Rivas—that's what you call him, right?"

"Yes."

"Well, that Don José Rivas must know what's happening in Cartagena."

"Of course."

"The harbormaster reports to him the arrival and departures of all the ships."

"Yes, he does."

"Then, your schooner the *Santa Catalina*..."

"She arrives in Cartagena this morning."

"From Vera Cruz?"

"Yes."

"Loaded with goods from Europe?"

"Yes. Goods that are consigned to me."

"So, you're really rich?"

"I'm a millionaire."

Barthélémy looked at his companion with an expression of unspeakable sarcasm.

"Ah," he murmured in a low voice, "the murder of that diamond merchant, reportedly committed by a Mexican, and the theft of his fortune—that story that was told in San Francisco de Campeche when we were there, was it true?"

Don Enrique Torribio became livid.

"What do you mean?"

"You already passed yourself for Mexican in Campeche."

"What does that prove? Am I not French?"

"True—and Low Norman, to boot," Barthélémy replied with a smile. "But there was no lack of Mexicans in Campeche, so let it rest and I won't breathe another word about it."

"Oh, I'm not concerned."

"Of course, you're not. Besides, it's none of my business, so let's get back to our affairs. So, if I understand correctly, the schooner does exist, it does come from Vera Cruz with a cargo that does belong to you, and it did enter the port of Cartagena this morning, and it is called the *Santa Catalina*."

"I'm glad to see that you haven't forgotten anything."

"Yes—but that ship, she didn't come alone from Vera Cruz, I presume. She had a crew—a captain?"

"Certainly! A captain and a crew of six men."

"So what became of them? Did they, by any chance, desert *en masse*?"

"Alas! my poor friend,"? said the fake Don Enrique Torribio Moreno, taking on a fatherly air, "we are all mortal in the end…"

"A proverb as wise as it is true."

"So here's what happened…"

"I'm listening."

"The schooner arrived too late last night to venture into the harbor channel, so it was forced to cruise for part of the night, in order to wait to enter the port at sunrise. Around midnight, while turning the ship around, the captain fell into the sea."

"Poor man!" Barthélémy said with great seriousness. "And he was not fished out of the water?"

"They tried."

"Ah!"

"…But, look at how cruel fate can be! A boat was put to sea, four men got in it. Unfortunately, the heat had melted the pitch of the seams of the canoe, and the boat sank like a stone."

"And the four men?"

"Drowned. The night was dark, the sea rough. Only two men remained on board, and they couldn't help their comrades."

"That's what's called unlucky! And just in sight of the harbor too!"

"Barely two leagues away. Had it been daylight, they would have been seen."

"Yes, but it was dark," said Barthélémy, in a mocking tone. "You will agree that the two men who were left alone on board must have been quite embarrassed."

"Luckily for them—and the *Santa Catalina*—the schooner had been reported at sunset. I had been waiting for her, and, knowing her precious cargo, I was eager to find out why she hadn't docked yet. So I chartered a boat manned by six sailors, and at about four o'clock in the morning, I boarded the ship, which was standing idly in front of the harbor entrance, waiting for a rescue."

"It was like an inspiration from the Heavens."

"Yes. And just as I was having the sails set, another ship was leaving Cartagena on its way to Cadiz."

"Ah! ah! What a coincidence!"

"The only two survivors of the original crew had been so struck by the dreadful events of the night, that they begged me to let them transfer onto that other ship.

"Naturally, you took pity on these poor devils and you agreed?"

"Indeed! I paid them what was I owed them, I even added a small gratuity to console them for the unhappy death of their comrades, and I took them to the Spanish ship, whose captain, whom I knew a little, agreed to take them on board."

"How everything fits so well together, my God!" Barthélémy cried, raising his eyes.

"So I hired the six men I had brought with me. These six were completely unaware of what had happened on board. Moreover, before leaving the port, I had told them—I don't know why—an idea that had suddenly caught my fancy—that the captain of the *Santa Catalina* had already left his ship the day before to come and announce her arrival to me earlier."

"I see. As a result, they were not surprised to see only two men on board, and they were convinced that their captain was ashore."

"As you can see, it's all very simple."

"If it had all been done on purpose, it couldn't have been more successful."

"What are you hinting at?" Don Enrique Torribio said haughtily.

"Me? Nothing at all."

"It's just that you have a way of insinuating things..." he replied, feeling queasy in spite of himself.

"Not at all! I take things as they come! I admire how much luck favors you. All you told me is very natural. Feel free to interpret my words as you wish, but remember this: I am in no way responsible for your actions, nor am I in any way responsible—thank God!—for your conscience. Therefore, none of this is any of my business, and I wash my hands off it."

"Excellent!"

"I just wanted to be well informed in order to not make any mistakes, or suffer from any misunderstandings, which may be regrettable in the difficult role that you've asked me to play in this comedy of yours, which, if it continues as it began, may well turn into a tragedy. Now, I know what I needed to know, and you can rest easy. You won't have to reproach me, I'm ready. What do we do next? And look at me. Tell me if I look the part."

Don Enrique Torribio examined Barthélémy with the most serious attention. The metamorphosis was complete. Absolutely nothing remained of the hirsute figure that, an hour earlier, had appeared on the threshold of the *jacal*. The captain, a man of excellent education, wore his new clothes with perfect ease. He made a very presentable *caballero*, one that no one would suspect of being anything else but.

The fake Mexican was thrilled. He shook his hand with effusiveness.

"On my faith, you are marvelous!" he exclaimed.

"But expensive," replied Barthélémy with his mocking cold-bloodedness, "as you'll soon find out," he added, putting in his pocket the purse his friend had given him. "Now, I repeat my question, what do we do next?"

"We are leaving."

"So be it, but first, dear friend, let me hide my rifle. It's a Gelin which, I confess to you, I hold very dear. Tomorrow or the day after, I'll come to get it."

While Barthélémy carefully hid his rifle under the dead leaves that had served him for so long as a bed, Don Enrique Torribio, after closing the suitcase, went out, cast a glance around, and then whistled twice in a certain way.

A whistle similar to his own answered him almost immediately. He then returned inside the *jacal*.

"Are you done?" he asked Barthélémy.

"I am," replied the other.

"Then do me the pleasure of bringing my horse in front of the *jacal*... Ah! Another word…"

183

"Speak."

"Remember that from now on, you are Captain Gaspar Alvarado Bustamente, commanding the schooner *Santa Catalina* from Vera Cruz."

"As you are Don Enrique Torribio Moreno, a wealthy Mexican and my consignee."

"Very good. Make no mistakes and always speak in Spanish in front of others."

"Understood. If you have nothing more to say, I'll go and fetch your horse?"

"Go."

The Captain disappeared for just five minutes, then returned with the horse.

"The horse is ready," he said.

At that moment, there was a hurried gallop on the road. A black man was coming, riding a horse and driving another one by its bridle. He stopped in front of the *jacal* and respectfully greeted the fake Mexican.

-"Don Gaspar," said Don Enrique Torribio, "I think it is pointless to wait any longer for that man I told you about. No doubt, he will not come."

"I believe you are correct, Don Enrique," Barthélémy replied, immediately entering into his role. "Moreover, it is impossible for me to stay here any longer. I must return to my ship."

"I am at your service, *señor*. Please, mount this horse that I had set aside for you, and accept this sword to replace the one you broke."

"A thousand graces, *caballero*."

All this had been said in the purest Castilian Spanish.

The two men saddled up and galloped to Cartagena, where they arrived shortly before five o'clock in the evening.

The black man, who one of Don Enrique Torribio's slaves, had followed them at a respectful distance, without trying to understand what had taken place.

CHAPTER XI
How the Trickster *met the* San Juan Bautista

We left the *Trickster* tossed in every direction by a furious sea, whose gigantic waves were breaking over her bow almost without interruption.

The storm lasted forty-eight hours, constantly increasing in intensity, and finally took such proportions that the ship was forced to take the extremely rare step of tightening all the sails and folding back the protruding masts. The ship was now controlled only from her helm, which four men, the sturdiest in the entire crew, maneuvered only with great difficulty.

The *Trickster* was exhausted; her deck, constantly swept by the waves; her crew, overwhelmed by fatigue. They began to make murmurs of complaints that her officers could hardly manage to stifle.

The expedition was beginning under dark auspices; already the fatal figure of thirteen was being whispered about, and, in light of the superstitious credulity of the sailors, things threatened to take on very serious proportions.

Only Captain Bearcub Ironskull, L'Olonnais, the Poletais and two or three others remained calm and impassive, their eyes fixed on the sky. They waited with confidence for the end of the hurricane.

On the third day, during the watch from four to eight in the morning, the storm seemed to want to abate; the wind dropped in intensity, although the sea continued, according to maritime slang, *to eat the ship*. At nine o'clock, the wind became manageable. At noon the

Trickster was making good progress, and the topsails were unfurled. For the first time in three days, the officers measured the elevation of the sun and calculated their position.

They were on what was known as St. Christopher's Passage, a route taken by most ships coming from or returning to Europe.

By then, the crew had regained all its cheerfulness; the sailors were cleaning their weapons and restoring order and cleanliness neglected during the gale on board. They were now making fun of their earlier panic and, with their usual carelessness, they spoke only of their future shares of the loot and the riches they would soon seize.

At around four o'clock in the afternoon, Pierre Legrand, who was on watch, was walking from the poop deck to the main mast, watching the sails, looking at the sea which was becoming calmer, and occasionally, at the helm, when the lookout at the top of the mizzen mast cried out:

"Ship!"

Pierre Legrand rushed to the bridge.

"Hey, lookout!" he shouted, making a megaphone out of his hands.

"Yea?" answered the sailor.

"Where do you see that ship?"

"By our starboard quarter, four miles upwind."

"Is it a three-masted ship?"

"No, it's a small brig."

"Let's tell the Captain," said the lieutenant to Alexander who, with his bosun's whistle in his hand, was standing next to him.

Alexander passed the order on to a sailor, who immediately ran towards the cabins.

"What route is she following?" resumed Pierre Legrand.

"She's coming upon us," replied the lookout. "They've seen us."

"Are you sure?"

"Yes, they've turned two quarters."

"Then it must be a *gavacho*."

At this moment, the Captain appeared on the bridge, holding a telescope. With it, he glanced at the point on the horizon where the ship was supposed to be. Then, without uttering a word, he dashed up into the swell and, in an instant, found himself on the great mast. From there, he climbed to the top, adjusted the focus on his telescope, and looked up again.

The entire crew stood motionless and silent on the deck. This magic word: *ship!* had galvanized even the slowest and most reckless. *Ship!* that is to say: prey, spoils, rich spoils perhaps; a fight against their implacable enemies… So the anxiety and impatience of the freebooters was great, while the captain continued coldly and meticulously studied the other vessel.

A few minutes passed. Finally Bearcub Ironskull climbed slowly down back to the bridge.

"Gentlemen," he said, raising his hat, "this ship is a Spanish brig. It has just come about, but, with God's help, before sunset, we will be in her wake. She is far from running as well as we do. Lieutenant, start the hunt!"

The maneuver was executed with extreme enthusiasm and speed. In a few seconds, the *Trickster* unfurled all her sails and soon she was flying over the sea with the speed of a gull.

The Captain, after making sure that his orders had been correctly executed, went back down to his room, followed by the Poletais and L'Olonnais.

The *Trickster* was perhaps the best of all the French, English, Dutch and Spanish ships that, at that time, crisscrossed the Atlantic in every direction.

This time, again she did not disappoint. Her unfortunate prey tried to change her course, turn around, but nothing helped. She was forced to admit defeat.

Soon, she could be seen on the horizon as a white spot, as big as a seagull's wing, then this spot grew, the canopy appeared, the whole ship was revealed, and, around six o'clock in the evening, she was no more than half a mile away from the formidable privateer.

The brig, recognizing the impossibility of escaping from the claws of her enemy, had now resigned herself to her fate, a characteristic of the Spaniards, who had lived for eight hundred years under the yoke of the Moors, and had, in spite of themselves, acquired the fatalism of the East.

The brig had retracted her sails and was bravely continuing her route under a small canopy.

Bearcub had returned to the bridge, and, climbing on a bench, he took up the megaphone:

"Everyone to their battle stations," he shouted.

"Stand firm!" ordered L'Olonnais.

Immediately, there was a great movement on the deck and in the battery; the grenadiers and the most skillful marksmen climbed into the masts. Then a deadly silence reigned over the ship.

"Captain!" said L'Olonnais, "everyone is ready and at their post."

Pierre Legrand, standing near the forecastle with a fuse in his hand, stood motionless behind a cannon, his eyes fixed on his Captain.

Bearcub made a gesture; the lieutenant lightly brought the wick of light down. A cannon shot rang out.

At the same time, the freebooters' flag rose majestically in the air. This standard, as noted in all the books on freebooting, was blue, white and red, arranged in the same way as those of the French flag today.

However, in the middle of the white band, the Captain had added a gold bear's head, using the privilege that freebooters had of adding, if they wanted to, their own insignia on the flag of their ships.

The cannon shot was only a warning shot. No cannonball ricocheted on the water. But this threat was understood very well by the other ship. A large Spanish flag immediately appeared on its stern. A cheerful hurrah, shouted by the entire crew of the *Trickster,* erupted like a funeral knell, to the ears of the brig's crew.

However, the hunt was still on. Soon the *Trickster* took advantage of the wind to cruise alongside the brig, and the two ships were within earshot of each other.

"Ahoy!" shouted Captain Bearcub Ironskull in his megaphone.

"Hola!" they answered immediately.

"Slow down or I'll sink you!"

The maneuver ordered by the freebooter was executed on the brig with a speed that was like magic. The brig continued to move forward for a few minutes, then slowed down to a crawl. Both ships were now at close gun range.

Bearcub resumed the conversation.

"What's the name of your ship?" he asked.

"The *San Juan Bautista*, of three hundred and fifty barrels."

"What cargo are you carrying?"

"Indigo, coffee, *plata piña*[51] and silver ingots."

At this dazzling enumeration of the riches contained in the brig, a shiver of joy ran like an electric current through the ranks of the freebooters.

"Where do you hail from?" resumed Bearcub.

"From Cartagena de las Indias, going to Cádiz."

At the name of Cartagena, the Captain repressed a gesture of surprise.

"How long since you left Cartagena?" he asked.

"Eleven days."

"Send a boat with your captain onboard."

This second maneuver was executed less quickly than the first one; the Spaniards had a terrible fear of the freebooters, whom they literally regarded as demons vomited by Hell. However, it was executed.

A boat was lowered into the sea, and several men went down to it with obvious repugnance. Then it headed towards the privateer, delaying, by all possible means, the moment of the dreadful meeting.

Bearcub turned toward his crew.

"Let everyone remain at their posts," he said. "No shouting, no grumbling. I want the utmost order and the deepest silence to reign on board for as long as this Spanish captain is here. Crew master," he continued, "have four men stand guard at the starboard gangway. Let's show these *gavachos* that we know the maritime

---

[51] Silver vases, dishes, plates and cups, previously smashed with hammers, and therefore subject only to very low customs duties. (*Note from the Author*)

customs. Let's be ready to cast a mooring line to their boat as soon as she docks."

In spite of its calculated slowness, a slowness that any other freebooter captain would probably have severely punished, the Spanish boat nevertheless reached the frigate.

The Spanish captain, who held the helm, was a forty-year-old man, with soft and unaccented features. An expression of sadness and despondency was widespread on his face.

He boarded the ship alone. Military honors were paid to him. He greeted them with a bitter smile and went towards Bearcub, who then descended from his watch seat and came to meet him.

"By Jove!," said the freebooter with a gesture of friendly surprise, "if it isn't Don Ramon de la Cruz!"

"Alas, yes, it is I again, noble commander," replied the other with a humble greeting.

"Again? Is this a word of reproach, Don Ramon?"

"I take it rather personally indeed, Captain. It seems to be written that I can't make a journey without being captured by your honorable lordship. I complain about fate, not about you."

"I understand! It seems to me that we have met three times before."

"Four times, Captain."

"Really?"

"Alas! I am sure of it," Don Ramon replied, with a sigh.

"Four times it is then, so be it! In light of our old acquaintance, tell me what I can do for you?"

"I could only ask for one thing, Captain."

"To give you back your ship, right?"

"Indeed."

"Unfortunately, this is impossible. However, God is my witness that I have the desire to accommodate you! I believe I have found a way. Do you have anything of your own on your ship?"

"Alas! All my fortune."

"How so?"

"The indigo and the coffee belong to me."

"What recklessness, Don Ramon!"

"I recognize it now."

"Well, let's see what we can do about it! How much is the purchase price of this indigo and this coffee?"

"Five thousand piasters. That's everything I own."

"Hmm! That's a lot. That's too bad. But by my faith, what is said is said. I shall buy your cargo for six thousand piasters, in my name and that of my companions. Furthermore, I will allow you to take two boats in which you can put all your personal belongings and those of your men. How many are they?"

"Fourteen, noble captain," replied Don Ramon with a bewildered air. "Plus two passengers whom I took when I left Cartagena."

"So seventeen men in total. In addition to water and food for eight days, you will take ten rifles, eight sabers, eight pistols, and a hundred and fifty powder charges to defend yourselves if necessary. We are in the middle of the West Indies. If you can't manage to reach a Spanish port, then it will be because the Devil interfered. Also, for greater safety, in case you encounter another freebooter from Tortuga Island, I'll give you a safe conduct. Are you satisfied?"

"Oh, noble captain," cried the poor man with tears in his voice, kissing Bearcub's hands in spite of himself, "how shall I ever repay you?"

"By telling your compatriots, my dear Don Ramon, that we, freebooters, are not as devilish as they believe, and that we have hearts like any other men. Now, a word of advice…"

"I'm listening."

"First, try not to cross my path again."

"By my faith!" naively replied Don Ramon, half laughing, half crying, "if I were to be captured a fifth or sixth time, I'd rather it be by you."

"Thank you! Now, while the move is taking place, come and refresh yourself in my cabin, and let's chat."

"It will be my pleasure, Captain!"

"L'Olonnais, you heard my orders," said Bearcub to his second. "See to it that everything is carried out as I have decided."

"Don't worry, I'll take care of it."

Bearcub and Don Ramon entered the cabin where refreshments were prepared. The two captains sat down. The freebooter, as we know, was very sober, which did not prevent him from doing the honors with a lot of spirit and grace.

After Don Ramon had emptied his glass two or three times, Bearcub took a fairly large diamond from a small leather bag, hung around his neck by a steel chain, and showed it to the Spaniard.

"Do you know anything about diamonds, Don Ramon?" he asked.

"A little," replied the other. "I've been trading them for some time."

"So take a look at this one and please estimate its worth."

Don Ramon took the diamond, examined it with the most serious attention, turning it over in every way, then said:

"I'd say this diamond is worth at least eleven thousand piasters."

"Or fifty-five thousand pounds," said Bearcub, pushing away the hand of the Spaniard who was trying to return precious stone to him. "Keep it in memory of our encounter, my dear Don Ramon. Now that our business has been settled, let's talk, shall we?"

"But," Don Ramon objected, "this diamond..."

"That's for your indigo and your coffee. You've just sold them to me at a hundred percent profit, that's all. I'm giving you a diamond because it's easier to carry than gold. Take it and let's not talk about it anymore. Rather tell me, who is the Governor of Cartagena right now?"

"Don José Rivas, Count of Figueroa, a worthy gentleman with a most charming daughter."

"Ah! So he has a daughter—a child, no doubt?"

"No, noble captain! Doña Elmina is almost sixteen years-old, as far as I can tell."

"The Governor's daughter is called Doña Elmina?" asked Bearcub, shuddering. "And beautiful as you say she is, this young lady must surely be highly courted?"

"I don't know if she is being courted. The only thing I know is that there was a lot of talk about her upcoming wedding when I left."

"Doña Elmina is getting married!" cried Bearcub who became livid.

"At least, that was what was being said," Don Ramon continued in a placid tone, far from suspecting the import of his words.

"And who is the happy mortal?"

"By my faith, noble captain, that 'happy mortal,' as you put it, seems to me to be a rather nasty character;. He's a Mexican who, one fine morning, burst like a bombshell in the city, without anyone knowing who he was or where he came from. They say he's enormously rich. He keeps an open house and is a very skilled gambler. It is, in fact, that skill that opened to him the palace of the Governor, with whom he is now intimately connected—so intimately even, that he must, on the first day of next month, marry his daughter—the poor dear child!"

"So you feel sorry for the girl?"

"From the bottom of my heart, yes, my dear captain! For I am convinced that she is being sacrificed, and that it is impossible for her to love this man, about whom, by the way, people whisper many singular and even sinister stories."

"Tell me about them."

"I told you, didn't I, noble Captain, that I took in two sailors onboard when I left Cartagena?"

"You did."

"Well, these two sailors were conveyed to me by Don Enrique Torribio Moreno himself."

"Don Enrique Torribio Moreno?"

"Yes; that's the name of the Mexican."

"I see. Very well. Please continue."

"Don Enrique Torribio Moreno was waiting for a schooner named the *Santa Catalina,* which came from Vera Cruz and belonged to him. This schooner was manned by seven men, including the captain. Well, the Mexican arranged things so that, during the night, before entering the port of Cartagena, the captain and four men drowned. Then, sometime after that terrible accident, Don Enrique Torribio arrived aboard the schooner with a new crew. The two surviving sailors were so frightened by what had happened that they wanted to disembark at once. As I was going out with my ship, Don Enrique

Torribio, who no doubt wanted nothing better than to get rid of embarrassing witnesses, offered me to take them on board. I agreed."

"Are they still there?"

"Of course! They know this murky affair from the tip of their fingers. Now, what interest could Don Enrique Torribio could have had in this drowning of his men? That's what I would like to know…"

"I'll find out," murmured the freebooter. "Could you hand over these two men to me, Don Ramon?" he then asked aloud. "I solemnly swear that no harm will come to them—quite the contrary."

"As you please, my dear Captain, but may I ask why?"

"Curiosity, my dear Don Ramon, nothing else. Here is your safe-conduct," he added, handing him a piece of paper on which he had written some words and signed. "Now, come."

"Oh! Captain," cried the Spaniard, squeezing the precious paper, "I really don't know how to thank you…"

"Well, we are old acquaintances after all, and I don't want anything bad to happen to you. Follow me."

They left the cabin almost immediately and returned to the deck.

L'Olonnais had carried out his chief's orders to the letter: the two largest boats of the brig had been loaded with trunks containing all the belongings of the crew. These had been distributed amongst the two boats, along with water, food and weapons. In the larger boat, intended for the captain, had been stored everything that belonged to him personally. About ten freebooters had remained on board the brig to guard it.

The two Spanish sailors gladly accepted Bearcub's offer and boarded the *Trickster* happily.

Apart from the information that Bearcub hoped to obtain from them, these two men, by their knowledge of the country and the port where they were going, could be of great use to the expedition. Therefore the freebooters, who understood the intention of their chief, were pleased to welcome the two newcomers.

Captain Don Ramon de la Cruz, after bidding farewell to Bearcub Ironskull and showering him with blessings, finally got into his boat, and the two embarkations set off under full sail, heading for the island of Cuba, where, if the wind stayed steady, they hoped to arrive in less than three days.

Bearcub Ironskull chose one hundred fifty men, whom he put on the brig, as well as twelve guns of 18, which he had kept in reserve in the hold of the *Trickster* and which were immediately installed on the deck of the captured ship. Then he debaptized the *San Juan Bautista*, which he now christened the *Rake*. He entrusted her command to L'Olonnais, and the two sailors, orienting their sails, set sail for Cartagena.

CHAPTER XII
How Doña Lilia gave hope back to her cousin

After the door of the room had closed on Don José Rivas and his friend, Doña Elmina dropped her head and two tears fell silently down her cheeks, while a deep sigh escaped from her chest.

Doña Lilia approached slowly, sat down on a chair next to her, grabbed one of her hands and gently pressed it between hers.

"My poor cousin!" she murmured in a voice full of tenderness.

Doña Elmina did not answer; she remained still and somber, her eyes fixed distractedly on the floor.

"Elmina, dear Elmina," said the young girl, kissing her cousin on the forehead, "don't let yourself be overcome by pain. Come back to yourself, regain courage. Your misfortune is great, but the power of God is infinite."

"No, Lilia! No, my darling! God himself can't save me now. I am under the mighty claw of the tiger, and, as you know, the tiger is relentless. I will die."

"Die, you!"

"Yes, Lilia, I would rather die rather than be subjected to the awful sacrifice that my father seeks to impose on me."

"Is that you I hear? You were so brave, so resolute, so full of hope just two hours ago!"

"I was hoping, you're right, but for what? I don't know myself. One always hopes, alas! when one suffers; and I do suffer, Lilia, my darling."

"My poor and dear friend, come back to yourself. I repeat, don't let yourself get so down. What happened during your father's visit should not surprise you, you were expecting it; so be strong. Let's resume our conversation so unfortunately interrupted, finish your barely started confidence, and perhaps..."

"Don't insist, my dear Lilia," Doña Elmina sharply interrupted, straightening her head. "This was only follies created by my own delirious imagination. I am lost, I feel it, nothing will hold me on the edge of that abyss into which I am ready to fall."

"Don't talk like that, Elmina, I implore you! On the contrary, take courage."

"Courage, you say? But what's the point of fighting an impossible struggle? Alas! my fate is irrevocably set."

"Who knows, by God, if such an event is even fated to occur..."

"Don't try to comfort me, my darling cousin," Elmina said bitterly. "You can't give me hope when you don't have any yourself."

"No! Let's be strong, my dear Elmina, let's be brave and for a moment, forget, if it is possible, your pain, or rather let's try to focus on something else. Let's talk heart to heart. Reveal to me this secret whose burden weighs you down, and which, until now, you have stubbornly carried alone."

Doña Elmina seemed to reflect for a moment; a pale smile appeared fleetingly on the corners of her lips, then she resumed with a tone of sadness and resignation that could not be expressed:

"My dear Lilia, why should I remain silent with you, my only friend? This secret that you ask for in the name of our friendship, I can give it to you in a few words: I'm in love. But the one whom I love ignores my love. He is far, very far from here. I will likely never see him again. He hardly knows me, but he would love me, if it weren't impossible, because so many obstacles oppose our union; such an impassable barrier separates us that I could never be his! So this love, ultimately, is a foolish dream."

Doña Lilia had listened to her friend with the most serious attention, sometimes nodding her head and shaping her cute lips in a charming pout.

"Elmina," she murmured, when the girl fell silent, "the French say that the word impossible does not exist in their language. Why shouldn't it be the same in Spanish?"

Doña Elmina stared at her.

"Why are you talking to me about the French?" she asked her with a slight tremor in her voice.

Doña Lilia smiled.

"The French are men of great heart," she replied in an insinuating voice.

"Yes. Some of them proved it to us," Doña Elmina answered, choking a sigh.

Doña Lilia rested her head on her companion's shoulder.

"I don't know if you've noticed it," she continued, "but this Don Enrique Torribio, when he is with us, seems..."

"Not a word about this man!" Doña Elmina cried out loudly. "I beg you!"

"Well, but while he was talking to you, I took a good look at him, and just like you said..."

"You felt as I did, right? You thought you recognized him?" interrupted Doña Elmina, whose nervous shiver suddenly caused her to shake.

"Yes, I did. It is him. The freebooter, the *ladron* of Santo Domingo!" resumed Doña Lilia. "Oh! What a strange resemblance... and yet, the man we're talking about must be dead..."

"Can't a demon come back from the abyss?"

"But what if it is him? You must warn your father, Elmina. Tell him everything."

"How?" replied the daughter of Don José Rivas, shaking her head with discouragement. "What do we know exactly? Nothing. Besides, this man has completely taken over my father's mind. He directs it, dominates it, does with it as he pleases. We would need a proof, just one; unfortunately, we can't get it; it is impossible for us to get it."

"Perhaps not!" Doña Lilia cried out loudly.

"What do you mean?"

"Listen to me, Elmina, because I, too, have something to tell you," the other said in a firm voice.

Doña Elmina looked at her cousin with surprise.

"You?" she said.

"Yes, I, Elmina. You know how crazy I am, and with what pleasure I like to wander around the countryside; often you yourself have reproached me for my wandering mood."

"That's true," murmured Doña Elmina, smiling through her tears.

"Well, my darling, it's probably to this wandering mood that we owe the only help that can save you."

"How so?"

"One morning, about six weeks ago, I was out riding my horse away from the village, running through the woods with no determined goal, happy to breathe in the open country air and feel the morning breeze play in my hair. All of a sudden, my horse swerved so that I was almost thrown from the saddle. I looked: a man was lying on the ground across the path, blocking my way. This man, dressed in rags, with a long beard and pale features, had the most miserable appearance. I got off my horse and leaned over him. His eyes were closed and a death rattle came out of his chest. I managed to revive him; the poor man was starving. I hurriedly went to the *pueblo* to fetch him some food. When his strength had returned, he confessed to me that he was a Frenchman, a *ladron* who had miraculously escaped from the Spanish prisons. Knowing that if his enemies caught him, he would be killed without mercy, he had dragged himself into the forest, where for a few days, he had lived on roots and wild berries. Although he had his rifle, he lacked powder and could neither hunt, nor defend himself. I gave him a knife and an axe that I had brought from the *pueblo* and I emptied my purse on the grass beside him…"

"You did! Lilia, my darling!"

"He said only one thing to me: 'You saved my life, it belongs to you.'"

"Have you seen him again?"

"Often. He told me his story. He was a famous *ladron* on Tortuga Island. So I told him about..."

"Who?"

"The one you know well, my dear," Doña Lilia resumed with a smile. "He said he knew him and loved him. Then a thought came to me…" she added hesitantly.

"What thought?"

"I was so sad to see you so unhappy, and not knowing what to do to help you, about a month ago, I asked Barthélémy—that's his name—if it would be possible for him to send a letter to Port-Margot."

" 'Is it very important, *señorita*?' he asked me.

" 'It is a matter of life and death,' I replied.

" "Then it is enough,' he said to me. 'I don't know how I will do it, but the letter will go, I swear to you. Give it to me.'

" 'You'll get it tomorrow.'"

"So, this letter…?" asked Elmina in a panting voice.

"I gave it to Barthélémy the next day. It contained only three words: *Cartagena*, *Luego*, *Peligro*. But the person for whom it was intended had to know who was sending it. Then I remembered a certain ring that never leaves you, that you always wear there in a scented skin bag, on your heart. I took it off while you sleeping and stamped the letter with it."

"You did all that, Lilia?"

"Yes, I did, my beloved cousin. Was I wrong?"

"Oh, Lilia, my dear Lilia," cried Doña Elmina, throwing herself into her arms. "Thank you, thank you a thousand times!"

"Three days later, Barthélémy, whom I had not seen since, although I had looked for him everywhere, came to find me here.

" 'The letter is gone,' he told me. 'In ten days at the most, it will reach Port-Margot.'"

"As long as he gets it," murmured Don José Rivas' daughter.

Doña Lilia smiled.

"That was fourteen days ago," she resumed. "One morning, Barthélémy said to me:

" 'The captain received the letter. He will come; watch. On my side, I will also watch.'"

"So he's on his way?"

"Yes! Are you happy now, darling?"

"Oh, my God, will you have mercy on me" cried Doña Elmina, sobbing.

The two girls remained embraced for a long time, mixing their tears with their smiles.

CHAPTER XIII
Where Don Enrique Torribio Moreno and his friend talk business

A few days had passed since the presentation of the fake Captain Gaspar Alvarado Bustamente to the governor of the city of Cartagena, Don José Rivas de Figueroa.

Barthélémy had played his role well; he had spoken pure Castilian, claimed his deep horror toward the *gringos* and *ladrones* of Tortuga Island, and above all, won with such charming ease the piastres of his new friends, that all the people who had attended each time the Governor's *tertulias* had, at first sight, recognized him for a *cristiano viejo* and a true *hidalgo* of Old Castile.

We will note in passing that, in Spanish America, and even in the Peninsula, the title of *cristiano viejo,* i.e.: Old Christian—and it was a real title—was only given to people of pure white race, whose blood has never mixed with that of the Indians in America and that of the Moors in Spain.

Don José Rivas, amazed at the sight of such a skilled player, had been drawn towards him by an instinctive sympathy, and had opened the doors of his house to him. So everything smiled at Barthélémy: he was rich, well regarded, and moreover, now had a beautiful ship under his feet.

However, in spite of all this happiness, Barthélémy was not entirely happy. There was a dark spot on this blue horizon, a spot that was nearly imperceptible to the eye, but which, similar to the *pamperos* of Argentina, could take on immense proportions in a few seconds and turn into a hurricane.

That day, around seven o'clock in the morning, the worthy captain was sitting pensively in the cabin of his ship, the *Santa Catalina,* his elbows resting on a table, his head in his hands, looking sadly at a huge glass of spiced wine in front of him.

"It can't go on like this any longer," he murmured. "I'm no longer a man, I no longer belong to myself, I have become—the Devil takes me if I lie—a toy to be spun around and fired at will. It's got to end; I'm fed up with it!"

He got up, emptied his glass in one go and climbed on the bridge.

"Get a dinghy ready!" he ordered the sailor on watch, who was walking along the gangways.

His order was immediately executed and, a few minutes later, the dinghy with him aboard was headed for land.

Just as Captain Barthélémy was setting foot on the first step of the stone stairs leading to the quay, he suddenly saw the high stature of his supposedly close friend Don Enrique Torribio Moreno standing in front of him.

The Mexican was smiling. Barthélémy, on the contrary, frowned. He knew the man and understood that this smile did not bode well for him.

"Where are you going?" Don Enrique Torribio asked him, reaching out his hand.

"Ashore," Barthélémy replied laconically without taking it.

"Do you have any plans?" Don Enrique Torribio continued, without taking offense.

"None."

"Then come and have lunch with me."

"I am not hungry."

"You haven't tasted the local *tostones*."

Barthélémy made an irritated gesture.

"What's with you?" Don Enrique Torribio asked, staring at him.

"I don't know, I'm annoyed. Let me go."

"Where are you going?"

"I'm going to get my Gelin, since you want to know."

"So you really care about that rifle?"

"I do."

"Well, then, fine, let's go together. I'll take this opportunity to go and check my *quinta* in Turbaco."

"I'd rather go alone."

"I understand, but I need to talk to you, dear friend."

"We can do that later."

"No, we must do it now. What I have to tell you is very urgent and very important."

"Ah!" said Barthélémy, stopping and looking at his interlocutor in turn. "Is anything going on?"

"Nothing yet, but soon something will."

"What?"

"I'll tell you. Come on, let's go."

"Since you insist..."

A slave, with two bridled horses, stood motionless a few steps away. Don Enrique Torribio made a sign to him; he approached.

The two men got into the saddle. Five minutes later, they were galloping through the countryside.

Don Enrique Torribio, seeing that his companion was obstinately remaining silent, finally decided to begin the conversation.

"You've taken the ten men I sent four days ago, haven't you?" he asked Barthélémy.

"Yes, although I confess I don't understand why you put a crew of sixteen on a boat that could easily maneuver with four."

"How do you feel about it?"

"I don't care. But I warn you; I don't know if you did it on purpose, but you had a happy hand: they're real scoundrels."

"Bah! You will tame them; it's only a matter of knowing how to do it, and you do know it. Did you also receive the powder and the four pieces of eight?"

"Yes. They're all carefully stowed in the hold."

"Are you ready to sail?"

"At the first signal. I've been whiling away the time doing nothing in the harbor. The ship's ready to go."

"Very good."

"So you're happy. That's good."

"You will be too when I tell you what you'll be doing."

"Taking part in some devilish scheme, no doubt?"

"A magnificent one! You know that the Governor has a daughter…"

"I also know that you're supposed to be marrying her."

"Only fools believe it!" said Don Enrique Torribio, shrugging. "I've been married for ten years to the Villequier woman. By the Devil! I don't want to be a bigamist."

"So what do you plan to do then?"

"Listen! Tonight, you're having dinner at the Governor's house, aren't you?"

"Yes, that's right."

"When the *dulces* are served, you will invite the Governor, his family, Don Lopez Sandoval, the commander of the garrison, and all the other guests to a party that you've planned to give on board your ship before leaving Cartagena, meant to thank them for the generous hospitality that you have received here. Do you follow me?"

"Not really."

"Everyone will eagerly accept. You'll start the party. While your guests are having fun gambling, drinking and dancing , you will quietly set sail and leave the harbor. Once you're two or three leagues offshore, we'll ransom our guests and that will be it."

"A good plan! But what about your fortune here? You're prepared to leave it all behind then?"

"My poor Barthélémy, you'll never be anything but a fool," Don Enrique Torribio said, with a mocking smile. "How many barrels did you take on board?"

"Thirty, I think. But you do know that, don't you?"

"Yes, your count is correct. Well, twelve of these barrels are full of gold. I have realized my fortune here slowly and carefully, under the pretext of making large purchases of land, houses, etc. It is now all safely stored aboard the *Santa Catalina.* Do you understand?"

"I do now."

"What do you think of my plan?"

"It's a rather dastardly scheme!" answered Barthélémy frankly.

"Bah! *Gavachos* are fair game, my dear friend!"

"Perhaps, but what about the girl?"

"Girls, you mean, because there are two of them."

"Two girls?"

"Yes—and very pretty too!"

"Ah! And what do you intend to do with them?"

"The girls?"

"Yes."

"I don't know yet; I'll see," replied the other with a salacious smile.

For a few minutes the two riders had been climbing a rather high hill, from the top of which the eye could see the calm and azure sea on the horizon.

All of a sudden, Barthélémy uttered a scream.

"What's wrong?" Don Enrique Torribio asked, surprised.

"Me? Nothing! But my horse stumbled, and I didn't expect it; that's all," replied the freebooter coldly, while searching with an anxious look the extreme limit of the horizon, where an almost imperceptible white spot, as big as a seagull, had just appeared.

"What a sad rider you are," Don Enrique Torribio said ironically.

"Hey, I'm only a sailor."

"And therefore a bad rider, right?"

"Guilty as charged. So what?" Barthélémy said with a certain harshness.

"Let's not get angry now."

"I'm not angry, but I find it annoying that you keep making fun of me."

"I didn't know you were so touchy."

"What do you want, I'm like that, take it or leave it!"

"*Caraï*! What a prickly rose you are! You're not in a good mood today."

"Perhaps not," said Barthélémy, who wanted above all to divert his companion's attention and prevent him from looking at the sea, where the white dot, almost imperceptible at first, seemed to grow in size.

"Forgive me, I was wrong," said Don Enrique Torribio.

"You're forgiven," replied Barthélémy gruffly.

"So let's get back to our business."

"What business?"

"The one we were discussing, *pardieu!*"

"Ah, yes."

"So, we're agreed, right? You will issue your invitation tonight."

"For what day?" asked the freebooter, his eyes stubbornly fixed on the sea.

"Let's see," Don Enrique Torribio said, thinking. "Today is Friday."

"An unlucky bad day," said the other with a mocking smile.

"I'm not superstitious! Still—invite them all for next Tuesday."

"So be it. Now, if you have nothing else to say to me, goodbye and see you tonight. Here we are in Turbaco."

"See you tonight."

They separated. They were then in front of the narrow path that led to the *jacal*, previously inhabited by Barthélémy.

Don Enrique Torribio Moreno continued on his way slowly and entered the village, while the other headed towards the forest.

"Once I don't need him anymore, I'll get rid of him," murmured the fake Mexican, watching his so-called friend disappear among the trees.

"Won't God's patience ever grow tired of this rascal's crimes?" grumbled Barthélémy as he sank into the forest.

CHAPTER XIV

Where Barthélémy puts his eye to a slit to see better, and his ear to a partition to hear better

An instant after leaving Don Enrique Torribio Moreno, Captain Barthélémy made a detour under the woods, came back in a circle and followed the trail of the fake Mexican whom he followed from a distance without being seen.

He saw the man enter, not his *quinta* or country house as he had announced it, but on the contrary an ill-named *pulqueria* where one usually met the usual assortment of villains and bandits whose Spanish colonies, from the very first days of their existence, seemed—one does not know why—to have acquired in great numbers.

Don Enrique Torribio set foot inside with a deliberate step, as a man who felt at home in such a dubious establishment.

We forgot to mention that, during the thirty minutes or so since Barthélémy had left him, the fake Mexican, before entering the village, and behind a bush, had taken advantage of the complete solitude that reigned around to change his clothes, making himself totally unrecognizable to any eye less interested or less penetrating than that of another freebooter.

Arriving a few minutes later in front of the door of the *pulqueria,* Barthélémy stopped.

He had a moment's hesitation; it was obvious that from the first step he took in the room, his friend's gaze would fall upon him and he would be immediately recognized.

This was exactly what he wanted to avoid.

Unfortunately, the Brother of the Coast was facing one of those challenges that luck suddenly brings up to thwart the best conceived plans, and which are almost impossible to solve.

But Captain Barthélémy was one of those energetic, iron-willed men who, when they want something, get it, and when they have made a resolution, would rather get killed on the spot rather than give it up.

"Bah!" he murmured, shrugging. "One who risks nothing gets nothing. However clever he may be, I won't take any lessons in subtlety from him. Besides," he added with a sarcastic laugh, "the good Lord owes me some compensation!"

He had his horse rear and gambol in order to attract attention, but when he saw that no one was coming out, he shouted:

"Ahoy there, *mozo*! By the Devil! Will you come out, wretch!"

Almost at once, a skinny, scrawny, twisted native with a starving look, but whose round gray eyes were surprisingly piercing, appeared on the threshold.

This charming man, took off his filthy cap, cast a wily glance at the traveler, and decided to come forward to meet him.

"What does Your Lordship desire?" he said, bowing respectfully and grasping the horse by the bridle.

"I want," replied Barthélémy, "you to take my horse to the *corral* and bring me a glass of *mezcal*."

"Here?" asked the other with a devious look.

"Of course not!" replied the freebooter. "In the common room, or, if it's too crowded, in a private room. I'll pay what it takes."

And he made a movement to set foot on the ground.

"You will be perfectly comfortable in our common room, Your Lordship," replied the innkeeper obediently. "The other clients won't disturb you."

"Why is that?" asked Barthélémy, jumping down from his horse.

"Because, Your Lordship, we have no clients at the moment, and the *pulqueria* is completely empty."

The freebooter cast a penetrating glance at the innkeeper, a glance that the man bore without lowering his eyes or looking away.

"Then it's different, my friend," said the freebooter, putting his hand on his arm. "Do you want to earn an ounce of gold?" he added, lowering his voice slightly.

"Er, if Your Lordship don't mind, I'd rather earn two," replied the other immediately, winking significantly.

"Really? I see that we're going to get along fine."

"Your Lordship, a poor devil like me, who earns barely eight piasters a year--when luck decides he should be paid other than with a stick—always gets along with the *caballeros* who deign to honor him with their trust, and show him some gold."

The word *show* was pronounced with such an accent that Barthélémy could not miss its meaning. So he took out of his pocket a red silk purse, through the stitches of which the gold could be seen to sparkle. He then inserted his right hand into the purse and pinching with mathematical precision two ounces between his thumb and forefinger, he made them shimmer before the poor man's eyes sparkling with avarice.

"What would you do to earn this and even double it if I'm happy with you?" he asked with a smile.

"Alas, Your Lordship," replied the innkeeper with an expression impossible to convey, "I have no father or mother, otherwise I would gladly swear upon their sacred souls ... but, in their absence, dispose of me. What is to be done? I belong to you, body and soul."

The freebooter closed his hand.

"Where is the corral?" he asked.

"There, Your Lordship, behind the house. You can see it from here!"

"Very well! Listen to me. You have five minutes, not a second more, to take my horse to the corral and come back. If you say one word to any living soul while you are doing this, there will be nothing between us. Do you understand? Go!"

"*Caraï*! Your Lordship, I will be mute like a possum."

And he took the horse. Three minutes later he was back.

"I am pleased with you," said Barthélémy. "Now, pay attention to what I am going to tell you. A quarter of an hour ago, a horseman entered your inn. You took his horse to the corral as you have just taken mine. I want you to let me in in a spot where I can see this man and hear everything he says, without him being able to suspect that I am there. If you follow my instructions, there will be not two ounces of gold, but four. And just so that you are certain that I do not want to cheat you, here are the first two ounces."

He then dropped the gold into the innkeeper's quivering hand. The native then made them vanish with such skill that it was impossible for the freebooter to know what had happened to them.

"By the way, I forgot to warn you for your own good," Barthélémy added. "At the slightest hint of betrayal, I'll blow your brains out like a dog!"

And lifting slightly one of the corners of his *poncho,* he let the innkeeper see the heavy pommels of two pistols stuck in his *faja.*

"Your Lordship," answered the innkeeper with some majesty, "if Tonillo had the honor of being better known to Your Excellency, Your Lordship would know that he is not a traitor. My boss is taking a *siesta*; I am therefore at this moment the only master in the house. I promise you, on the place that I hope to earn one day in Heaven, that you will see and hear everything that the man you want to observe say. Besides, he and his friends are bad customers," he added in a tone of mocking contempt. "They've been there for an hour already and have not spent anything, not even a *real*, and after all, the interest of our fine establishment must come first."

"That's right!" replied the freebooter with a smile.

"Come then," said the other.

Barthélémy followed him.

Tonillo—since that was his name—instead of entering the main room, went around the house, crossed the corral, opened a door closed only with a latch, and led the freebooter into a kind of cellar where there were some bottles of *pulque* and *mezcal* stacked on top of each other, and about forty stacks of hay.

He spread seven or eight stack slightly apart, then leaned against the wall and showed the freebooter a wide slit in the wood.

"Here, you'll be perfect," he told him.

"That's perfect; you can go now," replied Barthélémy. "See that my horse is not seen. When these *caballeros* are ready to leave, come back."

The innkeeper bowed respectfully and went out of the cellar, closing the door behind him.

Barthélémy was then plunged into almost complete darkness. The only glow that illuminated the cellar came from the wide crack in the wall revealed by the native.

"*Pardieu*!" grumbled the freebooter, with that sarcastic air that was particular to him. "I was certain that the Good Lord never abandoned honest people!"

And, accommodating himself as comfortably as possible, he applied his eye to the slit. Then, one of those picturesque paintings, like those of the immortal Callot,[52] offered itself to his sight.

In a room that was large enough, but poorly lit by narrow windows with leaded glass lined with cobwebs, where the smoke from cigars and cigarettes massed in heavy clouds below the ceiling, absorbing almost all the light, about twenty individuals, with sinister faces, receding foreheads, crooked noses, shifty eyes, and outrageous mustaches, were gathered together.

These individuals, dressed in sordid rags arranged on their bodies with that talent that the Spaniards possess so well which, if necessary, would allow them to drape themselves in a string, were scattered here and there around tables, lying, sitting, standing and affecting the most fantastic poses and attitudes.

But they were all armed to the teeth. Not only did they have long rapiers with shell handles on their hips, but they all carried pistols on their belts and large horn-sleeved daggers in their right boots.

---

[52] Jacques Callot (c.1592-1635) was a baroque printmaker and draftsman from Lorraine. He played an important role in the development of the old master print, making more than 1400 etchings that chronicled the life of his period, featuring soldiers, clowns, drunkards, Gypsies, beggars, as well as court life.

Barthélémy looked for a moment for Don Enrique Torribio in the middle of this colorful crowd of high-waymen. He soon spotted him, sitting on the only chair in the room, his back resting on the backrest, his head thrown back and smoking, as was his habit, an excellent cigar.

As the freebooter was looking through the crack in the wall, Don Enrique Torribio was speaking. The bandits listened to him contemplatively.

"*Caballeros*!" he said nonchalantly, dropping huge tobacco puffs through his nose and mouth. "I don't understand your hesitation! What is it all about? *Por Dios*! This a very simple thing..."

"A very simple thing?" replied in a hoarse voice a tall man with a sour face, who had lost his right eye and whose left eye squinted. "Your Lordship must be joking. I don't find it simple at all!"

"The Devil takes you, Matadoce," replied Don Enrique Torribio in a friendly tone. "You always raise objections to the least of things."

The worthy Matadoce, who, judging by his face, seemed to have deserved his name, which meant "Killer of Twelve" in Spanish, answered immediately without emotion:

"I only raise objections, Your Lordship, because I am an honest man, and I wish to do the work I am hired to do well and conscientiously, and in such a way as not to attract reproaches later. As for the girls, it goes without saying. It's only a question of a noose, more or less tight—that is all! A child could do it. Poor doves! They won't even think of defending themselves... Also, we will be at sea, far from prying eyes... No one will dare interrupting our work... But that's not where my concern lies…"

"Yes, yes," Don Enrique Torribio replied with a sneer. "I know what your problem is."

"*Caraï*! I confess that it bothers me furiously. I saw that Captain Bustamente, as you call him, twice before, Your Lordship, and on my faith, he doesn't look like an easy customer at all."

"But there are twenty of you!"

"So what? Listen to this, Your Lordship: Three days ago, a dozen friends and I, we decided to ambush him, to wait for him near the Governor's house. They say he is very lucky at cards and we wanted to relieve him of some of his earnings of the night. It was dark as pitch. He walked by; we all fell on him; another man would have begged for mercy and would have surrendered, no? But not him! What did our mad captain do? He drew a kind of knife, as long as a sword, and, without saying a word, without throwing a challenge, he fell so hard on us that in less than three minutes, he has disemboweled five of my men, wounded two or three more, and then he walked away without a nick. No, no, Your Lordship, it is not as simple as that! Also, in my capacity as a swordsman, I like this man—he is a brave man. On my faith, I shall not kill him for less than thirty ounces of gold, that's my final word!"

"Yes! Thirty!" replied all the other bandits in chorus.

"Take it or leave it, Your Lordship," Matadoce concluded.

Don Enrique Torribio seemed to think for a moment.

"Deal!" he said, with a grimace that had the pretension of resembling a smile. "I don't know why I humor you! You're like a bunch of spoiled brats! I'll pay you each your thirty ounces, but this time, you'd better finish him off!"

"Your Lordship!" answered the bandit with dignity, "without honesty, there is no business. My friends and I are, thank God, known for being honorable men, who always earn our money faithfully."

"It is not your honor that I am questioning," Don Enrique Torribio replied with a sneer. "Now that everything has been agreed between us—it has been agreed, hasn't it?"

"Yes, Your Lordship, it has," replied one of the bandits.

"Except for the advance," Matadoce added in an insinuating voice.

"You will each get ten ounces in a moment; the rest after the deed is done. Just remember that you must always be at my disposal. I will only take you to the schooner at the last moment."

Barthélémy thought he had heard enough; he left the cellar. Five minutes later, after giving his two ounces of gold to Tonillo, he walked away from the *pulqueria*.

"*Mordieu*!" he said between his teeth, while galloping away. "The beast is even more venomous than I thought. I don't regret having spied on him, and especially having listened to him. It was the best way to find out what that snake was planning! Forewarned is forearmed, as they say!"

CHAPTER XV
Where Barthélémy goes to get his rifle

Captain Barthélémy thus galloped without slowing down the pace of his horse during the time it took to cross the village of Turbaco.

When he was about a rifle range away from the village, he put his horse back in a trot, and when he reached a narrow, leafy path that went deep into the woods, one before which he had passed an hour earlier, he resolutely set off on it.

This path led to the *jacal* that he had inhabited for a while; where we had met him for the first time, in a very different appearance.

Arriving at the *jacal*, he saw, in front of the door, a man on horseback, holding a second horse with a bridle.

"Thank God!" he murmured. "She had the patience to wait for me."

And he drove the spurs into the flanks of his mount, which went off like a rocket.

At the noise caused by this fast ride, a pretty young girl appeared on the threshold of the hut. It was Doña Lilia.

In an instant, Barthélémy was with her, having jumped off and thrown the bridle of his horse to his manservant. He respectfully greeted his charming visitor and followed her inside the *jacal*.

"You made yourself rare, *señor*," said Doña Lilia, with a mutinous pout that made her look particularly lovely. "Didn't you receive my letter? Or did you forget what was in it?"

"Don't believe this, *señorita*. On the contrary, you must always believe that a word from you is like an order for me, and that I will always be happy to obey you."

"Perhaps! But with so little eagerness," she mockingly replied.

"*Señorita*, I was on my way here directly when I found myself face to face, at the moment when I least expected it, with my honorable friend, Don Enrique Torribio Moreno, who seems—God forgive me!—to have been intent, during the past few days, on sticking to me like glue, so much so that I only managed to get away from him only an hour ago, just a few paces from here."

"Ah!" she laughed. "And it took you an hour to get here? You'd better get yourself another horse, my dear captain, for in truth the poor animal must be horribly furrowed."

"You may laugh, *señorita*," Barthélémy replied in a prickly tone. "You must have a good nature since the account of my little annoyances cause you so much joy!"

"Good! You're getting angry, Captain. It's a clever way to get out of it."

"Not at all, *señorita*. And the proof is that I want to tell you everything. First, I went to a *pulqueria*…"

"To refresh yourself?"

"No. To learn."

"You mean, to drink?" she mockingly replied.

"Still joking, I see, *señorita*, but that doesn't offend me at all, I assure you. I stayed in a dreadful cellar; I applied my eye to a crack in the wall, and I saw and heard things that would have made an *alcade* and even an *alguazil* tremble—and these people are notoriously brave."

"What was it, then Captain?" she asked, now curious.

"Ah, but I can't tell you."

"So you're trying to sell me just another kind of tall tale like sailors like to tell?"

"Me? Never, *señorita*!"

"So why all this mystery?"

"Alas!" Barthélémy replied with a tragi-comic air, "is it my fault, *señorita*, if the life we have been given is itself a mystery? Wherever we go, we eat, we sleep, that mystery is always with us, hovers over our heads, and moves silently under our very feet?"

"Are you going mad on me, my dear captain?" asked the young woman, scrutinizing his face.

"Me?"

"Yes, you!"

"Not that I know of! I'm only trying to answer your questions, *señorita*."

"You're not doing a very good job of it."

"But as I told you, *señorita*, it is a mystery..."

"Ah, no, please, Captain," she interrupted sharply, "let's not do that again."

"As you wish."

"I think it's better if I give up wanting to know anything about you. "

Barthélémy bowed respectfully to his pretty interlocutor, but did not comment.

"So you really don't want to say anything?" she persisted. "Do you even know what's going on?"

"Oh, a lot is going on, *señorita*!"

"Yes—including this piece of news."

"What news?"

"That of my cousin's wedding to your Don Enrique Torribio Moreno, now set for next Thursday. What do you have to say about that?"

"I have to say that it's rather funny."

"You evil man! How can you find that terrible news funny?"

"Allow me to explain, please, *señorita*! If this union, rightly hated by your charming cousin, were to be consummated, I would be, like you, desperate. But as it will not be consummated, on the contrary, I find this news rather funny."

"I should scratch out your eyes, Captain. You're toying with me!"

"Me? Not at all, *señorita*!"

"I come here, with despair in my heart, to seek consolation from you, to tell you of our sorrows, and this is all you find to say? This union will not be consummated? Are you clairvoyant? Who on Earth will stop it?"

"Eh! eh! That, we don't know yet," he said with a sarcastic smile. "But, if it's not me, it will be someone else I know."

"Ah, yes! Your illustrious friend, the famous Captain Bearcub Ironskull!"

"In the flesh, *señorita*."

"The illustrious Captain," she said with a scathing look, "who always comes but never arrives?"

"Ah, but there, you're mistaken, *señorita*. He is arriving."

"Is he?"

"Yes."

"Captain Bear?"

"Bearcub Ironskull, the same, *señorita*."

"Have you seen him?"

"Well, not exactly, *señorita*."

"So what are you saying then?"

"Be patient!"

"I *am* patient, but you're irritating me! It's as if you take some kind of malicious pleasure in tormenting me!" she cried, angrily stomping the ground with her foot.

"How can you say that? Me, who am doing everything I can to please you, *señorita*!"

"Well then?"

Barthélémy sighed.

"In two words, here's the deal, *señorita*. Just now, while climbing the mountain, always in the company of my honorable friend Don Enrique Torribio Moreno... That's one with whom I'll get even soon…"

"Go on, Captain! For Heaven's sake!

"Well, *señorita*, just then, I saw two large ships, a frigate and a brig, which were beginning to appear on the horizon..."

"Is that your only clue?"

"That's all I needed, *señorita*, and this is why: the frigate had its lower gallant sail all clewed up, and its upper one was made of red canvas."

"You know, I didn't understand a word of that."

"I'm sure you didn't, *señorita*, but to me, it means clear as day that Captain Bearcub Ironskull is near, as clearly as if his name was written in six-foot letters."

"Oh, my God," she cried, stumbling and turning pale at the same time.

"What? Did you just get bit by a snake?"

"No, Captain—it's the emotion."

"I like that better, *señorita*, it's less dangerous."

"It's because you have such a way of announcing things!"

"I see! If I don't speak, you want to scratch out my eyes, but if I speak, you faint. What a quandary!"

"Shut up!"

"I couldn't wish for a better command."

"I want to know…"

"What?"

"When will Captain Bearcub Ironskull arrive?"

"Tonight, very probably."

"Can you communicate with him?"

"I could, that is to say... But no, I can't!"

"Why not? Please, explain!"

"It's quite easy, *señorita*. I could, if I had a boat, a canoe, a pirogue of some kind; but I can't, because I lack the aforementioned embarkations, and it is impossible for me, despite all my good will, to swim at least four leagues—not to mention that I would probably be caught by sharks that have the bad habit of continuously strolling along the coast."

"So the lack of a boat is the only thing stopping you?"

"Yes! Any type of boat, as long as I can fit inside."

"If I were to get you an Indian canoe, would that do the trick?"

"It would fit me like a glove, *señorita*!"

"What?"

"Don't pay attention: I'm mixing my metaphors. I meant that it would suit me perfectly."

"Well, I can get you one."

"A canoe?"

"Yes."

"Right away?"

"Pretty much. When do you need it?"

"Damn! Let me think, *señorita*... The sun sets around seven, seven-thirty... It won't be completely dark until eight... Ideally, I should have that canoe around eight-thirty—but no later."

"Why?"

"Because, calculating the time necessary to take that canoe to the place where I'll embark, then, the time necessary for the trip, I won't reach the frigate before midnight."

"Won't it be too late?"

"On the contrary, *señorita*, it will be just right. The Moon does not rise until eleven, and when it does, I'll be far enough away from the coast not to be seen."

"Well, that's your business, Captain, you know it better than I do."

"Yes, yes, take it easy, *señorita*, leave it all to me, I'll take care of everything."

"Decidedly, Captain, you are a most charming man, and I like you very much."

"Ah! If only that were true!" Barthélémy replied with a tragicomic look. "But it doesn't matter. It seems the wind has changed, and I like that better."

"And the captain, when shall we see him?"

"Who? Bearcub?"

"Ironskull, yes."

"When do you want to see him, *señorita*?"

"Not me. You understand, don't you? It'll be my cousin who will be happy to see him as soon as possible."

"Let me think, *señorita*..."

"You seem to do a lot of thinking when I'm around."

"True! But that's the only way of avoiding making stupid mistakes. Can you visit the *huerta* [53] of your house at any time?"

"Of course! Who would stop us? My cousin and I are perfectly free to go as we please."

---

[53] Garden, orchard.

"Well then, go there and walk about, both of you, without attracting attention, tonight, around three... And stop by the little door—you know the one?"

"The one at the top of the garden, near the forest?"

"The same."

"Ah!"

"It's likely that, around that time, someone you know will knock at that door..."

"Ah! Captain, if you can manage to pull that one out, I will..."

"You will what?" Barthélémy interrupted eagerly.

"I will... I will consider you to be a most charming man whom I respect very much," Doña Lilia replied, blushing.

"Then it is agreed. I will bring Captain Bearcub Ironskull to you, dead or alive.

"My cousin would prefer it very much if he were alive!"

"I understand. And you, do you have anything to ask me while we're at it, *señorita*? Don't be shy."

"No, nothing. "

"Well, then, *señorita*, I will now ask you for my pirogue."

"Indeed! I will leave right now. You will follow me discreetly at a distance. I will tell you where the canoe is. Above all, don't forget your promise?"

"*Señorita*, I would rather die than disappoint you."

"Here is my hand. Goodbye, Captain."

"Goodbye, *señorita*!" Barthélémy replied, kissing the pretty hand she held out to him.

The young woman made a graceful curtsy and, with a seductive smile, walked out of the *jacal*.

A moment later, the precipitous gallop of two horses riding away was heard on the hardened earth.

As soon as he was alone, after casting a suspicious glance around him, Barthélémy stooped down, rummaged through a pile of dry leaves piled up in a corner and removed his buccaneer rifle that he had hidden there when, some time earlier, he had met Don Enrique Torribio Moreno.

"Here is my Gelin rifle," he said sarcastically. "It is good to plan for every eventuality, and if I meet that trustworthy Don Enrique again, I can prove that I told him the truth."

At about half past ten that same evening, Captain Barthélémy got out in a pirogue and rowed towards the buccaneer ship he had first spotted during the day.

As an added precaution, in case some invisible spy was watching, he had lined his oars with wool so that the boat made no noise on the water.

CHAPTER XVI
How Barthélémy met some old friends

The night was dark, the wind cool for two days already. Bearcub Ironskull's freebooters had reached Cartagena but did not dare to approach the coast until they knew for certain what was happening ashore; so they cruised at about five leagues off the harbor.

The helmsman on watch aboard the *Trickster* struck two double blows, i.e., ten o'clock. This was immediately repeated aboard the *Rake*.

At this moment, a man stepped forth on the bridge of the *Trickster*. He was carefully wrapped in a heavy coat, whose raised hood made it difficult to distinguish his features.

On seeing him, the officer of the watch gave a low whistle. The men jumped into action and lowered the topsails. Soon, the ship stopped.

The man in the heavy coat silently got into a boat, in which a dozen Brothers of the Coast, all well-armed, sat already. The boat was then gently lowered into the sea. The sailors started rowing and the boat moved away from the ship, which had begun to sail away again.

As we have said, the night was dark, the sea rough and choppy. The top sail of the frigate and the lower sail of the brig soon disappeared in the darkness, and the boat found itself alone, plunging straight towards the land which stretched out like a huge black snake on the horizon.

Two men sat at the stern: L'Olonnais, and the man in the coat, Bearcub Ironskull.

"Tuck in the oars, brothers," commanded L'Olonnais after a moment. "Raise the mast, hoist the sail."

Five minutes later, the boat was running portside, riding smartly over the top of the waves, which it barely seemed to touch.

Two hours passed during which, apart from a few orders given by L'Olonnais, not a word was spoken on board.

Soon, they were so close to the land that, despite the darkness, it was easy to distinguish its capricious contours. The two Brothers of the Coast consulted each other for a moment in a low voice; then L'Olonnais ordered to tighten the sail, to lower the mast and to take up the oars again.

Suddenly, as this maneuver was being executed, a reddish dot appeared a short distance from the boat, and a hoarse voice shouted in French:

"Ahoy! Of the canoe!"

"Ahoy!" replied Bearcub immediately.

"Who is this?" murmured L'Olonnais. "It's strange, but it seems to me that I recognize that voice…"

"I, too," added Bearcub. "We shall see."

Putting his hands to his mouth to make a megaphone, he shouted:

"Who goes there?"

"Brother of the Coast!" was the immediate reply, with a joyful accent that could not be mistaken.

"Where are you?" asked Bearcub.

"In a native canoe; I'm alone."

"Come closer."

"I am."

The freebooters, whose curiosity was now aroused by this singular encounter, were on the lookout. Soon they spied another canoe, which glided over the water silently to come side by side with their embarkation. Without waiting for an invitation, the man inside that canoe climbed out and jumped into the stern of their own rowboat.

L'Olonnais immediately unmasked their lantern:

"Barthélémy!" he cried with surprise.

"L'Olonnais! Bearcub!" joyfully replied the new-comer. "By my Soul! I am so very happy to see you!" he added, extending to them two hands that the freebooters pressed affectionately.

"So, you recognized us?" asked Bearcub.

"*Pardieu*! I've been watching you since yesterday. Unfortunately I could only come tonight."

"What are you doing here?" asked L'Olonnais.

"It's a long story; too long to tell you right now."

"We thought you were dead!" added Bearcub.

"It was a close call; but, thanks to God, I am alive, ready and at your service, Brothers."

"We're counting on it," the two freebooters said to-gether.

"For our part, if you need our help, tell us," added Bearcub.

"I accept with a grateful heart," Barthélémy replied "Now, where were you going?"

"We're looking for a favorable place to disembark without being seen, to orient ourselves and to get some information," replied L'Olonnais.

"In that case, give me the helm. "Step aside, you others," he added, addressing the crew. "In a quarter of an hour, you'll be set."

"But what's the point of going any further, since you're here and you can give us all the information we need?" observed L'Olonnais.

"I can, indeed provide you with all the information; you need, but if it's all the same to you, believe me, Brothers, I recommend going ashore."

"Very well! Then, by the grace of God, let's do it!" said Bearcub.

The sailors bent over their oars, which bent like willow branches, and the rowboat flew like a seagull over the sea. One of the freebooters had transferred to the smaller Indian canoe and was following in the wake of the larger boat.

"Now, tell us..." started Bearcub Ironskull.

"Hush!" Barthélémy interrupted peremptorily. "We shall talk once on land. Right now, I need all my concentration not to make a mistake."

A moment later, the rowboat was sailing in still waters. Soon, a dome of foliage spread over it. They were in the midst of a mangrove bush. A slight shock was felt at the bow, then a squeak, and that was it. The boat remained motionless.

"We have arrived," said Barthélémy. "We are so well hidden here that we could stay for a fortnight without being discovered. Besides, this section of the coast is completely uninhabited. Tie the boat to the trunk of a tree, leave a man to guard it, and follow me."

The freebooters obeyed and groped their way forward, for the darkness was thick, but soon, they felt the earth beneath their feet. L'Olonnais handed his lantern to Barthélémy.

"It appears we're in some kind of cave," remarked the freebooter. "How clever."

They were indeed in a natural cave.

After making several detours, the glow of a fire suddenly appeared in the distance. The freebooters hesitated, not knowing whether it would be prudent to go further.

"Step forth without fear, Brothers!" said Barthélémy. "It was I who lit this fire before setting sail. Warm yourselves with it."

The night was cold and the freebooters needed no further invitation. Barthélémy knew the duties of hospitality. The Brothers of the Coast made joyful exclamations when they saw several baskets full of food and liquor which, at the invitation of their buccaneer friend, they hurried to share.

"Now, Brothers," said Barthélémy, "drink, eat, sleep without fear. You're safe here." Then, turning to Bearcub, he added: "Just now, Brother, you asked me for information. Now, I am ready to provide it to you."

"Speak," replied the Captain immediately.

"But not here. What I have to tell you is for your ears only."

Bearcub looked at Barthélémy with surprise.

"Follow me," said the other. "You will soon understand the meaning of my words."

Bearcub, after having made some last-minute recommendations to L'Olonnais, took his rifle and said:

"I'm ready, Brother."

"Come along."

They left the cave and, almost immediately, found themselves in front of a mountain at the top and on the sides of which stood the houses of a charming village.

"Before going any further," said Barthélémy stopping, "I have a few questions for you. Are you willing to answer them?"

"Certainly! I know that you are a loyal heart and a true Brother of the Coast."

"Thank you! Did you receive, about a month ago, at Port-Margot, a note containing only three words and bearing the imprint of a stamp known only to you?"

"I did."

"Is your coming here related to this note, or was it pure luck alone that brought you here?"

"As soon as I received this note, I organized an expedition and left for Cartagena."

"For what purpose?"

"To not waste any time in rescuing the person who was asking for my help, and sacrificing my life, if necessary, to save her," answered Bearcub with emotion.

"Good, Brother! I now know what I wanted to know. Follow me!

"Where are we going?"

"Be strong. I will take you to the person who wrote that note. It was I, acting on her instructions, who sent it to you."

"Oh! Could that be true, Brother?" cried Bearcub.

"Do you doubt my word?"

"No, of course not. Forgive me, Brother. I'm going crazy."

They then walked with great strides along the path that led to the village.

It was two o'clock in the morning.

CHAPTER XVII
How Bearcub Ironskull
had a very pleasant surprise

The two men walked at a quick pace, so it took them only a few minutes to reach the village. The streets were dark, silent and deserted.

Only a few dogs, disturbed in their sleep, greeted the passage of the two Brothers of the Coasts with a few howls, and then went back to sleep.

Barthélémy arrived at the Governor's house and, after a few minutes, stopped in front of a low doorway erected inside the garden wall, half-buried under the vines which, from the top of the wall, fell in green spirals almost to the ground.

"Here we are, friend," he said to his companion.

"Let's go in," replied Bearcub Ironskull sharply.

"There is no hurry. The person I want you to meet us will not be behind this door for another fifteen minutes yet."

"So they're waiting for us?" asked Bearcub whose heart skipped a beat.

"I, Brother, am expected. As for you, we dared not hope for your presence so quickly. But come with me to this grove of orange and lime trees. We will be safe from prying eyes and we will be able, at our ease, to talk about our business."

Bearcub followed his companion without answering. After they had both sat down comfortably on the grass, Barthélémy resumed the conversation in a restrained voice.

"What was your intention in coming here with two ships filled with people and guns?"

"I will answer you honestly, Brother, and faithfully, according to my custom. I love Doña Elmina; she does not know this love. However, when we separated, I swore to her that if someday she needed my help, my life even, that life belonged to her; and that, on a sign, from her I would come to her aid. She called me, I have come."

"You do know that her father wants her to marry?"

"To a Mexican, yes."

"Do you know this Mexican?"

"How could I?"

"That's right, you couldn't. When you have accomplished the task you set for yourself, what reward do you expect for your dedication?"

"None, Brother," replied Bearcub, shaking his head with melancholy. "I hope for nothing. I dare not question my heart, for I would go mad. I love, I suffer, that is all."

Barthélémy shook his hand in silence. After a while, he resumed:

"By the way," he asked, "what has become of your former master?"

"Boute-Feu?"

"Yes."

"He was condemned by the Council to die on Shark Island."

"Are you sure he's dead?"

"How could it be otherwise?"

"I assume nothing. Brother, God forbid! Only, in my opinion, it seems to me that it isn't enough to stomp on the head of a serpent; it is necessary to cut it off completely to be certain that he has ceased to live."

"What do you mean?"

"Right now, I can't speak to you more clearly. I have given my word, and as you know, I never break it. So do not ask me any more questions, but one last piece of advice: whatever you do, be careful."

"Thank you, Brother."

"Now, let's get up and come with me. She must be waiting for me."

They immediately got up and approached the door, against which Barthélémy scratched lightly. A soft voice was heard from the other side, whispering a single word:

"Faith!"

"Hope," replied the Brother of the Coast at once.

The door opened and the two men slipped through the gap.

"You are not alone?" exclaimed Doña Lilia with a slight cry of surprise and almost fear.

"Don't worry, *señorita*," replied the freebooter respectfully. "As I almost promised you, I'm with Captain Bearcub Ironskull."

"You are good and I thank you, *señor*," the young woman replied with emotion. Bowing gracefully before the two men, she added: "Follow me, *señores*. Elmina did not dare to hope for such happiness. Don't be afraid of any surprises; everyone is asleep in the house."

The freebooters bowed and walked with great strides behind the girl, who almost ran before them.

They arrived at the entrance to a grove where Doña Elmina was standing motionless, anxious and pale, her head bent forward, her gaze fixed, no doubt trying to probe the darkness and decipher the vague noises that she'd been hearing for a few moments.

"You!" she exclaimed with unspeakable emotion when she saw Bearcub Ironskull.

He stopped, put one knee in the ground and respectfully tipped off his hat.

"You called me, *señorita*," he said. "Here I am."

The young woman held her hand to her heart and leaned against the bower. Doña Lilia rushed to support her, but Doña Elmina gently pushed her cousin away, and extended her hand to the freebooter.

"Please, rise, *señor*," she said in a trembling voice. "This posture belongs to a supplicant and not to my would-be liberator. My heart did not deceive me, I counted on you; you're here!"

Bearcub stood up after depositing a respectful kiss on the young woman's hand and bowed to her.

"Dispose of me as you please, *señorita*. Tell me how I can best serve you. I swear to you, no matter how insurmountable the obstacles, no matter how great the perils, God will be with me, and no matter what happens, I will deliver you from your enemies."

"I have only one enemy, *señor*," she replied sadly, "but alas! this enemy can do anything he wants in Cartagena."

"I thought your father commanded in this city?"

"It is true, *señor*, but that man, or rather that demon, has taken control over my father's spirit. Don José Rivas only sees and thinks through him. Just a month ago, in this very house where we stand, he gave him my hand in marriage."

"And you don't love this man, señorita?" Bearcub asked sharply.

"I hate him; he frightens me, I would rather die than belong to him," answered Doña Elmina shivering.

Bearcub stood up and looked around with eyes full of lightning.

"Then, rest assured, *señorita*, that you will not marry this man," he said. "He is already doomed. Isn't he Mexican?"

"At least he pretends to be."

"What makes you say that?"

"He looks like another man."

"What other man?"

"You knew him."

"Me?"

"Yes, remember that terrible game of dice you played against another buccaneer when I was prisoner at Port-Margot."

"But that buccaneer is dead, señorita."

"Is he? Are you certain?"

"Oh! captain," said Doña Lilia, pressing herself tremblingly against her companion. "It is him; it must be; such a resemblance is impossible."

A cloud passed over Bearcub's face. He turned slowly towards Barthélémy, who was standing two or three steps away, leaning on his rifle.

"Brother," he said sadly, reaching out with his hand, "you must know the truth. Why do you refuse to tell me?"

To this sudden and so clearly formulated question, the freebooter shuddered; a nervous tremor agitated his whole body; he turned pale and hit the ground with the butt of his rifle:

"Why ask me that, Brother," he said in a strangled voice, "when you know very well that I cannot answer you?"

"Forgive me, Barthélémy, I was wrong to ask," Bearcub said honestly, "but your silence speaks for itself. I now know enough to take action. *Señorita*," he added, turning back toward Doña Elmina, "what is this man's name?"

"Don Enrique Torribio Moreno."

"Yes, that's right," Bearcub whispered. "And when should this accursed union take place?"

"The time has not yet been fixed, but it won't be long now."

"I repeat, *señorita*: rest assured that this marriage will not take place, I swear it on my honor."

"Alas! What can you do against so many enemies, you, a foreigner, almost alone in this country? I was wrong to call you to my aid. Let me fulfill my sad destiny. Do not start a dreadful war, I beg you, Captain."

"*Señorita*, when a man like me has taken an oath, no power on Earth can prevent him from keeping it."

"But you will be risking your lives for me, who belong to an enemy of your country."

"*Señorita*, my life is worth too little for me to be concerned; I care far more about your happiness."

"But I don't want you to die!" cried the young woman.

"God alone will decide, *señorita*," the Captain sadly replied. "I swear this to you: I will save you, or I will perish in the doing! God protects you! Now allow me to take leave of you. Soon, I hope, I will have the happiness of seeing you again—at least, I hope so. Good-bye, *señorita*."

He then respectfully saluted the two young women and, with great strides, walked away, accompanied by Barthélémy, but followed by Doña Lilia, who showed them the way.

Doña Elmina remained alone, motionless for a moment, then suddenly she fell to her knees, joined her hands, and, raising her eyes to the sky, bathed in tears, cried out:

"O all-powerful and merciful God, protect him! Protect him—because I love him!"

And she rolled unconscious on the grass.

CHAPTER XVIII
Where Don Enrique Torribio starts to worry

Meanwhile, Don Enrique Torribio Moreno was starting to worry. Despite all the money he had lavished on others, and the precautions he had taken to ensure the success of his bold plan, the former freebooter felt, through one of those instinctive presentiments that never fails to deceive, that the horizon was shrinking around him and was beginning to become laden with threatening clouds. Yet nothing around him seemed to have changed.

His friends were always attentive; his acquaintances always greeted him with the same self-serving obsequiousness, the Governor and the Commander of the garrison received him with the same smile. Twice he had visited Doña Elmina, and twice the girl, abandoning her usual reserve, had received him with a smile on her face and had chatted almost amicably with him.

What was really going on? And where did this vague feeling of anxiety come from that bothered Don Torribio Moreno in spite of himself? He would not have known how better to express it.

To suppose such a man capable of feeling the first signs of remorse would be to commit a grave error. Don Enrique Torribio Moreno was like a wild beast in all the meanings of the term; one of those savage natures cut out only for crime—fortunately rarer than one supposes—without a shred of morality, who do evil by instinct, almost for pleasure, without being aware of the crimes they commit, so much so that they seem to them to be part of the ordinary order of things.

Don Enrique Torribio, as a matter of principle, trusted no one. Forced against his better instincts to use Captain Barthélémy to ensure the success of his dark scheme, he had little confidence in the trustworthiness of his fellow Brother of the Coast, towards whom he knew that he had committed many wrongs in several circumstances.

His greatest desire was, therefore, to free himself as soon as possible from this troublesome accomplice, and as we saw above, he was already taking steps in that direction. But he was afraid of being somehow foiled by Barthélémy; so as the time he'd set for the abduction of the young women approached, he watched his accomplice even more closely, and tried to not lose sight of him for a single moment.

This fear of being betrayed by Barthélémy was the only reason for Don Enrique Torribio's concern. It was, in fact, a foreboding.

That evening, around five o'clock, he went aboard the *Santa Catalina,* which was anchored, as we have said, in the harbor of Cartagena.

As Don Enrique Torribio was docking the schooner on the starboard side, another boat that he could not see suddenly left from the port side. Captain Barthélémy, after exchanging a silent signal with the people in that other boat, hurried across the deck and rushed to greet Don Enrique.

But as everything at the moment made Don Enrique Torribio feel suspicious, the eager friendliness of Barthélémy—a man who cared little about etiquette—only made him feel even more distrustful. He frowned imperceptibly, cast a suspicious glance around, and asked:

"What were you doing?"

"What? Nothing of any importance, my friend," replied the other freebooter.

"Yes. I saw you leaning over the other rail, port side."

"Ah yes! I was waving good-bye to the lieutenant of that ship you see over there, anchored two cables away. She came in last night, from Vera Cruz. We'd moored a buoy to make it easier for her to enter the harbor, and he came to thank me."

Don Enrique Torribio looked at the ship.

"It's odd," he said pensively. "It seems to me that I've seen this ship before…"

"There would be nothing unusual about that," Barthélémy said. "It's not the first time he's been to Cartagena. What brings you here? Do you have something to tell me?"

"No, nothing. I came just to see you."

"That's all?"

"Yes," replied Don Enrique Torribio, distractedly. Then, he added almost as an *a parte:* "I know this ship…"

"It was a good idea you had to come," said Barthélémy smiling. "I was hoping you might."

"You were?"

"Yes, because if you don't have anything to say to me, me, I have something to tell you."

"Really? Speak then, but be brief."

"What I have to tell you is serious, Brother. No one must hear us. Follow me to my cabin."

Don Enrique Torribio looked at the other freebooter and smiled.

"It's really that serious?" he asked, whispering.

"Very serious," replied the other in the same mode. "So serious that if you hadn't come to see me, I would have had to go ashore to see you."

"Uh-oh! What's is it all about?"

"Come to my cabin, and you will know."

Don Enrique Torribio Moreno finally decided, rather reluctantly, to follow Barthélémy to his cabin, but not without having taken a last long look at the unknown ship, which seemed increasingly suspicious to him without knowing why.

Once in the cabin, Barthélémy took a bottle of rum and two glasses from a cupboard, offered a seat to Don Enrique Torribio, and, after pouring two large glassfuls, said:

"To your health!"

"And to yours!" replied the fake Mexican.

Barthélémy stuffed his pipe, lit it, and reclined in his chair.

"Now we can talk," he said.

"So, let's talk," replied Don Enrique Torribio.

After these initial words, there was a rather long silence. Barthélémy seemed to have completely forgotten his friend. Don Enrique Torribio waited for a few moments, then realized that the other freebooter, no doubt absorbed in his own thoughts, was no longer thinking about him.

"So?" he exclaimed, banging his fist on the table.

"So what?" said Barthélémy coldly.

"What are those serious things you wanted to talk about?"

"Don't worry. I'll take care of it."

"So, is it a big deal?"

"You'll be the judge of that, Brother."

"How can I if you don't tell me what it's all about?" replied Don Enrique Torribio on the verge of losing his cool.

Barthélémy looked at him ironically; then, finally deciding to speak in that mocking tone that he always used when talking with his former associate, he began:

"Here I am. Is our business still on?" he asked, wrapping himself in a thick cloud of smoke.

"More than ever."

"For the day after tomorrow?"

"The day after tomorrow, yes. Why are you asking me this?"

"Because it seems to me, dear friend," Barthélémy said sarcastically, "that the time has come to settle our account."

"Settle our account! What account?" shouted the other, surprised.

"The one you have with me. Do you imagine that I'm going to serve you with my eyes closed, without knowing what I'll get out of it? I told you I would cost you a lot of money, didn't I? Well, business is business, my dear associate, and the business you've got me into seems to me, to speak frankly, to be of a rather dubious nature, so I'll take precautions and ask for payment in advance."

"If it is only to talk to me about this that you have brought me here," replied Don Enrique Torribio with a sneer, "I am quite angry about it, companion. I have a lot of things to do tonight, so I can't stay any longer;. But later, tomorrow if you want, I will be at your disposal to discuss all this."

He emptied his glass and stood up.

"As you please," Barthélémy said without moving a muscle, "but on my word, I think you're wrong, Brother."

"Bah!" said Don Enrique Torribio, taking a step towards the door.

"Goodbye, friend. Oh, by the way, I was warned yesterday by a pearl fisherman returning from the high sea that a freebooter fleet had been spotted nearby."

"What?" cried Don Enrique Torribio, hurriedly retracing his steps. "What are you saying, Barthélémy? A freebooter fleet?"

"Yes."

"Are you certain?"

"Of course! I saw it with my own eyes! You understand that this was much too important for me not to take the trouble to immediately check for myself if it was true. But why, Brother, do you suddenly look so dismayed when you should be rejoicing?"

"I, dismayed?" Don Enrique Torribio said, trying to recover his composure. "Come on, you're crazy, companion, why should I look dismayed? But, tell me, can you guess at what these freebooters' plans might entail?"

"Certainly! Not only can I guess, but I know their plans, my friend! Their expedition is at least fifteen hundred men strong, chosen from among the bravest of our brothers. They simply want to raid Cartagena."

"To raid Cartagena? Now, come on!" Don Enrique Torribio exclaimed with a jump of surprise. "That is madness!"

"That opinion is not shared among the Brothers of the Coast, I assure you. On the contrary, they hope to succeed."

Don Enrique Torribio had fallen back on his seat; he was shaking with all his limbs; his face had grown

249

pale. But Barthélémy pretended not to notice his friend's condition.

"It's a daring enterprise, eh, Brother?" he said, re-lighting his pipe that had gone out.

"Very daring, yes, but how do you know so much about this?"

"Oh, my dear friend, it's very simple! I talked to their leaders. You do understand that, abandoned for more than a year in this country where I am virtually a prisoner, I didn't want to let slip a providential opportunity to become free again. So I went quietly to their flagship last night…"

"Continue."

"Ah! So you don't want to leave anymore? I see that you're becoming interested, in my story eh, companion?"

"Yes, very much so. Please, continue."

"These leaders, who, by the way, are all my old friends, received me in the most gracious way, and then. they asked me some information, which naturally I hastened to give them…"

"Who are these leaders? What are their names?"

"Well, there is L'Olonnais, the Poletais, Pierre Legrand, and two or three others."

"Is Bearcub on board?"

"Bearcub Ironskull?"

"Yes."

"I don't know. I didn't see him."

Don Enrique Torribio breathed a sigh of relief.

"Keep going," he said.

"I'm almost done. We talked, they asked me if I could be useful to them, I answered affirmatively and put myself at their disposal to help them with their plan.

I even added that we were two Brothers of the Coast here in a position to be useful to them, didn't I do well?"

"So they know I'm here?"

"Well, they know that there are two Brothers of the Coast in Cartagena—me and another one."

"But that other one is me!" exclaimed Don Enrique Torribio. "A thousand devils!"

"Why?"

"If they succeed, I'm ruined!"

"Why would you be ruined? You're crazy! Nobody knows who you are in Cartagena. You've gotten into the skin of your Mexican personal so well that..."

"Yes, here, in Cartagena, but them, the freebooters, the Brothers of the Coast, our comrades, they will suspect!"

"They don't know you're here. Do you think I was stupid enough to tell them your name before I was sure their plan would succeed?"

"You didn't?" exclaimed Don Enrique Torribio, shaking Barthélémy's hand with gratitude. "So they don't know I'm here?"

"They don't."

"Listen, Barthélémy, old friend," Don Enrique Torribio cried, bewildered, "all this has upset me so much that I don't know yet what to do. Let me think, and I'll give you an answer tonight. But know this: earlier, you've asked me to settle our account, didn't you? Well, I give you my word that if you remain a faithful friend and a good comrade, your reward will be more than you could have ever wished for!"

"Thank you," replied Barthélémy sarcastically. "I'll take your word for it."

"But from your part..."

"Complete silence, I understand."

Don Enrique Torribio ran out of the cabin like a madman, got into his boat, and immediately left the ship without even saying goodbye.

"All this is wonderful," the freebooter murmured, giggling as soon as he was alone. "But two precautions are always better than one. I won't lose sight of him; he's a snake that shouldn't be trusted."

CHAPTER XIX
A Plan of Attack

After his conversation with Doña Elmina, Bearcub Ironskull had a long conversation with his friend, after which he rejoined his companions.

A council was held in the cave between the freebooters—one in which Barthélémy, in his capacity as a Brother of the Coast, had naturally been called upon to take part.

It was certainly no easy task to raid a city like Cartagena, well-fortified and guarded by a large and resolute garrison. But the very difficulty of the job excited the freebooters and pushed them to persevere in their project.

Barthélémy, who had lived there for a long time, and who, because of the life he had been forced to lead, knew the region very well, gave precious information on the state of the city's forces, its weaknesses, and the means that would have to be used in order to take control of it.

That information was further confirmed and supplemented by the pilot brought from Guantanamo and the two former sailors of the *Santa Catalina* who all also knew the city well.

Cartagena, like most Spanish-American cities at that time, was actually defended only on the sea side, for it was by sea that any enemy was likely to come; on the land side, there was no attack to fear; so a simple *adobe* wall, about ten feet high, three feet thick at the most, and in poor condition in many places, made up the city walls.

Four gates, which were never closed, had been cut through it.

Following Barthélemy's advice, it was on the ground that the most serious attack would be attempted. This was the plan that the freebooters agreed on:

Three hundred elite men, chosen from among the most skillful marksmen, commanded by L'Olonnais, would be disembarked with supplies and would remain hidden in the cave, until the moment chosen to launch the attack. (The cave was only two leagues away from Cartagena.)

One hundred Brothers, under the command of the Poletais, would be infiltrated one at a time into the city by Barthélemy, who would gradually position them inside the vast warehouse owned by his rich Mexican friend, Don Enrique Torribio Moreno, to which he had a key. These one hundred men would be ready to act at the first signal.

Twenty freebooters, commanded by Alexandre, Bearcub's own *engagé*, would hide in the woods and keep watch over Don José Rivas' house.

At the time of the attack, these twenty freebooters would seize this house, where they would take refuge, in order to watch over Doña Elmina and Doña Lilia, who, if the attack failed, would serve as hostages for the Brothers of the Coast.

The *San Juan Bautista*, which would be restored to its honest and peaceful appearance for the occasion, would anchor in the port of Cartagena, just a stone's throw away from the *Santa Catalina*. It would be placed under the command of Pierre Legrand and would have a crew of one hundred fifty men, fifty of whom would remain hidden in the hold until further notice.

Finally, Captain Bearcub Ironskull would attack the harbor with the *Trickster*. While the frigate would be under fire from the first fort, the second and third forts would be seized by the men from the warehouse, so that the three forts, being attacked simultaneously and from different angles, would not be able to support each other.

This audacious plan, which could only succeed because of its very boldness, would throw disorder among the Spanish forces. It had been conceived and proposed by Bearcub Ironskull, based on the recommendation from Barthélémy. The Brothers of the Coast joyfully accepted it, and the decision of the council was unanimous that it should be put into effect immediately.

Bearcub Ironskull was even more eager than his companions to begin his daring attempt. When all was well agreed and settled, he and Barthélémy bid a fond farewell to each other, and the freebooters returned to the frigate, where they arrived just before sunrise.

Barthélémy, after having left his companions, immediately returned to Don José Rivas' country house. During Bearcub's earlier conversation with Doña Elmina, he had not wasted his time.

He had known for a long time the garden into which he had introduced his friend. He knew, for having visited it several times, that it was very large and, above all, very bushy, ending on the forest side with an old cabin that no one ever visited. Barthélémy then thought that it would be better to hide Alexandre's twenty men in this very cabin, instead of in the woods, where some stroke of bad luck might expose them.

As soon as he found himself near the house, instead of entering it, he quietly walked along the wall outside and finally reached the cabin. It was a rather large building, but almost in ruins, with two grilled windows with a box-shaped enclosed balcony, following the Spanish custom, which opened onto the countryside, at a height of about fifteen feet.

After making sure that he was alone, the buccaneer took a long rope rolled around his belt. He tied a heavy stone to one end of it and threw it over the balcony so that the stone passed through the iron spirals of the railing before falling back to his side.

Barthélémy then grabbed it, and after making sure that it was securely held, he climbed up and, within seconds, he stood on the balcony. Then, with the tip of his dagger, he unlocked the large door, which opened without the slightest difficulty. The freebooter then stepped inside the cabin.

He performed a thorough inspection of the cabin, which consisted of a fairly large single room, still furnished with a few chairs, tables, benches and sideboards, all in poor condition, but not broken. Two large windows overlooked the garden; they were shut, but it was easy to see outside through their shutters.

Barthélémy looked around. The garden was deserted. The freebooter happily rubbed his hands together. He opened the door in front of the balcony and found himself on a sort of landing with a staircase. He walked down, opened a second door, and entered another room much like the one above, but even more crowded with old furniture.

After he struggled to make his way through, he made sure that the door to the garden was locked. As an added precaution, he secured it internally by means of two metal bars.

Then he returned to the upper room, went out onto the balcony, closed the shutter, jumped to the ground, removed his rope, and cheerfully resumed his way to

Cartagena, where he arrived around eight o'clock in the morning without having been noticed.

That same day, Don Enrique Torribio came aboard the *Santa Catalina* and had the interesting conversation with Barthélémy that we reported in our previous chapter.

The following night, Bearcub Ironskull's plan of attack began to unfold. By dawn, everything was in place. The freebooters were just waiting for their leader's signal to attack.

They knew they wouldn't have long to wait.

CHAPTER XX
Where Don Enrique Torribio Moreno discover that his presentiments did not betray him

As soon as he had returned from the *Santa Catalina* and disembarked Don Enrique Torribio Moreni went to the Governor's palace.

Don José Rivas de Figueroa's trusted valet let him in at once, but told the fake Mexican that his master, after having waited for him for a while, not seeing him arrive, and supposing that some serious motive had detained him, had finally decided to go to his country house, where he asked Don Enrique Torribio to join him as soon as possible; for he had news of the utmost importance to tell him.

Don Enrique Torribio Moreno had a horse saddled up and immediately set off at a gallop, hoping to catch up with Don José Rivas, who, according to the same valet, had only left Cartagena twenty minutes earlier.

While galloping, Don Enrique Torribio was thinking. What was the important news that Don José Rivas wanted to communicate to him? Was the Governor already aware of the arrival of the freebooters in the waters of Cartagena?

His horse was galloping fast and gaining ground. When he arrived some distance from the village, however, he was forced to slow down because of the steepness of the road. He turned his head and distractedly looked at sea, whose immense blue waters extended to his right all the way to the horizon. He suddenly let loose a cry of surprise and stopped, pale and trembling.

At almost three-gun ranges from the coast, a magnificent frigate, all sails to the wind, was cruising. It only took a glance from the former buccaneer to recognize it.

"The *Trickster*!" he murmured in fright as he wiped away the sweat that flooded his pale forehead. "Bearcub Ironskull's ship! Barthélémy's lied to me! He's betrayed me! It is Bearcub himself who commands that expedition! So he knows I'm here! I should have listened to my hunches! There's no longer any need to hesitate. I must get ahead of him at all costs. Otherwise I'm doomed!"

Enraged, the former freebooter drove the spurs into the flanks of his horse, which neighed in pain, and resumed his journey. However, he reached the house without having encountered Don José Rivas.

As he entered the patio, he saw several horses being bridled by servants. He jumped down and inquired:

"Palombo, is the *señor gobernator* here?"

"Yes, *mi amo*,"[54] replied the slave. "He just arrived with Señor Colonel Don Lopez Aldao Sandoval."

"Is the Colonel here?

"Yes, *mi amo*."

"This is strange," Don Enrique Torribio whispered to himself. "Where are they, Palombo?" he asked the servant.

"In the living room with *las niñas*."

Don Enrique Torribio threw the bridle of his horse to the slave and ran into the house.

As he opened the living room door, a hand came to rest on his shoulder.

---

[54] My Master.

He turned around and saw the sarcastic figure of Barthélémy leaning towards him—the last man he expected to see there.

"What are you doing here?" he exclaimed.

"You're here too," replied the other buccaneer with a mocking smile.

"I know that, but what about you? Explain yourself!"

"Soon, soon, my friend," Barthélémy answered in the same mocking toner. "But first, let's go in. I have more news for you."

"Oh, so everyone has news today?"

"So it seems," Barthélémy replied lightly.

And without further ado, he opened the door himself, smiling with that knowing and ironic air that gave Don Enrique Torribio the shivers.

They entered. The Governor and the Commander of the Cartagena garrison, Don Lopez Aldao, were standing in the middle of the room, talking to Doña Elmina and her cousin, Doña Lilia. The conversation seemed very lively and carried in an almost threatening tone.

Upon seeing Don Enrique Torribio, Doña Elmina turned sharply towards him.

"In front of this man," she exclaimed, "since chance, or rather God himself, has brought him here, I will tell you, Father, that I will never consent to be his wife."

"Beware, daughter!" Don José interrupted, angrily kicking his foot. "Beware!"

"*Señorita*! In the name of Heaven!" murmured Don Enrique Torribio Moreno. "What's going on? I've just arrived... I don't understand..."

"Silence, *señor*!" shouted the young woman violently. "You have no right to raise your voice here!"

"Enough, daughter!" shouted Don José. "You will marry Don Enrique Torribio because I said so!"

"Never, father," cried the young woman with increasing energy. "I would rather die than consent to become the wife of such a wretch!"

"But *Señorita*!" exclaimed Don Enrique Torribio, who was taken aback by such a harsh attack and did not know what to say.

Barthélémy slyly laughed at his friend's pitiful appearance. Doña Lilia was trying to give courage to her cousin and protect her from her father's anger.

Don José, at his daughter's last words, had a terrible moment of rage and made a threatening gesture.

"Woe to you," he shouted, "if you dare resist my will!"

"I don't want to marry this man," she replied in a voice broken by pain.

"You will marry him, I tell you, or else..."

"Kill me then!" she cried with an accent of inexpressible despair.

"I repeat to you," shouted Don José, clutching her arm tightly, "I repeat to you that you will marry Don Enrique Torribio Moreno!"

Suddenly the door of the living room opened with a bang; a man appeared on the threshold, escorted by two enormous dogs and two wild boars.

All those present shouted a cry of surprise and fear when they saw him.

This man was Bearcub Ironskull!

He wore his buccaneer outfit and held his rifle in his hand. He took two steps forward, and in a calm voice, announced:

"You are wrong, *señor*. Doña Elmina will not marry this wretch."

There was a moment of amazement.

At the Captain's entrance, Barthélémy had gone without affectation to stand in front of the door in order to block the passage.

"A freebooter! A *ladron* here!" cried the two Spaniards, grabbing their swords.

"No shouts, no threats," resumed Bearcub, still impassive. "Don José Rivas, how well do you know this man whom you want to be your son-in-law?"

"But I believe..." murmured the Governor, tamed in spite of himself by the firm and loyal accent of the Brother of the Coast.

"You have a short memory, *caballero*," continued Bearcub sternly. "This man who has impudently stolen your fortune by cheating at cards, and who today pretends to your daughter's hand, is deceiving you. He has been married for a long time in his country. I will now tell you who this man truly is..."

"Before you do that," Don José said haughtily, for he had regained all his composure and power over himself, "tell me who you yourself are, *señor*, and by what right you have invaded my house."

"Who am I, *señor*?" Bearcub replied coldly, "I am a freebooter, as you yourself have recognized. I am the man to whom you owe your freedom and your daughter's honor. What right do I have to be here? The right that every man of heart takes upon himself to protect the weak when they are persecuted by those who should defending them."

"Such audacity will not go unpunished, *señor*," Don José shouted angrily. "I will know how to punish you as you deserve..."

"Enough with threats; they are useless, *caballero*. *Señoritas*, I beg you to withdraw to your apartments.

Fear not, Doña Elmina, you are now under my protection, I will defend you against all, even against your father."

The Brother of the Coast saluted the girls, who bowed and left slowly without saying anything.

Don José wanted to run and stop his daughter, but Barthélémy suddenly stepped in front of him.

"Please, go no further, *señor*," he said. "Believe me, listen instead to Captain Bearcub Ironskull. On my soul, it's worth it."

While doing this, Barthélémy had been forced to unblock the door in front of which he had been standing until then for barely two or three minutes.

Don Enrique Torribio, always on the lookout and desperate to escape, took advantage of the path that had been so providentially cleared for him to rush outside.

Almost immediately, they heard a horse galloping away. The fake Mexican, seeing that the situation would soon be no longer tenable, had judged it prudent to flee as soon as possible.

All this had taken place so quickly that the astonished spectators had not been able to stop him.

Where was he going? We will find out soon.

"Have a good trip," concluded Barthélémy laughing.

"*Señores*," Bearcub Ironskull said with nobility, "the city of Cartagena is currently under attack by land and by sea. Go and lead your soldiers. I will not violate the laws of hospitality by holding you prisoner in your own home. Give thanks to Doña Elmina, for it is for her alone that I am doing this."

"Miserable wretch!" Don José cried out in rage. "I will take revenge for this infamous betrayal."

Bearcub smiled disdainfully.

"The one who betrayed you," he said, "is the man you wanted to make your son-in-law, your former captor in Santo Domingo, the renegade buccaneer whom his brothers had condemned to die and whom the Devil himself saved—Boute-Feu!"

"Boute-Feu!" cried Don José at the awful revelation.

"Blood washes away all faults, *caballero*, so thank me, for I leave you the opportunity to die as a soldier."

Don José hesitated for a second; a burning tear that immediately dried off moistened his eyes.

"My daughter!" he cried.

"Whatever happens, I will return her to you safe and sound after the battle. She and her cousin are under my protection, you have my word of honor on it."

"Goodbye then. We may see each other again in the fires of battle. God willing, I shall find death there."

The door suddenly opened again and the two young women ran in.

"Father! Father!" cried Doña Elmina as she fell to Don José's knees.

The Governor seemed to hesitate for a second.

"Father!" repeated the young woman in a sad voice. "Have mercy on me."

But pride had now regained the upper hand in the soul of the haughty gentleman; the devil had defeated the angel. He stared at the poor child for a moment with a strange expression on his face, then leaned towards her.

"If I forgive you, will you now obey me?" he asked in a low voice with a cruel ironic accent.

"Oh, father," she cried with pain.

He stood up, a bitter smile on his pale lips:

"Back!" he said, pushing her back hard. "I don't know you anymore!"

And he rushed out of the room.

Don Lopez Aldao Sandoval made a movement to follow him, but at the last minute, paternal love overcame his will. He stopped, pressed his daughter Doña Lilia to his heart, before pushing her into the arms of Bearcub Ironskull.

"Look after her!" he cried with a sad accent of pain.

And he left, choking a sob and hiding his head in his hands.

The two young women almost passed out.

"Alexandre!" shouted Bearcub.

The *engagé* appeared.

"Your life depends on these two ladies' safety," said the freebooter.

"Understood, Captain," replied the man.

"What about us now?" asked Barthélémy.

"We shall win—or die with our Brothers."

A few minutes later, the two Brothers of the Coast had left the house.

CHAPTER XXI
Where Don José Rivas de Figueroa confesses to Don Lopez Aldao Sandoval

The two Spanish officers, mounted on excellent horses, were racing over the land in the direction of Cartagena. Don José Rivas, with a pale forehead, frowning eyebrows, tight lips, no hat, sword in hand, was constantly pressing his mount.

"Scorned!" he murmured, "betrayed, abandoned by all! Owing only to the pity of that miserable *ladron* the favor of dying a soldier's death!"

"That man is not a wretch, and you know it well, my friend," replied Don Lopez Aldao, nodding his head.

Don José turned around suddenly.

"You, you, too, also betray me!" he cried in painful anger.

"I do not betray you, Don José, since I am at your side, ready to die with you. But your sorrow leads you astray."

"You are right! It is true! I am mad! I am wrong!" Don José replied bitterly. "Forgive me, my friend, but you do not know—you cannot know all that I suffer."

"And I, am I not suffering too, Don José? Is my honor as a soldier not as compromised as yours? Am I not a father, too? And God knows how much I love my daughter! Poor dear, sweet child! Well, on my honor, I swear to you, I am convinced that Doña Lilia is as safe in this man's custody as if she were right next to me."

"Eh!" cried Don José Rivas impatiently, "do you suppose by any chance that I don't know all this as well as you do?"

Don Lopez Aldao looked at him in amazement.

"If this is so, then I don't understand you, my friend," he said.

"You cannot understand me, indeed," Don José Rivas whispered with a bitter smile.

They quickly but silently continued on their way.

Soon, the two Spanish officers were within sight of the walls of Cartagena. All was calm because, despite what the buccaneer had said, and he believed to be true, the attack had not yet begun.

The two horsemen crossed a small, dense guava wood that almost touched the city wall, which was, as we said, in poor condition and had large gaps here and there.

As far as the view extended in all directions, the countryside was deserted; an unusual gloomy silence hung over this scenic landscape.

Don José stopped and stepped onto the ground. His friend watched him with surprise; he didn't understand his behavior.

"Let our horses rest a little," said the Governor in a somber voice. "There is no hurry; the enemy is still far away.

Don Lopez Aldao bowed without answering and dismounted in turn; they tied their horses to the trunk of a tree.

The Governor was extremely pale; he let himself fall to the ground and remained there for several minutes, with listless eyes, tense features, sweat on his forehead, seemingly unaware of what was going on around him. He was prey to a terrible inner emotion that, despite his efforts, he could not manage to overcome.

"What's the matter, Don José?" the commander finally asked. "Are you feeling well?"

"No," replied the other. "But it's only my heart that suffers. Listen to me, Don Lopez, I want to make my last will."

"Your last will?" Don Lopez exclaimed, with surprise.

"Yes, and as you are my only friend, you are the one I place in charge of executing it."

"But…"

"Do you refuse?" Don José exclaimed violently.

"No, of course not!"

"Then, let me speak, Don Lopez Aldao, time is running short."

"But, my friend..."

"Do not interrupt me, my friend," said Don José in a dark voice. "The battle that is coming will be fatal to me, I have a premonition of it. I don't want to take to the grave with me a secret that is killing me and that I have kept for far too long in my heart. Listen. When I am dead, you will act as you deem appropriate, or rather, as I am certain, as your honor will require. If you do not let me speak as I want to now, I will not have the courage to make the confession that is killing me; so I will be brief. Two implacable hatreds have for twenty years torn my heart: I hate the *ladrones*, and I hate Doña Elmina."

"But she is your daughter!" exclaimed Don Lopez.

"No, she is not!" Don José said curtly.

His voice was hoarse, his accent jerky, his anger rushed, as if he had been eager to finish the strange confession he was making, and that, perhaps, in his heart of hearts, he was already regretting having started.

Don José Aldao listened to him, with an astonishment mingled with horror.

Don José Rivas resumed after a moment:

"I was twenty-five years-old at the time; I had been married for three years to a woman I had wed against my parents' wishes. You know that my family belongs to the highest Spanish nobility," he continued. "I lived with my wife and daughter, then two years-old, in a house in the town of San Juan de Goyava on Santo Domingo Island. One night, the buccaneers raided the town and set it on fire. My house, after a desperate resistance, was stormed; all my servants were mercilessly massacred by the *ladrones*; only I miraculously escaped through the fire; my wife and daughter perished in the flames…"

"It's horrible," exclaimed Don Lopez.

"Yes, it is, isn't it? But I'm not finished. I love gold, not for itself, but for the pleasures it provides; gold is everything to me. According to one of the clauses of my marriage contract, my wife's entire fortune was to be returned to her family in case she or her children died. This fortune was immense, amounting to more than two million piasters. Their deaths meant my ruin, and I wanted to remain rich, to keep my wife's fortune at all costs. I had married her only for that purpose.

"In the tumult that followed the sack of the city, I managed to get out into the countryside without being seen. I met a drunken buccaneer sleeping at the foot of a tree. I approached him, killed him and took his clothes, which I put on. Then I walked straight ahead, at random, on an expedition, with no plan in mind; stopping only when fatigue overwhelmed me, but somehow managing to remain alive. I was almost mad with despair.

"On the third day, I entered a city which, as I learned later, was Port-Margot. The clothes I wore disguised me so well that no one noticed me. My family is from Navarre, and therefore I speak French almost as well as if it were my mother tongue. I stopped at the first house I saw and asked for hospitality; it was granted. My host was a poor Breton who had recently arrived in Santo Domingo with his wife and daughter—a girl who was the same age as the one I had so sadly lost…"

"So Doña Elmina…?"

"Is the daughter of my host, yes. This is how it was done. My host's name was Guichard and he was very poor. A few days after my arrival, he joined a ship commanded by the famous Montbarts, and left, entrusting me with the safety of his wife and daughter. Remaining alone, sole master in this house, the demon tempted me and breathed a horrible thought. The very night that followed my host's departure, around midnight, I entered my hostess' room silent as a wolf. She was sleeping. I went to the child's cradle. But somehow, sensing the sound of my footsteps, the mother woke up. Why did she wake up? I didn't want to harm her!

"When she saw me, no doubt enlightened by one of those presentiments that never deceive a mother's heart, she guessed my plan, and rushed at me, shouting and calling for help. So I killed her; then I coldly wrapped the little girl in my coat and ran away. Four days later, I arrived in San Juan de Goyava. And it was just about time," Don José continued with a strident laugh that was barely human. "My heirs were already taking my property. My unexpected return disconcerted them. My wife was dead, but my daughter was alive; so I kept my fortune. A month later, I had sold all my possessions and left for Mexico…"

"Oh, how awful!" Don Lopez Aldao cried out in horror.

Don José Rivas continued without worrying about this protest, which perhaps he hadn't heard.

"Well, my friend, in spite of all that I have done for her," he added with an expression of unspeakable bitterness and spite, "the child never loved me. Her instinct always kept her away from me, and seemed to have revealed to her that we are not of the same blood. She is drawn, so to speak, in spite of herself, to these wretched *ladrons*."

"But what happened to her father?" asked Don Lopez Aldao, who was interested in this strange story despite himself.

"I never heard of him afterward; but, you understand, I never tried to hear from him. That man didn't matter to me; undoubtedly, he must have been killed in some expedition. This is the secret I wanted to confess to you before I die."

"Poor child!" Don Lopez Aldao sadly murmured.

Don José Rivas laughed with supreme disdain.

"Don't pity her," he said bitterly. "It will be easy for her, if she wants it, to locate her real family. Who knows? Perhaps I am wrong and that Guichard still lives? I forgot to tell you that the *ladrones*, exposed by the lives they lead to be often unexpectedly separated from their families, have the custom of tattooing their children. Doña Elmina wears a blue tattoo on her right arm, big as a *réal* coin.

"Now you understand, don't you, my hatred for the *ladrones*, those eternal enemies that I have always met and who have always defeated me. You understand how much I suffered from the heroism of that wretch who, after rescuing me from shameful slavery in Santo Domingo, forced his protection on me only an hour ago, in my very house, and so disdainfully let me go when I was in his power. I have finished, my friend. Let us leave now."

Then he got up and untied his horse. His friend followed him mechanically, in unspeakable horror. This dreadful revelation had dismayed him.

"One last word," said Don José.

"What is it?"

"I had recognized this wretch Boute-Feu who sought to become my son-in-law," said Don José with an awful snicker. "I knew who he was. The marriage I tried to force on Doña Elmina was to be my last and most complete revenge!"

"Enough!" cried Don Lopez. "You are a monster!"

The Spaniard laughed devilishly and, driving in his spurs, snapped the reins. The two riders took off.

No sooner had they gone away that a man slowly rose from the middle of the bushes, where he had hitherto been hiding. After following them for a moment with his eyes, with a peculiar expression, he muttered:

"I did well to follow these two worthy Spanish officers. What a dark rascal that honorable hidalgo is! On my soul, my excellent friend Boute-Feu is almost a saint compared to him!"

Speaking in a mocking tone, he went into the woods, untied his own horse that he had left there, mounted it, and galloped off toward Cartagena.

This man was Captain Barthélémy.

CHAPTER XXII
The Last Battle

In spite of what had been decided at the council of the freebooters, Captain Bearcub Ironskull had taken command of the landing troops, leaving that of the frigate to L'Olonnais. He hadn't wanted to entrust anyone else with the task of watching over Doña Elmina.

The *Trickster,* which had not picked up enough wind, had not been able to get into the harbor at the agreed time; she had been forced to tack, hence the delay in attacking the city.

However, when the buccaneers appeared and the battle finally began, the Spaniards, who had not had time to organize the defense, and who were surprised by the unexpected sight of the enemies appearing from all sides at once, put up only a rather feeble resistance.

The city would have fallen then and there if the Governor and the Commander of the garrison, who had just arrived, had not managed to withdraw the elite troops to Fort San Juan, and, by their very presence, raised the morale of their soldiers and their determination to continue to fight to the bitter end.

Then, the battle became hard, fierce; if the defense had been as energetic everywhere else, the freebooters would never have succeeded in taking Cartagena.

Fort San Juan controlled the city; it had to be taken at all costs.

Ten times, the freebooters, annoyed by its resistance, bravely mounted an assault, and ten times, despite their best efforts, they were repelled from its walls.

Night was approaching; it was time to end it all.

Bearcub Ironskull gathered his bravest companions around him, and, followed by L'Olonnais, the Poletais and the other leaders of the expedition, he decided to attempt one last, supreme assault. But before giving the order, he called Barthélémy.

"So?" he asked.

"Nothing," replied the buccaneer.

"We must find that man! He is probably planning some betrayal."

"I fear as much," Barthélémy nodded. "According to my information, he went back to Cartagena, where he gathered the scoundrels he had placed on board the schooner, and has since disappeared with them."

"This Boute-Feu is my curse," murmured Bearcub Ironskull, pensively. "Listen, take fifty men with you, get on a horse and run to the house. That's where he's going to be."

"Yes, of course, you're right," exclaimed Barthélémy, hitting his forehead with his hand. "It's there and not anywhere else where he'll strike! I'm leaving at once," he added with a sigh of regret. "But I would have liked to see the last battle. The assault will be superb."

"I believe it. They fight like lions. But who knows if you, too, will not have a good fight over there?"

"Who knows? Do you want to come?"

"I can't! I must stay here with our men. Good luck, Brother, and may God watch over you!"

"Farewell, Brother, and good luck to you too!"

As Barthélémy was walking away in a somber mood, he heard Bearcub's behind him shouting:

"Last assault, brothers! To your swords! This time, we must end it!"

"May God watch over them too!" he grumbled.

A moment later, Barthélémy had gathered a large troop of horsemen, took command of them, and they rushed at full speed towards the village.

An hour later, he and his men arrived like a hurricane in sight of Turbaco.

Immediately after having escaped from Don José Rivas' house in the manner we described, Don Enrique Torribio Moreno—or rather, to call him by his true name, Boute-Feu—had gone to the *pulqueria* where Matadoce and the other bandits he had hired were hiding while waiting for his orders.

He burst into the *pulqueria*. The bandits were smoking, drinking mezcal and playing monte, without the least concern for what was going on in the world outside, patiently enjoying the state of idleness in which the one who had hired them had left them.

On the order of the buccaneer, they stood up, grabbed their weapons and, in an instant, were ready to follow him. There were now fifteen of them; two days before, the others had gone to Cartagena and embarked on the schooner, as per the original plan.

The fifteen bandits came out of the *pulqueria* separately and went into the woods next to Don José Rivas' house, where they hid in the bushes, waiting for the moment to act.

Boute-Feu, after recommending the utmost caution to his cutthroats, left them there and hurried back to Cartagena to bring the other bandits hidden aboard the schooner.

His hatred gave him wings. In less than two hours, his journey, round trip, was completed, and he rejoined Matadoce and his companions in the woods.

He was then at the head of nearly fifty determined bandits, men who would stop at nothing and, at a sign from him, would not hesitate to commit the most awful crimes.

Boute-Feu, no longer having any realistic hope of escaping the vengeance of the Brothers of the Coast, resolutely threw off his mask, and since he had to die, at least he did not want to go without revenge.

After distributing a large sum of money to his men, and explaining his plans in a few words, he prepared to play his last hand.

His goal was to enter the house that he supposed to be defenseless; to seize the girls; then—as in his heart he did not doubt the success of the freebooters and was convinced that they would manage to seize Cartagena— to entrench himself solidly in the house, withstand a siege if it was necessary; and to go only under good conditions, using Doña Elmina and Doña Lilia as hostages.

For the success of this project, he counted on Bearcub Ironskull's love for the young woman and on his generosity and greatness of spirit.

This plan was well thought out, boldly executed, and had a great chance of success.

Boute-Feu thus began to attack the house.

He first broke through the garden gate through which Barthélémy and Bearcub had entered two days earlier and the bandits rushed into the *huerta*.

Unfortunately for Boute-Feu, as soon as his gang moved forward, they ran into the freebooters commanded by Alexandre Legrand, Bearcub's *engagé*.

The surprise was severe. But the bandits outnumbered the Brothers of the Coast by twice as many, and were determined not to back down an inch.

The fight thus began and soon took on immense proportions.

Upon arriving at the village fountain, Barthélémy stopped his troop for a moment and listened with concern. Loud gunfire could be heard on the other side of the house.

"I hear gunshots!" he exclaimed. "Bearcub was right! Our brothers are under attack! Forward! Long live the Brotherhood! forward!"

They galloped into the courtyard of the house. There everything was quiet because the battle was being fought in the garden.

"Forward!" Barthélémy resumed, jumping down from his horse.

The freebooters followed him. The garden was littered with corpses. In the middle of a wide lawn with a huge *mesquite* in the center, Alexandre and eight buccaneers—the only survivors of the twenty left there by Bearcub—all more or less wounded, formed a circle around the trunk of the *mesquite*, facing attacks from all sides at once, defending themselves like lions against about twenty bandits, who surrounded them and attacked them with fury.

"Fire and stab at will, boys!" shouted Barthélémy.

A dreadful gunfire rang out and the freebooters rushed at the bandits, with their buttstock high, uttering their terrible war cry:

"*Flibuste*! *Flibuste*!" [55]

There was then a dreadful melee. The bandits, caught between two fires and seeing that escape was impossible, were killed to the last man. Not a single one escaped alive.

"Hello there!" shouted Barthélémy while aiming at a figure who was trying to slip unseen into the bushes.

---

[55] Buccaneering or freebooting.

"One moment! please! Don't leave like that, my good man!"

The shot went off; the man fell to the ground, uttering a cry of pain that sounded like the roar of a barking fawn.

The buccaneer rushed towards him.

"Hey! hey! You wanted to give us the slip, eh, Boute-Feu?" he said to him, with his mocking air.

He tied him up solidly and entrusted him to two of his companions. Boute-Feu gave him a hate-filled look, but did not answer. Barthélémy's bullet had broken his right leg. The old buccaneer had not wanted to kill the renegade, whom he had recognized perfectly when he was fleeing; he had only wanted to stop him from escaping, and he had succeeded.

With Boute-Feu under guard, Barthélémy joined Alexandre, who was busy dressing two rather serious wounds he had received, one in his right arm and the other in his head.

"The young ladies?" he asked.

"They're there," replied the *engagé*, "under this pile of foliage and branches."

"Safe and sound?"

"Yes, but it's high time you came, Brother."

"I bet!"

"Do you think the Captain will be happy with me?"

"By Jove! It's impossible to imagine how he could not!"

"Then all is well," exclaimed Alexandre happily.

"But you're wounded."

"Bah, it's nothing. "

And the *engagé* quietly continued to dress his wounds.

The young women had been so well buried under the leaves by their defenders that they had not received a scratch; but they were half dead of terror.

Bearcub Ironskull had been correct in supposing that Boute-Feu would attack the house and try to capture them. A few more minutes, and the wretched man would have succeeded in his odious project.

Barthélémy, without wasting a moment, organized everything to return as quickly as possible to Cartagena and take the two women with them.

"What about my father?" cried Doña Lilia.

"Soon you will see him again—at least, I hope, so" replied the buccaneer.

"Have you seen him?"

"From afar, yes. He is a brave soldier."

"And what about my father?" asked Doña Elmina with agitation. "Do you know what's happened to him, *señor*?"

"I'm afraid I don't know him, *señorita*."

"What? You don't know Don José Rivas, *señor*?"

"Forgive me, *señorita*, but..."

"Yes?"

"Well, er..."

The buccaneer stopped. He realized, but too late, that his tongue had been faster than his brain and that he had let slip some things he shouldn't have said.

"Speak, in the name of Heaven," Doña Elmina insisted, painfully. "My God, is he hurt? You don't answer... Say something, I beg you... Is he dead?"

Barthélémy made a violent effort and made up his mind.

"Bah!" he murmured. "Perhaps it's better to tell her everything now..."

"My God! You're making me tremble."

"Calm down, *señorita*."

"Is he hurt?"

"I don't know, I repeat, *señorita*, but what I do know, having heard him say it himself, is that he is not your father, not even a blood relative. You are the daughter of a brave Brother of the Coast, that's it!"

"Don José is not my father?" cried Doña Elmina, joining hands. "My God! What does this mean? I must have heard you wrong, or I'm going crazy..."

She collapsed and rolled unconscious on the lawn. Barthélémy looked at her with a frightened face.

"To Hell with women!" he shouted, punching himself on the head. "I thought I was giving her good news!"

"You are a fool, *señor*," said Doña Lilia, laughing.

"I'm beginning to believe it," replied the buccaneer with deep conviction.

Barthélémy returned to Cartagena at around eight o'clock in the evening in the company of the two young ladies and Alexandre's men.

The freebooters now occupied the city. The last assault had succeeded after a fierce hand-to-hand combat. The defenders of the fort, recognizing the futility of a longer defense, had finally been forced to lay down their arms.

Contrary to their custom, the Brothers of the Coast, thanks to the charismatic will of their leader, did not dishonor their victory with unnecessary cruelty.

Don Lopez Aldao, after a heroic resistance, had surrendered his sword to Bearcub Ironskull in person. The latter had forced him to take it back and, at the same time, gave him back his daughter.

As for Don José Rivas, he had taken justice into his own hands by shooting himself rather than falling into the hands of his enemies.

That same evening, the Spanish commander had revealed to the leaders of the freebooters the story of Doña Elmina. The young woman was immediately adopted by the Brothers of the Coast.

As a reward for his fine conduct during the attack on the house in Turbaco, Bearcub had declared Alexandre free of his commitment and made him a Brother of the Coast.

The occupation of Cartagena lasted eight days; then the expedition left for Santo Domingo, taking with it an immense booty.

It was in vain that Bearcub searched for Doña Elmina's parents; the poor Guichard had left very few traces of his brief stay in Santo Domingo. They had to resign themselves to never seeing the veil that enveloped this impenetrable mystery lifted.

One month later, Bearcub Ironskull married Doña Elmina. The bride's witnesses were Monsieur d'Ogeron, Governor of the colony of Santo Domingo, and Montbarts the Exterminator.

Thanks to an exchange negotiated by Monsieur d'Ogeron, in the name of the King of France, Doña Lilia and her father were able to attend Doña Elmina's wedding.

Don Lopez Aldao, asked by his daughter, decided to resettle in Port-Margot. Four months later, Captain Barthélémy became the happy husband of Doña Lilia.

As for Boute-Feu, he, too, traveled from Cartagena to Santo Domingo, but in a rather unpleasant way, that is to say, hung from the foresail mast of the *Trickster*.

As sooner or later virtue always finds its reward, Barthélémy inherited the fortune of his ex-friend, Boute-Feu, and the charming schooner *Santa-Catalina*; a fortune of which the worthy captain was all the more proud, as six months later it had almost entirely passed into the greedy hands of the merchants of Port-Margot.

But he had kept the schooner, thanks to which he became rich several more times, and his charming wife, he mockingly said, took the place of all that he had lost.

Towards the end of the reign of Louis XIV, Doña Elmina appeared at the court of Versailles, where she was presented to the King by Madame la Marquise de Maintenon herself; but by then her husband had reclaimed his original name and title.[56]

Certainly no one would have recognized in this elegant and proud gentleman Bearcub Ironskull, the fearsome freebooter who for so long had made the Spaniards tremble on the seas of the West Indies.

---

[56] Strangely, Aimard implies here that Bearcub's real identity was that of a French nobleman, but never bothered to spell it out or tell that story.